## MEMOIRS OF AN EX-PROM QUEEN

**A novel for every woman:**
"This book already has a substantial underground reputation in feminist circles, but it should appeal to a far wider readership. Funny, bitter and all too true, it chronicles growing up sexy in mid-America . . . Should appeal to virtually every woman!"

—Publishers Weekly

"Extraordinary . . . This is a sad and witty story, expertly conceived and executed . . . More than just another novel about woman's desperate lot . . . it is very good and . . . important!"

—Newsweek

## MEMOIRS OF AN EX-PROM QUEEN

A novel for every man:

# Memoirs of an Ex-Prom Queen

### A Novel by
## ALIX KATES SHULMAN

BANTAM BOOKS · TORONTO · NEW YORK · LONDON

A NATIONAL GENERAL COMPANY

All names,
characters, and
events in this book are fictional,
drawn solely from the imagination.
Any resemblance to real persons is unintentional.

This low-priced Bantam Book
has been completely reset in a type face
designed for easy reading, and was printed
from new plates. It contains the complete
text of the original hard-cover edition.
NOT ONE WORD HAS BEEN OMITTED.

MEMOIRS OF AN EX-PROM QUEEN
*A Bantam Book / published by arrangement with
Alfred A. Knopf, Inc.*

PRINTING HISTORY
Knopf edition published February 1972
2nd printing ........ May 1972      4th printing ... September 1972
3rd printing ...... August 1972     5th printing ..... October 1972
Time Inc. Book Club edition published April 1972
Literary Guild edition published May 1972
Portions of this novel have appeared in APHRA, Vol. 1, No. 2, Winter
1970, in Vol. 3, No. 1, Winter 1971; and in WORKS IN PROGRESS,
Vol. 6, April 1972
Bantam edition published May 1973
2nd printing

For
*MARTIN*

My gratitude
to the
*REDSTOCKINGS SISTERS,*
*APHRA,*
and
*DAVID SEGAL (1928-1970),*
who got me started.

I have learned to mistrust symmetry and the decimal system. There was once a time when I would do anything I chose for which I had ten good reasons, or again, anything for which I could find no reason not to, a time when I would not resist a dare.

I am more cautious now. I have children and responsibilities. I am suspicious of reasons and hostile to dares. The evidence suggests that nature is probably unbalanced, that ten is no truer than four, that reason does not prevail.

Accordingly, doubt is my motto. To share what I've learned (and to have something interesting to do now that I am past thirty and the children are in school) I shall compose a memoir. I shall begin my story neither at the beginning, moving forward as a reader expects, nor at the end, moving backward as a writer recalls, but rather somewhere in between, where the the truth is said to lie.

In a railroad station in Europe, then, about to cut free of my first husband, likely against all reason.

On the Sunday of my first lecture a sealed note was left at my hotel for me. The anonymous writer warned me of a plot against my life: I was going to be shot when about to enter the hall, he assured me. . . . I walked leisurely from the hotel to the meeting-place. When within half a block of it I instinctively raised to my face the large bag I always carried. I got safely into the hall and walked towards the platform still holding the bag in front of my face. All through the lecture the thought persisted in my brain: "If I could only protect my face!" . . . Surely no man would think of his face under such circumstances. Yet I, in the presence of probable death, had been afraid to have my face disfigured! It was a shock to discover in myself such ordinary female vanity.

—*Emma Goldman*
in LIVING MY LIFE

The girl was ugly. I was bored during the whole journey.

—*Casanova*
in HISTORY OF MY LIFE

# O
# N
# E

As the Orient Express lumbered into the subfreezing Munich Hauptbahnhof (and I fresh from Madrid!) to spew me onto the platform into the arms of my waiting husband, I was mistress of no grand schemes. I knew only that I had slightly under two minutes in which to bundle myself up, gather my dictionaries and belongings, fish out my ticket, and find the precise and perfect English words with which to shed my spouse. I knew he would be waiting, smiling, at the end of the platform, just one step beyond the ticket puncher, perhaps already holding out to me one of those sausages for which the Munich station was so famous and which—damn him—he knew I loved. There wouldn't be a moment to experiment with attitude or wording. By then I knew that to wait and see would be to hesitate, and to hesitate would be to lose. I had already in my four long years of marriage to Frank wasted too many

1

chances of getting free by taking aim at him. This time I had to get him square between the eyes on the first shot or he would get me.

The letdown of getting settled into a pair of glum furnished rooms in that dreary northern European city that lacked even the distinction of being a capital had catapulted me south. Frank had his work; I had my nothing. Munich was certainly no place to spend a winter cooped up with a possessive husband in one of those postwar windowless houses six blocks beyond the last stop of the streetcar line; a house with endless locks and keys, a spying landlady, and no telephone. Only Fulbrights for friends in a foreign land. A waste of my youth!

"All right, go on to Spain, then," he had said when I pestered him for my ticket. "I'll use the time you're away to polish my piece on the German Question now that *Intersection* has shown some interest."

I had been careful not to show my delight. He was clearly ambivalent about my traveling.

"I'll try to bring some books for you from the library. Maybe you can pick up a little Spanish while you're there. Enjoy yourself; get it out of your system."

But obviously if I had really enjoyed myself, how could I ever get it out of my system? I had enjoyed myself too much to answer the letters he sent me in care of every American Express office south of Munich. I would have had to answer them with lies, and I wanted to live open and clean.

Well, my chance to prove my honesty was coming up fast. If he would only give me half the money I'd clear out of his life. He could keep the apartment and the furniture, no alimony, finish out the year here, and wait till New York for the lawyers. Simply reroute. I would go to . . . Rome. Let him decide what to tell our friends; let him think of a story for the family. Let him save his face any way he could. Mine would take care of itself.

As the train screeched slowly to a stop, I took a final look in my mirror. Not bad, not good. I was losing my power to judge, now that I was twenty-four. I smoothed the bangs above my eyes, fluffed up my hair at the crown, flexed my smile. Looking good made everything easier. But I felt old—twenty-four and married and old; a has-been like last year's Miss America. Please God, I prayed, let me be beautiful at least until after my money runs out.

The rosy-cheeked clergyman with whom I had shared the compartment was saying *"Auf wiedersehen, Fräulein"* and extending his pudgy hand. Those hand-shaking Germans.

"Bye-bye," I said. They loved to hear you say bye-bye. His chattering away at me in German since just past Nancy had chased the Spanish rhythms from my ears and made me postpone my preparations until the last possible moment. And now he was insisting that I leave the compartment first, when I needed every extra second.

*"Bitte,"* he said, holding the door for me and waiting.

*"Danke,"* I said. And abandoning the last possibility of flight, I walked onto the platform into the lion's lair.

There was the lion himself, just as I had expected him, a step beyond the ticket puncher, grinning once he spotted me, and carrying an armful of anemones. As though I were returning from a short trip exactly on schedule.

*Get him!* But my words were not ready.

*Achtung! Achtung!* blasted the loudspeaker, as Frank glided up to me and gained the advantage by speaking first. Well, let him, I thought. I'll have the last word: bye-bye.

"Hi, baby. Welcome back. Did you have a good time?" All smiles, he held out the flowers to me. Flowers! They were the first flowers he had ever bought me; he was pulling something. Once when we were both students he had gathered a fistful of buttercups to turn our chins yellow. But that was different. These flowers were premeditated. How hateful of him to bring anemones that I loved, that open and close and grow taller so gaudily right before your eyes, like a time-lapse film. It was as though he knew ... But suddenly it struck me that of course he didn't know. At that moment I knew everything and Professor knew nothing. It was I who intended to act, I who had the advantage. I was ready to exert all my power—the only kind of power a woman has. Until the night before when I had wired him about my imminent arrival on the Orient Express, he had surely considered me one of the missing or departed; but now he thought me his wife come home from a little trip. He didn't even suspect that I intended to leave him forever. He thought I would let him correct my spelling and teach me German, that I would cook him *weisswurst* and entertain his friends and explore Bavarian churches while he did his work, and be flattered to belong to him. He didn't even suspect the truth. I avoided his kiss by thrusting my suitcase at him. He put it down. With one arm around my back he squeezed my shoulders and placed a husbandly kiss on my cheek. "Welcome home," he said tenderly with the joy of possession, each syllable visible as a puff of steam in the freezing air of the station.

His words were visible objects in the air. And where were my words?

It was all I could do to keep my knees from

trembling. Could he not have noticed how rotten I looked? It should have been so easy for me simply to blurt out the truth. Then why did it seem to be such a dirty business instead? Maybe because I knew Frank believed exactly what he wanted to believe, no more, no less. His cup of tea did not include the dregs, though the dregs are the tea. His brew was nothing but vapor.

"God, I missed you. Why didn't you write?" he asked. But of course he couldn't allow me to answer such a dangerous question. Quickly he asked instead, "What happened to you?" switching me over from active to passive.

How I wished I could tell him that nothing happens to me, that it is I who happen to them, true or not. How I wished I could tell him ... "A lot happened," I said. *Now. Tell him now.* But the loudspeaker interrupted with its *Achtungs* and I lost my nerve.

"I was worried about you. Didn't you get my letters? I wrote you everywhere I could think of. Well. Now you've traveled. I hope *that's* finished! I hope it's all out of your system. Now that you're back, I'll never let you out of my sight again. God, I missed you." A train starting up drowned him out. He squeezed my arm and yelled, "Come on. Let's get some sausages and you can tell me about your adventure. Here, take these." He succeeded finally in handing me the flowers; then he picked up my suitcase.

Why was everything nice he did for me a bribe or a favor, while my kindnesses to him were my duty? Now he was going to try to stall off my revelations with sausages, buy my silence with anemones. Out of the corner of my eye, I watched him bouncing too jovially along through the station carrying my bag, his long legs rushing ahead of him as though they had some place important to take him, and I knew it was only a matter of moments until the right words would come to me, the words with which to tell him the truth. I would use his words, his vaporous vocabulary.

"Frank. Wait. Before we go for sausages there's something I have to tell you."

"What?" he asked smiling at me. Always smiling. He didn't even put down my suitcase or slow his walking to hear what I had to say. He didn't seem to remember that all the while I was away I hadn't written him a single letter.

"I was unfaithful to you, Frank." Casually I brushed the bangs out of my eyes. "In Madrid."

He didn't move a muscle, not even to drop the smile. But I knew I had struck him. I could proceed, knowing the words would come easily. How much better to tell the truth than to try to hide it. After that I was sure only the formalities could keep me here and for only a little while, like waiting around after a funeral, and then I would be free to go.

But I took no chances. Solemnly, officially, I said, "I know how you feel about it. I know that's the end of us." His turn now.

Yes, he heard me. He began slowing down. Finally he stopped walking entirely. He stood looking at me, picking up my suitcase and putting it down again, like a twitch. His mouth hung open a little, letting the truth seep in. He wiped a hand on his overcoat. Then out he came with it, his simple, automatic response: "No!" Softly at first, then increasing in volume in minute increments of decibels. "No! No! No!" I knew him well enough to recognize each one of them. What a variety of *no's*, relieved now and then by a synonym or a paraphrase: "You didn't," "I don't believe you," "It isn't true," "You couldn't have." A barrage of negatives. The *no's* allowed me for another instant to hate him. *Listen to him!* I said to myself triumphantly, justifying. But there was really no time for that, and besides, justifying would be a trap. No, I needed simply to press my advantage and be gone.

"Yes," I whispered to him, unsure of its effect. "Yes," I repeated softly between bites at the station sausage stand, gently, trying to suppress the note of triumph. But there it was on the counter between us, gaudy as the anemones, our basic matrimonial dispute: "No!" "Yes!" "I won't let you!" "I shall!" "It's a lie!" "It's the truth!" "You didn't!" "I did!"

*Unfaithful.* It was a word he could understand, a concept he could manipulate, a clean, abstract, intelligible word, implying order. Order violated, but order all the same. Though he held his face in his hands while I finished my last bite of sausage, I knew he would be all right when I left. He would wring his hands and say to our friends, "She was unfaithful," and he would believe in my corruption and his purity, and then he would get himself another wife.

"You leave me no choice at all. That's it, you know," he threatened.

"I know," I said, accepting the gambit.

He looked at me hard, frowning and biting his lower lip the way he did when he was working, and then he risked asking, "Don't you *care?*"

Desperate question. What could I say to him? Poor guy, but it was him or me. "I guess I don't love you any more. I don't belong to you any more." Well, at least it was the truth. I looked down into my beer. After a suitable number of seconds had elapsed I took a swallow. (Any sooner and he would have said, *Put down your mug and listen to me!*)

"Haven't I allowed you everything? How could you do this to me? Why?"

*To him.* I shrugged.

"Why did you feel you had to do it?"

*Do it.* He was as slippery as sperm. No, no—I refused to defend! "I didn't *have to do it.* I felt like it."

"But why?"

"I don't know, I guess because there wasn't any reason *not* to."

"I'm the reason not to. Because you're married to me. Because you made a commitment. You promised me you wouldn't," he said puffing up. Puff. Puff.

Technically I had promised. But under protest. Now he would lose me on a technicality. I had promised only because he had insisted. To calm him. Lies.

"But I didn't have to tell you about Madrid, did I?" I said. "So the promise wasn't really a reason not to *do* it, was it? It was only a reason not to *tell* you."

"Quite right. Yes. You promised at least not to tell me. But now you've told me. And now it's too late. Why did you have to tell me? I wish we could wipe it out and forget about it." Again, he held his face in his hands.

Would it have been unkind of me to point out to him how often he had read over my shoulder my letters to and from my friends, trying to find out? Did he want to know or didn't he? Generously, I pointed out nothing.

"I told you because I know it will happen again. Because you won't let me breathe. It will happen again and you'll find out. I hate lies!"

He blew his nose, snorting loudly. I was embarrassed. It would make red veins on his nostrils and blue veins on his neck. Was he going to carry on in the

railroad station? On the radio someone was singing a
Dietrich song:

> *Ich bin von Kopf bis Fuss auf Liebe eingestellt*
> *Und das ist meine Welt, und sonst gar nichts.*

"If it's okay with you I'd like to go home now," I
said, getting out my mirror. "I have a lot to do. I feel
as though I haven't had a bath in a month. I'll try to be
out of here in a day or two, three at the most. That
sound all right to you?" I looked worse than I should; I
had to see a doctor. I put away the mirror and stood
up.

"We'll need to talk a bit first," he said, trying to
compose himself.

"Okay. We can talk if you want." It was the least I
could offer.

He gazed through to the back of my head, out of
focus, saying nothing. I started to walk toward the exit.
I knew he would follow me. He left some money on
the counter and caught up, lugging my suitcase with
one hand, the anemones, which I had forgotten, in the
other. He slid up in time to hand me back the flowers
and open the door. At the curb he took my elbow
commandingly and guided me through the insane Munich traffic to the narrow island where the trolleys
stopped. Never forgot his place or mine. Oh, well, I
was too weary to mind; I would let him protect me
from the traffic, Munich was such a cold and hostile
city.

On the island Frank gathered up his wits. "You
don't *look* changed," he mustered with a faint smile.

"Please. Let's not talk about how I look. I've been
sick. One of the things I have to do before I leave is see
a good German doctor."

"What's the matter?"

"I don't really know. I saw a doctor in Madrid, but he didn't help. These Catholic doctors . . ."

"What did he say?"

"Something about hormones. And he gave me some pills. I took them for a while, but now I'm afraid to take any more. I think it's crazy to play around with hormones, don't you? I just hope I'm not pregnant," I said laughing and pushing my hair off my forehead.

"Pregnant?" He blinked.

"It's really very unlikely; I always used my diaphragm. It's just that I missed my last period. But that could be for a lot of reasons."

He looked around to see if anyone was listening to our conversation. "How could you?" he whispered. As if anyone there could understand us or would care. All the people squeezed onto the narrow concrete island were straining to see what number trolley was approaching or trying to keep the wind out of their faces. No one paid the slightest attention to us.

A number-five trolley pulled up behind a number-six and stopped, bells clanging. Frank put down my suitcase and got out a sufficient number of pfennigs. The conductor punched two tickets methodically in several secret places and waved us on, giving the suitcase a shove.

Settled in the back of the car, Frank looked hard at me. "You planned it," he said.

"What?"

"You took your diaphragm with you. You planned to be unfaithful."

Oh Christ. "I did not."

"Of course you did. Don't lie."

I refused to answer. I was still saving my last word. It was not true that I "planned" it in the way that he meant. But when you came right down to it, what difference did it make whether I left him two months before or was leaving him then? Poor Professor, out of focus, worrying the wrong question.

"I never go anywhere without it—like you and your spare glasses. We all have to look out for ourselves. But that's not *planning* anything."

He didn't answer. Perhaps he didn't even hear me.

The trolley stopped short, throwing me momentarily against Frank. For an instant our eyes met and I saw that his were filled with hate. Was it the hatred of the lion facing his tamer or his prey? Something had gone wrong. Quickly he focused away. For the rest of the ride he sat in a pool of silence until we reached the end of the line. Not a word. But his silence didn't fool me. I had already seen the hate. I knew I must not let down my guard for an instant or he would spring. I suddenly felt afraid.

. When the trolley stopped at the end of the line we began our six-block trudge through the snow-piled streets to the dreary house we lived in. I carried the anemones; Frank carried my suitcase, his head bent in accusation.

How dare he accuse me! "What did you expect?" I shouted. But the only reply I got was the thump-thump of my suitcase against his leg.

Why was I so afraid? Wasn't I free? I swore to get out of there. Fast.

Too late I realized I ought to have gone to a hotel; too late I saw that the distance between the beds was not enough. Even in a separate bed I would be trapped under his ego.

I tried to keep the conversation calm, but Frank would not stay calm. I saw it all: first he would talk about principles and then he would call me names. And if the argument didn't go his way he would shift the grounds and latinize, exaggerate his consonants and patronize. Already he was whispering, *"Quiet! Do you want Frau Werner to know what you are?"* and I, losing my own control, was shouting, "I don't give a shit what Frau Werner thinks! Or what you think either! I care what I think! And what I think is I'm leaving this house and this country and you and Frau Werner!"

"Shut up, you whore! You bitch! You selfish, castrating bitch!"

The names they use! My God, I thought, how did I get into this? I had expected it to be so easy. Hadn't he threatened a thousand times to leave me if I was "unfaithful"? Talk about deceit! It was *his* word that was worthless. Always insisting that a bargain is a bargain—what about *his* side of the bargain? There should have been nothing to it: my confession and punishment, a quick D-and-C, pack up, back on the Orient Express, and out of there. Otherwise time would go by and money would be wasted. I had little enough money or time to waste any more of either on him. I refused to listen to his names. I would not let him manipulate me with assaults and arguments.

"You are trying to make me kick you out, but I won't," he threatened. "I'm still your husband. I have rights. If you want to leave me you'll have to do the leaving. I can't stop you, bitch. But I'm not going to help you. Not one cent! You can whore your way around Europe!"

I decided not to answer. I didn't need his permission, of course, but why point it out? The Fulbright money was his, but the rest was mine, earned on nine-to-five jobs he would never have taken, though he was willing enough to live off it. Perhaps after a night's sleep he'd be calm and more sensible.

I asked Frau Werner about getting a bath though it wasn't our night to use the tub. She said of course, she'd run my water. I slipped out of my clothes, and as I reached for the towel she had placed on the doorknob, Frank came up behind me, yanked the towel out of reach, almost knocked over the anemones, and unfastened my bra. The lion raises his paw. As the bra hung loose from my shoulders he slipped his hands underneath and started to fondle my breasts.

"What do you think you're doing?" I wanted to swat at his mosquito fingers and get on to my bath, but I hesitated. There was something desperate in his fast breath on the back of my neck, and I was afraid to fight. "You belong to me. You're my wife," he mumbled into my neck, at once proclaiming his strength and my duty.

"Stop it," I said. I tried to shake him off my shoulders, but he hung on, squeezing my nipples in his fingertips. I began to struggle in earnest. His breath on my neck made me very nervous. "Please, Frank. No fair."

" 'Please Frank, no fair,' " he mimicked, adding, "bitch!"

I tried to stay calm. He was very angry. Daddy. As I hesitated to use my nails on his wrists he pushed me onto one of the beds and deftly pinned my wrists over my head. With a wrench of his head he shook his glasses off; they dropped to the floor. I had a picture of myself as a comic-book victim, strangling on my own bra, which was flopping around my throat, and I felt an almost uncontrollable urge to laugh. But Frank looked so helpless without his glasses, dewy-eyed and unfocused, that bitch or no, I struggled not to laugh at him. Controlling my own impulse to be cruel, instead I said, "I'll scream!"

"Scream then," he mumbled. And transferring both my wrists to one of his hands for an instant, he prepared with a minimum of undressing to rape me.

There was no way out. I could hardly suppress the laughter any more. I tried to think of other things. I wondered if Frau Werner was listening at the door and if the bath would overflow. "Don't! You'll be sorry!" I cried mainly for the record, hoping not to smile, and then finally, as Frank ignored my wants and his kisses began to tickle unbearably, "For God's sake, Frank, at least let me take off the bra and put in my diaphragm!"

But nothing doing. "Forget the diaphragm," he said, and to the accompaniment of my finally unsuppressible laughter, off we went on our last trip together.

Well, so what? He'd done it so many times—what did one more matter? I'd be leaving soon enough. He could do what he wanted: I still had that last word in reserve.

Two days later, when the petals had started falling off the anemones, my last word was still there where it had always been—in reserve. Though I had spent my life trying to arm myself with final words, I had never been able to pull a bye-bye without having a big hello ready for the next guy. Even as a kid, the thought of spending a Saturday night alone could produce in me such anxiety that I'd go out with anyone just to have a date. In fact, from the eighth grade on, no matter how I talked up freedom, I had never managed to spend more than four consecutive months without at least one man to count on, and frequently two, in case one ran out. In high school they called it "boy crazy"; in college, where everything accelerated, "oversexed." To me it was life insurance.

If I could know for sure I was still beautiful, I thought, it would be easy to leave. If I had been certain of it in Spain, maybe I wouldn't have come back to Munich at all. Maybe I would have sent Frank a long letter and stayed in Madrid, or else got hold of a good mirror and a good doctor and gone straight to Italy. But as it was, I knew my looks were slipping. When I got a look in Frau Werner's bathroom mirror under a decent light I was appalled by my reflection. Was it the mask of pregnancy or worse? There was suddenly a pale, almost imperceptible fuzz on my upper lip that had not been there in America. Probably from those hormones I'd taken in Spain. I needed a cure. If I couldn't get rid of it or if it spread, I was finished.

Smug Frank didn't notice a thing. In his myopic eyes I was still as lovely as ever—that was his insidious power over me. I could tell from the way he took my arm proudly in public and looked around to see who noticed that he still thought me beautiful. Maybe I should have been grateful, like a junkie getting a fix, but I resented it. Not that I was squeamish about trading on my looks when there was nothing else around to trade on. No, it was just that I would need another fix and another, when all I wanted was out. It was impossible to get younger. My chances of leaving would only be worse next year. It was maddening to be stuck there with Frank on account of a faulty epidermis. I was a coward.

No doubt I had made a mess of things. There I was, after all my resolve, still in Munich. I kept thinking that if I could find one disinterested man to call me beautiful, maybe I could believe it and muster the nerve to leave. Since looks were everything, my only asset, I really had to be sure. Frank's word was not enough. All the other assets that I had so carefully cultivated in my youth I had abandoned somewhere, half-formed, in the flood of matrimony, and now at twenty-four I was too old and frightened to go back and reclaim them. My early promises had all been broken; now all my fragile eggs were in this one worn basket.

There had once been a brief time when I did know I was beautiful. Back in junior high, just after the War, I had had what I considered proof. But even then being beautiful mattered so much that I always suspected I was just passing my prime, like a miser who counts his riches every night and wakes up in the morning thinking himself poor. Even then mirrors told me very little: all I ever saw when I looked in one was me. The me I had examined in my bedroom mirror when I was a stringy, buck-toothed, pigtailed kid yearning to be beautiful was the same me Beverly Katz had cursed in envy in junior high ("You can't expect to get away with this shit forever! Someday you'll pay!"), the very me who was foolishly tweezing hairs in a seedy Madrid hotel the night before leaving Spain for Munich. My mirror image always had to be interpreted. And for that I sought my reflection in someone else's eyes.

♥

Mid-Depression, when I turned five, my family moved to Baybury Heights, Ohio, one of Cleveland's coming brick-and-frame neighborhoods sprinkled with vacant lots and apple trees. My arms were just long enough to reach bottom branches and I quickly took to the trees.

But even then, a carefree tomboy roaming free, I longed to be pretty. Every girl did.

"Climbing Sasha," my father called me as I sped through breakfast so I could race to the woods behind our house. Skinny and agile, I scaled the trunks with ease, spending my first summers in the green branches and on the moss beneath. All the kids could manage the apple trees, but only I could scramble straight up to the top of the Spy Tree, a lone slender birch, and see on a clear day all the way downtown to Cleveland's one skyscraper, the Terminal Tower. "Can you see it today?" my brother Ben would call from below. "Is it foggy or clear?" yelled up Susan McCarthy, who lived next door. And they would just have to take my word for it. I took my lunches in the treehouse with the McCarthy kids. After supper, if the boys let me, I played touch football on our quiet street or kick-the-can with everyone in the neighborhood.

Tomboy or not, I spent my indoor time dressing up in my mother's clothes and putting on lipstick and nail polish with the other girls. There was a hummingbird in the hollyhocks behind our house, the most delicate, lovely thing I had ever seen; I wanted to be like her. Even though it hurt when my mother brushed my hair each morning before school, it was worth it to have braids on which to tie pretty matching ribbons. I hoped the ribbons wouldn't get dirty as I climbed Auburn Hill to school past the boys waiting in the vacant lots to pelt us with snow or mud, depending on the season.

Once I started school I learned I would have to choose between hair ribbons and trees, and that if I chose trees I'd have to fight for them. The trees, like the hills, belonged to the boys.

Before and after school, the boys would fan out over the school grounds and take over the ball fields, the apple orchard, the skating pond, the "Mountain" for king-of-the-castle, while we stayed on the concrete playground in the shadow of the school building. There we played girls' games under the teachers' protective eyes. We could jump rope, throw rubber balls for a-meemy-a-clapsy, practice tricks on the bars nestled in the ell of the building, play jacks or blow soap bubbles—all safe, dependable, and sometimes joyous games which the boys disdained because we did them. Best of all, we could trade our playing cards.

When the recess bell rang, while the boys raced past us to the fields, we'd take out our card collections, separating the packs, slipping the rubber bands that divided them onto our wrists, fan out our cards for each other to see, and begin trading: the mate of a pair of kittens for a horse or Pinky; a pair of parrots for a drummer and a ship. Our trading cards were nothing like the boys' silly baseball cards, commercially manufactured for collecting and sold with bubble gum. Our girls' collections were made up of real adult playing cards, one of a kind salvaged from broken packs, which we valued for the charm of the pictures on their backs. Though my collection, being new, was one of the least impressive in the school, I treasured it all the same. It had few sets of four, hardly an unusual pair (though I had a better than ordinary collection of Shirley Temples), but there was at least one card in every category, and like life itself the collection had an open future. No card was so odd as to lack a fixed and perfect place in my endlessly adaptable collection. I loved them all.

And like my cards, I too was adaptable. Though in my summers and on my street I had wandered freely, taking to the woods and the very tips of the trees, in my first weeks of first grade I learned to stay uncom-

plainingly in my place on the steps or in the shadow of
the school. I learned masculine and feminine.

"Go on to the Mountain, girls, it's a gorgeous day,"
Mrs. Hess would urge as we stood on the steps at
recess trading cards. Or, "Why don't you play some
freeze tag? You need the exercise." But we knew
better. We knew that going near the ball fields or
behind the backstop or near the basket hoop or in
among the fruit trees or around the Mountain or near
the skating pond were extremely dangerous expeditions,
even if we went in a pack—for that was all boys'
territory, acknowledged by everyone. Despite Mrs.
Hess's prods and assurances, we knew that at any
moment out there a pair or trio or more of boys might
grow bored with their own game and descend on us
with their bag of tricks. If a girl was spotted on their
territory the boys felt perfectly free to: give her a pink
belly, or lock her in the shed, or not let her down from
a tree, or tie her to the flagpole, or lash at her legs with
reeds, or chase her to the ravine, or look up her dress,
or trip her, or spit mouthfuls of water in her face, or
throw mud at her, or "accidentally" knock her down,
or hold a hand over her nose and mouth, or pull her
hair, or pummel her with snowballs, or "wash her face"
in snow, or mess her books, or tear her clothes, or
scatter her trading cards, or shout obscene words at
her, or throw stones at her, or splash mud on her dress,
or invite her to play on false pretenses, or just hit her
or spit on her or twist her arm behind her back, or not
let her drink at the water fountain.

And it was not only the bullies like Mel Weeks and
Bobby Barr who did such things to us. All the boys did
them sooner or later, and some boy did something to
some girl every day. They did it for fun. They did it to
prove themselves. They did it because they hated us. If

sometimes a boy got it too, it was only from another boy, never from a girl; the terror went only one way. And every boy longed, if only secretly, to be as powerful as the feared and respected bullies.

We knew better than to tell Mrs. Hess. The one time I ran crying to her with my dress ripped after Bobby Barr had pulled me out of an apple tree, she hugged and comforted me with a double message: "I know, dear, those are rough boys. Why don't you play with the girls?" There was only one thing for a girl to do: stay in the shadow. Prudently I gave up football, trees, and walking to school unaccompanied for acceptable "girls' things," until, before I was ten, like everyone else I unquestioningly accepted the boys' hatred of us as "normal." Just as the Cortney kids wouldn't play with me because I was a Jew, the boys wouldn't play with me because I was a girl. That was the way things were. Like our trading cards, we were valued only in our place among our kind. In fact, from the moment we got kicked out of the trees and sent into the walk-in doll house back in kindergarten, our movements and efforts had been so steadily circumscribed, our permissible yearnings so confined, that the only imprint left for us to make was on ourselves. By the third grade, with every other girl in Baybury Heights, I came to realize that there was only one thing worth bothering about: becoming beautiful.

***

With the U.S. plunge into World War II the gap between the girls and the boys grew to a chasm. While *they* were learning to spot enemy planes, launching the U.S. fleet on the playground, and deploying platoons over the skating pond, *we,* bored breathless by the war, pored over movie magazines, made scrapbooks, joined fan clubs, and planned, should the war last long enough, to become U.S.O hostesses. Instead of collecting cards (somehow fewer and fewer people had time to play cards, and the cards themselves, like other luxuries, were beginning to disappear from circulation) we collected the foil inner wrappers of chewing gum, chocolate bars, and cigarette packs, which themselves all became scarcer and scarcer until they too, like the Cheshire Cat, finally disappeared entirely. We lived instead on the sweets of patriotism, quietly accepting the consolation of the decade: "That's tough."

"What's tough? . . ."

"Life."

"What's life?"

"A magazine."

"Where do you get it?"

"At the drugstore."

"How much does it cost?"

"Ten cents."

"I only have five cents."

"That's tough."

"What's tough? . . ."

My father, an energetic attorney, sat on the Draft Board, making our family eligible for a prestigious B-card, which entitled us to an extra monthly ration of gasoline, and weekly donned his Air Raid Warden's helmet. My glamorous mother rolled her own cigarettes using begged tobacco, served meat substitutes without complaining, and set up a cozy blackout shelter in the basement of our house, decked out with all the comforts of the surface. Once she gave a "blackout party." On the radio, newscasts were as numerous and tiresome as commercials; even my beloved Hit Parade was constantly interrupted with important bulletins and flash announcements of bombings and landings. At school we competed by grade and sex to collect, sort, stack, and reclaim old newspapers, magazines, flattened tin cans, toothpaste tubes, foil balls, rubber tires, rags, old clothes (for the Russians), canned goods, and scrap metal. (The girls seldom won.) Anti-Semitism became temporarily taboo. Life changed in a thousand little ways. But however distracting the regimen of war, the overriding change in my life was the addition to my face of unsightly orthodontal braces in the late spring of 1942, coincident with the Battle of Midway.

Until I donned my dental armor it had always been my mother's comforting word against everyone else's that I was pretty. Though I sat before my three-way mirror by the hour studying myself, I couldn't figure out whether to believe my doting mother or the others. I would scrutinize my features, one at a time, then all together, filling in the answers at the end of our common bible, *The Questions Girls Ask,* but I always wound up more confused than when I started.

*Does your hair swing loose? Do you tell your date what time you must be home when he picks you up? Do you brush the food particles out of your teeth after every meal? Do you avoid heavy make-up? Do you stand up straight? Do you see to it that your knees are covered when you sit down? Are your cheeks naturally pink? Do you consume enough roughage? Are your ears clean? Do you wear only simple jewelry? Do you protect against body odor? Do you powder your feet? Do you trim your cuticle? Are you a good listener?*

It seemed as impossible for me to know how I looked as it was important. Some people said I looked exactly like my mother, the most beautiful woman in the world; others said I resembled my father who, though very wise, was not particularly comely.

But once the grotesque braces were on, all my doubts disappeared. It became obvious that my mother's word, which she didn't alter to accommodate my new appearance, was pure prejudice. While to her, busily imagining the future, the advent of my braces only made the eventual triumph of my beauty more certain—indeed, it was for the sake of my looks that they had been mounted at all—to me they discredited my mother's optimism.

Sometimes at night, after a particularly harrowing day at school, after receiving some cutting insult or subtle slight, I would cry into my pillow over my plainness. My mother took my insults personally when I told her about them. "What do they know?" she would say, comforting me. "Why, you're the prettiest girl in your class." And when I protested between sobs that no, I was awkward, skinny, and unloved, she would take me in her arms and *promise* me that someday when my braces were removed they would all envy me and be sorry. "You'll see," she would say, stroking my lusterless hair, her eye on some future image of me or some past one of herself. "Just you wait."

I longed to believe her but didn't dare. Before bed each night I would walk to the gable window in my room that seemed to form a perfect shrine and on the first star I saw wish with a passion that lifted me onto my tiptoes to be made beautiful. I performed the rite just so, as though I were being watched. I thought if I wished earnestly enough my life would change and everything I wanted would come true. My grandmothers, teachers, uncles and aunts, and especially my father, were always encouraging me with their constant homilies: if at first you don't succeed try try again; hard work moves mountains; God helps those who help themselves. Nor was there any lack of precedent: from the seminal Ugly Duckling, a tale which never failed to move me to tears, to Cinderella and Snow White and Pinocchio, there were deep lessons to learn. All those step-daughters and miller's daughters and orphan girls who wound up where I wanted to go likely started out having it even worse than I. I wallowed in fable, searching for guidance. White-bearded Aesop stretched his long bony finger across the centuries to instruct me in prudence, while from Walt Disney's Hollywood studio I learned how to hope. "Someday my prince will come" echoed in my ears even as it stuck in my throat. From my first glimpse of the evening star until the ritual wish was over I would not utter a syllable; but pressing my hands tightly together like a Catholic at prayer to dramatize my earnestness, I would summon a certain Blue Fairy, blond-haired and blue-eyed and dressed in a slinky blue satin gown, to materialize. "Star bright, star light, first star I see tonight, I wish I may I wish I might, have the wish I wish tonight." I believed she would one day grow before my eyes from the dot size of the star to life size, and landing on my window sill reach out with her sparkling wand, which would glint off my braces and illuminate my darkened room, and touch me lightly, granting my wish. I had actually seen her only once, in Walt Disney's *Pinocchio*, but I believed in my power to summon her. If it wasn't ludicrous for my simpering brother Ben to see himself a general, it couldn't be ludicrous for me to wish for a minor miracle of my own. When I had finished wishing, I would stand in my gable until I could spot five other stars (on a clear night ten), then climb solemnly into bed.

If during those years I wore braces there was ever any sign that I might turn out lovely, no one except my mother noticed it. Certainly not I. Each morning I examined myself anew in the mirror for the fruits of my wishes; each morning I saw only the glum reality of my flaws. Faced with my reflection, I shuddered and looked inward. Those steel bands that encircled my teeth like fetters and spanned my mouth like the Cuyahoga Bridge were far more remarkable, more dazzling, than any other aspect of my countenance; exhibiting obscenely the decaying remains of the previous day's meal, no matter how thoroughly I had brushed my teeth the night before, they completely monopolized my reflection. The pain they produced in my mouth was nothing to the pain they caused in my heart.

At night I scanned the sky for stars; by day I studied them in the world. Hurrying home from school, I would pore over the movie magazines, cutting out the photos of the stars I loved and pasting them lovingly in my scrapbooks. Like the boys with their total recall of batting averages and lineups, I knew by heart the films, studios, ages, husbands, and measurements of every star I loved. I had my favorite studio, my favorite actress, my favorite singer, my favorite actor; and my preferences, like those for trading cards in years past, were strong and inexplicable.

With my classmates I would play guessing games about the stars until dinnertime.

"I'm thinking of a certain movie star whose last initial is B."

"Is it a woman?"

"Yes."

"Is she at Warner Brothers?"

"No."

"Is she famous for her legs?"

"No."

"Is her first initial J?"

"Yes."

"Is it Joan Blondell?"

"No."

"Is it Joan Bennett?"

"No."

"Is it Janet Blair?"

"Yes!"

On weekends, standing in the tub shampooing my hair, in secret I would pile my frothy curls high on my head before the mirror in the style of Joan Fontaine or Alice Faye for long magical moments while the bath water grew cold around my shins. Then rinsing out the soap at last and rendering my hair limp again for another week, I would return as my poor self to the tepid tub. There was no getting away from me for very long.

I placed all my faith in the miracle. I wished nightly on my star and daily on dandelion puffs to be beautiful. I wished on fallen eyelashes, on milkweed, on meteors, on birthday candles, on pediddles, on wishbones, on air. Seeking some sign of the coming miracle I told my fortune with cards and drew prophecies from tea leaves. "Rich man, poor man, beggarman, thief, doctor, lawyer, merchant, chief": only a beauty could land one of the desirables. I examined my palm, my horoscope. I avoided stepping on cracks. I depetaled daisies. I knocked on wood, set the knives and forks on the table exactly so, whispered magical syllables and incantations. I ate gelatin to make my nails hard and munched carrots to make my hair curl. I crossed my fingers, bit my tongue, held my breath, and wished steadfastly for the single thing in the world that mattered.

Then suddenly, in August 1945, as the boys of Baybury Heights reeled in ecstasy over the impact of the A-bomb and the girls of my class assembled their wardrobes for the coming encounter with junior high—on the very eve of my entering a new world—the Blue Fairy, that lovely lady, came through. My braces came off, and the world was mine.

☆

My problem was, when I looked in Frau Werner's mirror, I couldn't be sure what was the matter. The symptoms of my malady were elusive. Nothing so dramatic as a pimple stared back at me—only a much less promising reflection than I was used to: wearier, older. Even the fuzz on my lip was visible only sporadically, depending on my mood and the light.

It had all started in Spain—I think. I had gone there to fulfill myself as a woman and had come away wondering if I was turning into a man. My body, after only a few doses of hormones, was playing tricks on me as it had at puberty, and I could do nothing but sit by and watch. Growing a mustache at twenty-four was serious; I was unequipped for a man's life. Would I need electrolysis? Were my barely adequate breasts diminishing? Should I get a padded bra? If a few artificial hormone pills could transform me like this, imagine what a pregnancy would do! I would never, never have a baby. It was unjust that the slightest alteration of my chemistry might ruin me for life. My twenty-fifth birthday was rapidly approaching; I ought to have had five years more to prepare for old age. But at the rate I was deteriorating, I might not have five months.

If only my "hormonal imbalance" were nothing but a severe attack of insecurity. But no, I had had tangible symptoms in Spain, aside from my looks. Something had happened. I had missed my period, and felt pain when I urinated, and experienced incontinence. Wetting my pants could not, at my age, be attributed to insecurity.

"You've got to find me a doctor, Manolo. I've got to have a pregnancy test."

"Yes, yes. Next week we go to Madrid."

"I can't wait for Madrid. There must be a doctor in one of these towns! People have babies everywhere!"

Our life was so slovenly that the simplest task was impossible to accomplish. Always, next week in Madrid. No program, no discipline, no sightseeing since I had been traveling around with the little Teatro Clásico Español. Three weeks of nothing but eating, drinking, fucking, Flamenco, and getting high, stealing an occasional extra hour of sleep while Manolo was rehearsing or on stage. No bath, no mail. If I wrote letters, no stamps. All my planning for nothing. I was going out of my mind with indecision and restlessness, thinking always, *I must leave tomorrow,* but always unable to pack today. It was a bad life for me.

When I'd left Munich to test my independence and soak up Spain, I had thought nothing bad could happen to me there. I had crammed Spanish history and Spanish art, read travel books and Frank's *Don Quixote,* preparing to make of the trip an Experience—and an opportunity. If I could somehow manage on my own, I thought, then I would leave Frank; but if I found after a month that I really couldn't manage, I would resign myself to staying wifely home for good. A simple, economical plan: the worst that could happen was I would enjoy a month in the south and be back where I started, no different than before.

It hadn't turned out that way. I had not been able to manage on my own—couldn't even mail a letter or visit the Prado. But if I could feel for a man what I felt for the stranger Manolo, then how could I possibly return to my dreary husband? Compromise was one thing, hypocrisy another. I couldn't do it: couldn't stay in Spain, couldn't return to Frank, couldn't survive alone. That left me nothing. *Nada.*

Manolo was impossible. He sapped my will and made me ill besides. He was in the midst of a life I could have no part of, except as a spectator. When my symptoms did not improve on their own, I started nagging him to find me a doctor. His intentions were lofty, but his memory was like a child's. As we never stayed more than two nights in any town, we were always ready to leave before Manolo decided to act. It was not until I had wet four different beds in four different villages that, pulling into the middle-sized city of Valladolid, Manolo agreed to go in search of a doctor.

"I have found a doctor, Sasha. We must take him your piss."

I jumped all over him. "Manolo, *amigo, amor. Gracias, gracias.*" I was halfway out the door, dragging him after me.

"There will be time for me to take it to him after dinner. Now I am hungry." He clapped his hands loudly and rubbed his palms together.

We all ate together around a long wooden table in the *pensión* the troupe had taken over. Sixteen of us, like a family. The meal was as long as the table. First soup, then eggs, then fish, then rice with chicken, then a few leaves of salad—all digested with mounds of bread and gallons of wine. The Teatro Clásico Español seemed unaware of drinking water. And, finally, the smooth golden custard that ritually ended every Spanish meal, flan.

After the flan I excused myself and went upstairs to pee in a bottle. When I returned to the table, everyone was already steeped in the seductive rhythms of Flamenco, accompanying Pepe's high minor falsetto and José María's and Tonio's sensuous dancing with *las palmas* and castanets. Of course Manolo wouldn't leave the table. He poured out more wine and struck his cupped right hand with the fingers of his left, Flamenco-style. "We have time for the doctor. I promise it," he said. I could do nothing but clap too.

It was the music and the meals, oddly both jubilant and solemn, which gave ceremony to our disjointed life. The meals always began in a hush, as though the crude plank or earthen floors of the rooms we gathered in were cathedral stones, and always ended in a passion of Flamenco, a communion. Everyone helped teach me how to eat eggs by jabbing the yolks with bread, how to drink wine from skins, how to clap out the *palmas,* stomping and clapping faster and faster until the music exploded in a frenzy.

It was almost time to set off for the theater before Manolo suddenly remembered the doctor. *"Dios mio! El doctor!* Come!" he yelled, jumping up and draining his wineglass. Though of course it was too late, we set off.

Fade-in on a muddy cobblestoned back street of a poor Castilian town, five minutes past curtain time with three figures, two on stiletto heels, hobbling along in search of the Teatro Principal, which seems not to exist. The figure in the center is the drunken leading lady, supported on one side by a Spanish youth who resembles the young Brando, and on the other by an American girl too far from home. She carries a bottle of urine in one hand. The street is filled with screaming, running children. The leading lady is babbling something about her heart; the bottle, lacking a top, is sloshing urine over everything including the leading lady, who, believing it wine, grabs for it.

THE YOUNG BRANDO: Pugh! (dashing the bottle to the gutter).

Oh, well—it doesn't matter: the doctor has gone home, and the next morning the company is leaving town for good. There will be other towns, more urine.

In Palencia at last we saw a doctor. ("Palencia? I'll send Frank a postcard and he'll think I'm in Valencia, right on schedule." We had another good laugh, but I never got around to mailing a card, as I never managed to finish writing a letter.) The doctor reported that I was not pregnant. He diagnosed my malady as inflammation resulting from excessive sex, and prescribed large white pills and abstinence. As I sat across a desk from the doctor, afraid, Manolo translated his words to me proudly, sentence by sentence, allowing the doctor to admire his English and his *cojones*. A very accomplished young actor.

I took the pills. But Manolo, living on an excess of everything, would not practice abstinence. *"O mi amor,* do I hurt you? I never want to hurt you. I am truly sorry," he would say, aghast, his belly moving over mine. But he couldn't stay off me. Whenever I got angry and threatened to leave, he'd leap around the bed laughing and grabbing at me, and maybe twisting my arm or dealing me a provocative slap, until I promised to stay; then we'd make love again. Once he stole my passport, threatening to tear it up unless I

promised. I forgave him every time. I imagined he did
it because he needed me to stay, as I needed him.

I was sorry to need him, disgusted to know that I
had thrown away my one Big Chance not five minutes
after entering Spain. Unable to manage for five minutes
on my own! As the train crossed the border from
France and the entire motley Teatro Clásico Español
had climbed on board, I had attached myself to this
troupe. When Manolo, Veronica, Pepe, and José
María had straggled into my compartment with guitar
and castanets, I had imagined they were simply my first
Spanish sights. Musical, like the movies. But after
Manolo, as young as I and with my kind of looks,
began trying out his English on me, it wasn't half an
hour before I knew that all he had to do was ask me to
stay, and I wouldn't leave the train in Madrid as
planned. Maybe love at first sight is always desperation.
Though I passed myself off as an adventuress, inside I
knew I was really a coward. Worthless without a man.
As the train pulled out of the Madrid station a few
hours later, I leaned back on the plush seat in Manolo's
care. We squeezed hands until Madrid and all her
guidebook wonders seemed as distant as Munich. What
difference did it make, I thought, if I see Madrid now
or later? There was all of Spain to see. Wasn't it better
to see it through native eyes, accompanied by Spanish
music and Spanish love?

***

I was not, as I had expected to be, an outcast. Rather,
whoever didn't accept me as just one more member of
the troupe took me as something of a celebrity. I was
in a class apart, too strange to need explaining, too odd

even to need to remove my wedding ring. Americans were still a rarity in Spain in the fifties, especially female Americans traveling alone, and I was shielded by the sheer glamour of being *la norteamericana loca*. I was a wondrous creature who knew someone who knew someone who knew Tennessee Williams. To Manolo I was more: like some visiting mogul I was powerful, rich, worldly. An exceptional woman, like their own idols Ava Gardner or La Pasionaria. As notable as a man.

My celebrity carried advantages. As an outlandish American I could, for the first time in my life, be as abandoned as I liked in bed. I could direct everything for my own satisfaction, and Manolo took great pains to please me.

"You like that? *Bueno!* I will do it all the night long!"

He caressed me all over for hours and hours, or kissed me exactly where I wanted for longer than I asked, while I lay back and let him; he did not find my breasts too small; he knew exactly when to enter me; he let me lead, let me set the rhythm, refusing to stop unless I commanded it. In a week I was more intimate with Manolo than I'd ever been with any man—partly, perhaps, because of the freedom the language barrier imposes; partly because of the sheer number of hours we logged in bed together; but mainly because for the first time in my life I was as much a person as my man. We were like Martians to each other, incommensurable and therefore equal. Ordinary standards simply didn't apply to me. A creature apart, a Martian-American, I carried my own standards. I didn't worry about how I looked to Manolo; I felt no need to hide from him the imperfections of my body: a Martian-American was more than beautiful enough for him, sufficiently blinded by love. No one dominated: we just circled around

each other, coming together for our dance. No games to
play, no roles to fit; neither rivals nor adversaries, we
were two creatures exploring each other. Anything
went.

"Say dirty words," he ordered, mounting me.

"I don't know any," I laughed.

"In inglés. Say them in inglés. I will say to you the
names in español, and you will say to me the names in
inglés. Then we will see."

It was too ludicrous to be humiliating. I was a new,
important person. We called each other dirty names
until his erection dissolved in our laughter and we went
to sleep.

Each morning after the company nightcap at three
A.M. or so, Manolo and I would get into bed, taking
with us wine, my Lucky Strikes, the Spanish marijuana
he called "yerba," and my dictionaries. Then we would
start to talk. Manolo wanted to know everything about
me and America. Mostly I told him about New York,
for which he had a passion, but we talked also about
Spain, Franco, the Church, evil, everyone in the
troupe, Broadway, words, my husband, Manolo's
fiancée María, prices, prostitutes. He taught me Spanish songs and I taught him English ones. For the
singing lessons sometimes Pepe and Pilar and Tonio
would come into our room and sit on the sagging bed
with us—all the rooms seemed to belong to everyone—and then the next night we'd march through the
dusty village streets with a crowd of children behind us,
chanting our songs. Pepe could never learn to pronounce the "j" in "Jingle Bells," as I could never
pronounce the "y" in *oye*.

"Sasha, *oye*," he would say cornering me hopefully,
while everyone got ready to laugh. "Yyyyingle bells?"

"No, Pepe, *oye*. Jjjjingle bells."

Once Manolo and I retired to bed, there was no idea or subject we were willing to forsake for lack of vocabulary. Instead we wore out the dictionaries. Manolo would perch my reading glasses on his nose and attack the pages of the dictionary until it yielded up his meanings. He would curse loudly if his word wasn't there, then try a substitute word instead. For both of us our English was getting better and better, while my Spanish remained nonexistent. "Wait for Madrid." he'd say. "*There* you will see a dictionary!"

When we woke at dinnertime, Manolo went straight to the washstand in the corner of the room where earlier a black-frocked maid had placed a fresh pitcher of water; then picking up the heavy pitcher and pouring a hard stream over his black hair, he would let out a mocking scream. I would wake to wash more decorously, splashing water first into the basin and from there to my face. He laughed at my strange Martian ways, but sometimes he copied me, as sometimes I copied him. Neither of us had a corner on virtue, though the maid, glancing back at me sprawled naked in bed across Manolo in the middle of the afternoon, found only me, to our amusement, wicked.

Week after week of one- or two-night stands, long days in bed, going out for air only at night, hour after hour of teaching camp songs to Pepe and Pilar and the rest of the troupe, nights of finding where the gypsies sang on the stark edges of Castilian villages, making endless love, coming and coming—it was all very romantic in retrospect or in a letter. But at the time it was positively unhealthy. I was suspended over Spain like a puppet: no will, no baths, no drinking water, no clean underwear, no daylight. I began to neglect myself, then to languish. There was nothing for me to do but tag along. Help with the sets? No energy. Write a

play? No discipline. Learn Spanish? No necessity. I
taught Manolo English, but when it was time for him
to teach me Spanish, we'd make love again. The troupe
performed twice every night, at nine and again at
midnight, and went to sleep at dawn. Knowing no Spanish, it was too boring for me to sit through the plays.
But I couldn't read, either, in the dark. The villages we
played were seldom listed in the guidebooks. They
almost never had churches worth looking at, and when
they did, we'd leave before I could see them. The Spain
I had crammed for was as distant as Frank. The post
office was never open when we were awake. And what
else was there for me to do in Spain but write letters
and look at churches?

  I was superfluous. Learning Spanish or helping out
with the sets was hardly different from rearranging the
furniture or adopting a new hair style. Or buying a
dress, giving a dinner party, having a baby. Love was
always supposed to be enough, but it could hardly even
replace sightseeing.

  If there had not always been that promise of
Madrid, maybe I would have found it in me to leave.
Several times I checked the train schedule and once I
packed my bag. But there was always next week in
Madrid. And Manolo.

  We traveled around Castille for more than a month
before Veronica finally announced we were going to
Madrid, and a seance Pepe held that night confirmed it.

  "Now," proclaimed Manolo, projecting his voice to
the sky, "I will show you Madrid! Now you will know
España!"

  It was going to be worth all that waiting. We would
bathe, walk the broad avenues "as grand as those of
Paris," sit in the luxurious parks, eat the renowned
seafood which trucks rushed to Madrid from the coast

every morning to delight a populace of very particular taste. We would tour the churches, the palaces, the museums. "Now you will see," said Manolo, lifting me in the air.

The first day in Madrid I had a bath and Manolo got his motorbike out of hock. After that he had no money left, not even for gasoline.

On the road the company had paid for his bed, board, and bus or train fare from town to town (I, of course, had always paid for my own), and he had needed money only for wine, cigarettes, and dope. But in Madrid, unless he stayed with his family, he needed money to live, and unfortunately his meager pay was such that to live with me for only a week he would have had to be three actors. It was fine for me to pay my way as Martians might, but not his way too. Yet he had had to spend his entire accumulated wage in a single night, just getting his *moto* and showing me his old hangouts. Now he had no choice but to accept money from me.

It ruined everything. By his standards of honor we were no longer on a par. Now he faced my dilemma.

We checked into a cheap hotel near the railroad station. It was understood that I would finance everything. Then we drove all over the city at top speed on the *moto*, Manolo calling back the sights to me. As we whizzed past the Prado, circled the Royal Palace, and bounced through the serenely beautiful Plaza Mayor, where, I remembered from the books, Ferdinand and Isabella had held their court, Manolo shouted back the names and drove on. It was useless; even Madrid was beyond my reach. I looked, but saw only an enticing city receding at the rate of fifty miles an hour. Though I didn't complain, Manolo felt my disappointment; he even resented it. Without the troupe, we were but one

more poor *madrileño* and one rich tourist, living off
each other.

We began to hurt each other like ordinary earthly
men and women. Manolo sulked and refused to bathe
with me. I brooded, and planned to go sightseeing
without him. With my cleanliness restored, I wanted
more than ever to go to the Prado, to the Royal Palace,
to Goya's chapel, to a bullfight. Now that my urine was
under control I wanted to go out clean early in the
morning with guidebooks and an itinerary, and come
back to bathe at dinnertime. But though we fought, I
couldn't leave. We were afraid that if we broke the
spell even for a day we would discover feelings we
didn't want to acknowledge. Hoping to recapture what
we had had on the road, we stayed in bed with our
wine and dictionaries until hunger drove us out, and
then we simply sat around in a café or tore through the
streets of Madrid on the *moto*. In two months I had
seen nothing of the land but the buff dusty hues visible
from a bus window, and nothing of the towns and cities
but the insides of cheap hotels. I hadn't managed to
visit a single museum. The longer I stayed, the more
desperately I needed to leave. But our efforts pulled us
deeper and deeper into our dilemmas, like quicksand,
and we clung to each other.

One evening in a well-lit bar off the Puerto del Sol
where the whole company reassembled to plan the next
tour, suddenly everything was settled. After he had
ordered our wine and I had paid, Manolo looked hard
at me and said, "Sasha! You are growing *mostachos*!
*Oye,* Pepe!" he called across the room. *"Ven a ver los
mostachos de Sasha!"*

I showed no emotion at the time, but when we
reached the hotel later that night, I packed my bag for
good.

"Do not go, please," said Manolo sitting quietly on the bed watching me pack.

"I have to go."

"Please stay."

"I can't."

*"Porqué?"*

"You know why. My husband is waiting for me. And I want to go to Italy." I thought: *hypocrite*.

"Stay. One day we will go together to Italy."

"I can't."

"Stay until Thursday. We will see all the sights. I promise it. We will go to El Prado tomorrow at ten o'clock in the morning. Thursday we will go to Escorial. There are storks sitting on the chimneys. I swear it on my mother. I will take you there. On the Virgin. Thursday. You will see it. Please do not go."

But it was no use. I had to leave.

On the train Manolo sat across from me in my dim compartment until the last moment. We held onto each other's hands, already turning to memories.

"Write to me. I will come to you in Italy if you leave your husband," he said. "Or maybe in the winter I will come to you in New York."

"Okay." I smiled. We had planned it so often. "I'll send you my address in Rome." But I knew that Franco's rare passports went to higher-ups than Manolo.

The train started.

"Goodbye," I said, clinging to his hands through the compartment window.

*"Adíos."*

We looked at each other through the window until we were specks in the distance. At least, I consoled myself as the train entered the hills, I wouldn't again be subject to such scrutiny.

# T
# W
# O

They say it's worse to be ugly. I think it must only be different. If you're pretty, you are subject to one set of assaults; if you're plain you are subject to another. Pretty, you may have more men to choose from, but you have more anxiety too, knowing your looks, which really have nothing to do with you, will disappear. Pretty girls have few friends. Kicked out of mankind in elementary school, and then kicked out of womankind in junior high, pretty girls have a lower birth rate and a higher mortality. It is the beauties like Marilyn Monroe who swallow twenty-five Nembutals on a Saturday night and kill themselves in their thirties.

Pretty or plain, by the time you survive puberty, your job in life is pretty much cut out for you. In either case, you must somehow wheedle back into that humanity from which you have been systematically excluded since you learned to walk. Among the ruling fraternity whose members can often barely hide their contempt for you, you must find one sponsor willing to brave ridicule for love of you. You must make him desire you more than manliness. For boys are taught that it is weak to need a woman, as girls are taught it is their strength to win a man.

When on the brink of puberty I emerged from behind my braces with a radiant smile, long black eyelashes, and a pink glowing skin, my troubles were only beginning. I suppose I should have expected a hitch: in the fairy tales too there was usually a steep price to pay for a wish fulfilled. The Blue Fairy had blessed my face all right, but suddenly there was my body. I loathed it. It frightened me, it was so unpredictable. It was nothing if not trouble. People were always ready to make fun of it. They made fun of it for not having breasts, and then they made fun of it for having them. It had once supported me in the trees and on the exercise bars, but I could no longer trust it. I hated walking on the street inside it. On the slightest provocation I blushed crimson, and then they made fun of it for that. My very blood betrayed me. What had my body to do with the me inside?

One day I got out of the bath bleeding *down there,* and from the nervous way my mother said it was "natural" after I screamed for her from the bathroom, I knew for sure I was a freak.

"Stay calm. I'm going to explain the whole thing to you," she said. "It's really nothing to get upset about, dear." She smiled and patted my cheek as blood trickled down my rippleless thigh to my unshaven calf.

I was way past being upset. I was so horrified by my

sudden wound that I was detached, as though I were watching a mildly interesting home movie of myself. My leg had known blood before—there were scabs and scrapes along the shinbone and around the ankles, and cinders permanently imbedded under the skin of both knees—but never blood before from *there*. That it didn't burn or sting like other wounds only made it more sinister. I was sure my curious finger had injured something. I was probably ruined. It was likely too late even to confess.

"Sit down on the toilet and wait a minute while I go get something. And don't worry, darling." She sounded almost pleased as, leaving the room and closing the door behind her, she chuckled to herself, "Well, well, well."

I examined the water still in the tub, lapping gently at the dirty ring. A faint trail of blood led from the tub to the sink where I, a good girl, had stood avoiding the bathmat. Was there blood in the bath water too? Oh, no! There was blood on my fingers and now blood smeared on the towel which other days polished to gleaming my sunburnt skin, cleansed in the chlorine of the public pool. What was taking her so long? Everything I touched was getting soiled.

Seated on the toilet, I looked down at myself. It was hard to see, not like my brother's. The mysteries were inside—to keep us, I guessed, from seeing them. To use a mirror, even in this crisis, would have been suspect (suppose she walked in and saw me?), though indeed it might have helped, as my father had taught me it helped to watch the dentist in a mirror drilling out tooth decay. I had always hidden it so carefully, a mirror now would be doubly suspect. I could hear my father urging over the hum of the drill: *watch and relax, reeeelax, let go,* and the pain had somehow slipped away. But my father couldn't advise me now. Anyway, if I relaxed now, wouldn't the blood come streaming out? I tightened up.

The blood wasn't flowing, exactly. Every so often, when I thought it had stopped and formed a scab, more would ooze out without registering as sensation at all. Like cells seen through a microscope, the blood moved slowly, surreptitiously. It wasn't the familiar color, either—it was ominously deeper.

At last mother came back, carrying equipment. She locked the door behind her and shored me up with a smile. "Now," she began. "This is called a sanitary belt." She held it up. "It holds the sanitary napkin." Like a stewardess demonstrating the oxygen mask, she held them up, the long bandage dangling by its tail from her index finger and thumb. Sterile.

"Stand up, dear. Now, slip the belt around your waist. The tabs in the front and back. That's right. There. Now the napkin. It absorbs the flow. I'll keep them in here now, with the towels, so you'll know where to find them each month." (She smiled for the future: "I always tried to be a good mother," I would someday hear her say.) "I'll put it on for you this time, but you'll have to learn to do it yourself. The side with the blue thread goes on the outside, like this. First you fold the edges, like this, test it to make sure it's secure, like this, then turn it around to the back and do the other end the same way. Not too tight or it'll chafe. There. Now turn around. . . . Good! Now let me explain."

My mother's textbook words droned on and curdled like sour milk. *Every month?* If it happened once a month for a lifetime, why had I never seen these bandages before? If it happened to everyone, why hadn't my best friend Jackie, who had large breasts,

told me about it? Now I knew I was an anomaly. One
of my breasts was larger than the other, like one of my
feet. Some of the girls had hair under their arms and
between their legs, but not I. Instead of having hair
down there I would have this awful bleeding. People
would know. The sanitary napkin which hung between
my legs was already molding to the shape of my thighs,
a parasite sucking my blood. I shuddered. How could I
possibly go out of the house wearing it?

"... and passes through the vagina."

In our family we had never called it anything, and
now she was calling it a "vagina." Unutterable word. It
was better than "cunt" or "pussy"—boys' words—but
for me they were all unutterable. Twelve years old and
I had never called it anything but "down there."
Except for the one time I had furtively looked at it in a
hand mirror, I had never seen one. I had caught flashes
of my mother's large breasts, and a rare glimpse of her
pubic hair, but that was all. I had giggled over the
hygiene book of a friend's older sister (we too would
have hygiene in high school), but there were no pictures in it—only diagrams of inside organs, like liver,
uterus, bladder, and tubes, all as invisible as lungs, and
as disgusting.

Finished and self-satisfied, my mother put her arm
around me and kissed the tip of my nose. "My sweet
Sasha, one night you go to sleep a little girl, and the
next day you wake up a young woman. You'll be a
lovely woman, Sasha." But I knew I was not a woman.
I was a child, frightened, unable to comprehend what
was happening. Nothing had been explained; everything had at least two meanings. I tried to pass as
normal, but inside I knew I was a freak.

Submerging myself in junior high, I found all my

classmates plunging recklessly into the pulsing Baybury swim. They dived and surfaced and turned in unison with the precision of mackerel, as though their medium were the world. How was it, I wondered, that they all seemed to know exactly what they were about, following currents I never felt? They politicked at lunch hour, dipping their ears into one another's secrets, living on lemon cokes and loyalty, while I, watching from the edges, a starfish clinging to a rock, waited for the current to slow down enough for me to get the feel of it. One week they decorated one Barbara for her "perfect" legs and another week another Barbara, and I, studying those imponderables, couldn't even understand what they meant. Were my legs good or bad? There was no knowing. I pretended to understand, acquiescing in my classmates' verdict that Barbara H.'s legs were the best there were, like Susan S.'s sense of humor, and I whispered with the others as they swam by. But to me a leg was a leg, and, unsure of myself, I remained mystified. If I were really pretty, why, I wondered, did boys ridicule me? Why did girls whisper when I walked by?

Actually, there was plenty for them to whisper about if they only knew. Between my legs I had found an invisible button of flesh, sweet and nameless, which I knew how to caress to a nameless joy. I was pretty sure no one else had one, for there was no joy button in the hygiene book, and there was not even a dirty name for it. Though I listened carefully, I never heard anyone, boy or girl, so much as allude to it, nor was it pictured on the diagram in the Kotex box. Once, my anxiety overcoming my embarrassment, I had tried to ask my friend Jackie about it. But lacking a name or description for it, I couldn't even present the subject. When Jackie simply looked at me blankly, little beads of shame dampened my forehead, and I shut up. After that, I never dared question anyone. Evidently, only starfish like me had joy buttons. Accepting my difference, I scrambled anxiously to keep it secret as best I could. Suddenly swimming out of my depth, I felt weighted down by more and more shameful secrets until it was difficult just to stay afloat. At night in bed I would swear to caress my joy button only once, and then, breaking my promise, give myself up to it. I expected something terrible to happen, but I couldn't help it. Trying to control my controlling obsession, I led myself into strange nocturnal rituals and odd compulsions. The more I could prolong my caress before my joy button "went on," the more often I allowed myself to stroke it. I would count the strokes and try to break my record. I was torn between prolonging the joy and getting it over with before I heard my parents coming upstairs.

There were other secrets I was powerless to control. In the Majestic Theater where we congregated on Saturday afternoons to watch Frances Gifford in her leopard sarong enact another episode of *Jungle Girl*, the boys who scrambled to sit beside me sometimes tried to rest their hands on my thigh or, slipping their arms around my shoulders, dangle their fingers down on my breast. If they really liked me, would they handle me so? I knew I shouldn't let them, but I was afraid to stop them and cause a scene. If I sat quietly and held my breath, maybe the other girls wouldn't find out. The dilemma was too shameful to face straight on; nothing could make one scandal-proof. I crossed and uncrossed my legs, folded and unfolded my arms, and prayed the hands would go away but leave the boys.

It was the same at the swimming pool in the

summer: I was ashamed to be seen in a bathing suit, but more ashamed to be ashamed. I forced myself into the pool every day to disguise my shame, and blushed to be seen inside my body. And when I could I hunched my shoulders to conceal my breasts or hid under a towel.

On the way home from the pool, there was no hiding. Walking home with the other girls we would run the gauntlet among gangs of marauding boys from other schools who hooted at us from passing cars, pulled up beside us, or followed along behind making lewd remarks. Frightened, we'd tense up, step fast, and keep our eyes straight ahead, pretending to ignore them until they finally got bored and left us alone. We had no other defense. Sometimes we'd be followed all the way home; sometimes we'd be threatened and cursed. The worst of it was not knowing a tease from the real thing. After a while I decided it was safer to take a bus than walk home from the pool or the movies, even if I had a long wait for the bus by myself. I lived farther out than the other girls and always had some distance to walk alone. Better to be insulted at a bus stop than followed on a lonely suburban road.

One evening I was waiting for the bus alone, carrying my wet suit rolled up in a towel under my arm, when a station wagon full of boys pulled up beside me. As usual, I pretended not to see them, until someone called my name.

"What's the matter, Sasha, stuck up?"

I looked up. Inside the wagon I saw Al Maxwell, an older boy from my block, and what seemed to be half the football team.

"Want a ride, Sasha? Come on, we'll take you home."

"No thanks," I said politely, "I'll wait for a bus." I didn't trust them.

"What's the matter, you scared?" said someone. They were all laughing. "Come on, we won't hurt you."

I was flattered and frightened at once, the old dilemma. I didn't want to go, but I didn't know how to refuse without appearing ridiculous or chicken or hurting their feelings. I wanted to be a good sport.

I hesitated and looked behind me. There was no bus in sight.

"You don't have to be afraid," said Jimmy Brennan, a star, opening the door for me. "Get in." When he smiled at me, I wavered. "Don't worry," he said kindly.

I swallowed hard and got in.

Ten minutes later we were driving on a road I'd never seen.

"Where are we going?"

"Oh, just for a little ride. Don't worry."

When we were all the way out to Sharon Falls, halfway to Akron, they parked the wagon in the woods and Jimmy Brennan unzipped his fly and took out his thing. I started to cry. They said if I didn't touch it they'd kick me out of the wagon and make me walk home.

I didn't know what to do. I wanted to stay a nice girl. Besides, I was terrified of Jimmy's thing. Part of me wanted to see it with an evil desire, but I was afraid if I actually touched it I'd throw up. I saw it gleaming white out of the corner of my eye while the boys were busy making jokes, and I could tell it was hideous and enormous. Oh, why me? I hated myself.

"It won't bite you."

"You better touch it soon, or we'll make you kiss it."

"If you don't touch Jimmy's, you'll have to touch Al's. His is much bigger." They all laughed.

"Touch it." "Touch it." "Touch it." "We won't tell."

I knew there were too many of them not to tell. I was going to have to touch it—there were so many of them and only one of me. I knew that the longer I waited the worse it would be. But even after my will had capitulated, it was a long time before I could bring myself even to look at it.

It was hairy and repulsive. Quickly I turned my eyes as far from it as I could and jabbed at it with a finger on an outstretched arm. The smooth, slippery skin brushed my hand, slimy as worms. I squeezed my eyes closed until, satisfied, they drove me home.

Inside and outside I was transformed by puberty. But though the evidence of it was all around me, I couldn't understand my metamorphosis. The evidence was there in the corridors, on the telephone, at the movies, in Clark's Restaurant at lunchtime, after sorority meetings on Friday nights. Yet it was all strangely inconclusive. Could it be that the prettier I grew the worse I would be treated? Much likelier, I thought, I wasn't really pretty.

People whose names I didn't know said hello to me in the hall in tones I didn't understand. People called me on the telephone and hung up when I answered. Football star Iggy Friedman and jitterbug champion Larry Bruder came to my house, ostensibly to study math with me or to practice dancing, but something told me they really came for some other reason that I couldn't imagine. If I was really pretty I needed proof.

Like those who will always think of themselves as fat
no matter how many pounds they lose, I continued to
think of myself as freaky. To protect myself, I remained aloof, a starfish on a rock.

There were weekly opinion polls called Slam Books
which told in black and white what people thought of
each other; yet even they told me almost nothing.
Filled between classes in composition books from the
five-and-ten, one charm per page, when completed the
Slam Books yielded one perfect Composite Girl. As
early as the eighth grade my name began to turn up in
their pages, and by the ninth grade it appeared regularly. But it was usually on the NOSE page, or under
BEST COMPLEXION. True, my skin concealed me well
enough, and I was pert in profile, but what about inside
and straight on? My avowed distinctions were purely
negative; they did not even photograph well. The
excellence of my nose was its insignificance; the virtue
of my skin was its odd refusal to erupt. When everyone
else's pimples cleared up, what then? Could my looks
outlive the disappearance of their blackheads? Could I
base my future on anything so trivial as skin? Unlike
BUST, CHARM, SEX APPEAL, PERSONALITY, POISE, SENSE
OF HUMOR, and HAIR, which as they grew in mass grew
in value, my acknowledged assets were self-limiting.
While the girls with positive charms, even immaterial
ones, could look for daily gains, the best I could hope
for was relief that no flaws had yet surfaced. There was
nothing I could do to help. Baffled, I clung to my rock,
filtering data from the passing stream, and withdrew
further into myself. If I couldn't control my body, at
least I could control my mind. Self-control, my father
said, is the key to the world.

My father was proof of it. He had lifted himself
from a ghetto high school to a position of eminence in

Cleveland's legal establishment by sheer will, or so the family story went. Now I realize that my father was merely filling his destined slot in the professional scheme of things for hard-working sons of frugal and ambitious Jewish immigrants: his older brother had became a doctor, his younger brother a dentist, and all his sisters teachers until they turned into wives. My father, the middle son, had of course to be a lawyer. But close up it is hard to distinguish ambition from destiny, and I heard only my family's version. In high school my father had used his cunning to study shorthand and typing instead of shop, and landed a job as private secretary to one of Cleveland's industrial tycoons. He played chess with the boss, attended law school at night, and in between, with that single-mindedness he passed to me, he learned at least ten new multisyllable words a day, practiced oratory before the mirror, and studied the classics of literature in the tiny nickel volumes of the Little Leather Library series. When the time came for him to take the bar exam, he passed with the highest score in Ohio. It was predicted he would have a brilliant career.

My mother, as clever and ambitious as he, heeded the predictions and married him. Already loved by my father at a distance, my mother, the youngest and fairest of a family of lovely sisters on my father's ghetto block, had no trouble at all—so went the story. In America beautiful clever girls do not long remain schoolteachers.

They passed their hopes to their children. My mother, wanting happiness for me, gave me braces and dancing lessons; my father, valuing learning and success, gave me his library of Little Leather books. My brother Ben mastered the Baybury hills no-handed on his bike and managed a paper route; and I entered the

Little Leather Library. I read and reread each volume,
fleeing from my baffling outer life. Their contents came
in such small, sweet packages that I could digest them
piecemeal and savor them at length. I never suspected
that a book measuring three inches by four inches
might be considered suitable only for adults or that in
larger bindings those very treasures might have struck
me as impossibly difficult. Starting with the fairy tales
and the *Arabian Nights,* I moved easily through *Candide, Gulliver,* and *Rasselas* without noticing any difference in genre, and then on to the plays, stories, and
essays my father had studied. While my brother played
football and read baseball books, and my classmates
read beauty books and movie magazines, I went
through plays by Ibsen, Strindberg, Oscar Wilde, and
Moliére; stories of Tolstoy, Kipling, Balzac, William
Morris, de Maupassant; meditations of Marcus Aurelius; words of Jesus; addresses of Lincoln; essays of
Mill, Thoreau, Shaw, Voltaire, and Emerson; dialogues
of Plato; and even selected reflections of Madame de
Sévigné. They were so fanciful and cerebral that they
made me forget I was a piece of meat, albeit a prime
piece according to the specifications of my mounting
pile of *Seventeen* magazines. My father, glowing with
pride to see me following behind him, discussed the
classics with me as an equal, using long, latinate words
(a language I dubbed "lawish"); and my mother, imagining me in a better college, saw me marrying a better
man. To me, however, the little books imparted Truth,
all dipped out of a single vat of life's wisdom. My
one-time belief in miracles mellowed to a belief in the
printed word, and wide-eyed still, I read every romance
as a parable for the future, every essay as personal
advice. Coupled with looks, knowledge was surely
power.

A cunning freak, I learned to keep my knowledge and ambitions to myself. In school, I tried to pass as smart instead of studious. I refused to learn typing and shorthand out of the same wisdom that had led my father to study them. I wanted to be admired, not a secretary. I realized that for a girl "business skills" were sure to lock the very doors they had opened for my father. Instead, I cultivated other, more useful skills. Without neglecting to brush my hair assiduously according to the instructions in *Seventeen*, I used my electives on math and commercial law, and mastered forging my father's signature for report cards and excuses. I started a notebook, with sections for words to learn, quotations to contemplate, reforms to accomplish. Ten resolutions each New Year's Eve. In everything I set myself records to beat, as I did at night with my joy button. What I couldn't master, like spelling, I disdained, claiming I could always use a dictionary. I wouldn't compete unless I could win. Borrowing from Marcus Aurelius a philosophy of sour grapes, I hedged all my bets: I wanted to be the smartest since I couldn't be sure I was the prettiest; I wanted to be the prettiest since I couldn't be sure I was the smartest. With a vanity refined to perversion, I cut school to hide that I cared to be smart, telling no one about my books, and I affected sloppiness to hide how much I wanted to be beautiful, locking away my beauty charts in my desk drawer. I began to look for trouble so it wouldn't take me by surprise. If I asked for it, I thought, maybe I could control it.

Unlike other truants who cut school to shoplift, go to the movies or a burlesque show, miss a test, or play pool, I had another purpose. I went downtown where no one knew me and, standing at a bus stop on some busy corner, I tried to stare down strange men on buses that passed by, testing my audacity. I would stare at someone till I caught his eye, then force myself to continue no matter what he did, until I stared him down and made him look away. I wanted to beat the boys at their own vile game. I would rather hate them than fear them; best of all I would make them fear me. I wanted to pick my mark, hold his eye, control his mind, bend his will to mine. I didn't dare try it in Baybury. Instead, I cut school and went downtown to play my Bus Stop Game. It was a dangerous game, for I could never tell when a man would call my bluff by leering back and force my eyes into humiliating retreat. But I had to do it: it was part of my nameless joy-life. If I succeeded at the Bus Stop Game by outstaring my mark, I rewarded myself with my button's joy; but if I failed by looking away first, I forbade myself to touch it. My father's daughter, I was very strict.

Eventually I got so good at the game that I was able to board the buses and try it on passengers from whom I couldn't escape. I selected the most frightening men to root out my fear. I wanted to make my eyes into such powerful beams that I could bend strangers and enemies to my will. I studied audacity, determined that if I couldn't be sure I had the power that comes with beauty, I would have another kind of power.

But it all turned out to be unnecessary. One balmy Friday night in early October—a Round Table night—I suddenly got the proof I had lacked that I was indeed beautiful.

The seventeen girls of Sigma Lambda Tau (the best sorority? the second-best?) all sat cross-legged in a circle on the plush cranberry carpet of Maggie West's living room. The previous Friday and the following were for business; but this one was for Round Table only: pure confrontation. Around the circle clockwise the word would pass, exploding in scandal, wrath, or outrage. One at a time the month's transgressions and oversights would be named, complaints registered, warnings given, accusers faced.

In our pleated skirts and cashmere sweaters over white dickies, we sat fiddling with our charm bracelets and straightening our sox, waiting for the President to start. Some of us gave last-minute orders to the pledges, writing merits and demerits in their conduct books. Others of us checked our new breasts in their Carousel bras like tips of sausages in their casings, looking from one to the other: were the straps adjusted evenly?

Beverly Katz, President, whispered something surreptitiously in someone's ear, then, smoothing down the pleats of her baby-blue skirt, called the meeting to order. How was it, I wondered, that her pimples did not affect her eminence? Neither her big bosom (BEST BUST) nor her sly black eyes that so perfectly expressed disdain explained her mysterious authority. She ruled by mean glances, not good looks. I studied her, wondering why everyone laughed when she cracked those jokes I never got; why even I laughed.

"Okay, let's get going. You wanna start, Sally?" said Beverly Katz, turning to the girl at her side. And off went Sally, around the circle, loosing her rhetoric on us, passing compliments and hurling insults. When she finally came to me, she frowned and hesitated a moment; then, changing her mind as I held my breath, passed on to the next sister. I was still cringing when she began on my neighbor in a voice that, like everyone's, emulated Beverly's. "I'm not saying who told me," she said, "but I happen to know . . ."

I tuned out, relieved. Why had she even hesitated over me? How could I have offended her? From my

bayside perch I tried only to please, giving offense to
no one. I went to their meetings, observed their taboos,
admired their figures, studied their styles, always keeping my mouth carefully shut. My joy-life was secret. I
wanted only to belong.

Some of the girls—perhaps the guilty ones—hung on
Sally's words. Others scanned their notes, rehearsing for
their own turns to talk, soon to come up. Between turns
Beverly Katz popped bubbles or cracked jokes, though,
as everyone knew, she had little reason to be jovial. It
was already three weeks since she had received her
S.L.T. pin back from Iggy Friedman, tackle, with
whom she was certainly still in love and had probably
already gone too far. And without Iggy, as everyone
knew, she would never be re-elected President.

If Beverly Katz was at twelve o'clock, then I was at
nine o'clock. Around the circle passed the word, coming closer to me. Each girl in turn had a chance to
speak her mind to all or none, as she was moved. From
Sally to Sue to Maggie to May. Six o'clock, seven
o'clock, eight o'clock.

"Sasha?" said Beverly, popping a bubble.

I shook my head. My thoughts, questions all, were
too tentative to expose to them, the slightest of whom
seemed so certain, so powerful. As always, I passed.

On we moved toward the ultimate moment after
Round Table when the Cokes and potato chips would
be passed around, a record would be started on the
phonograph, we would separate, the doors would be
thrown open, and the boys, who had been waiting
noisily on the lawn outside, would at last be invited in.
We were all needles for that moment. Rumor had it
that the football team was gradually defecting to Alpha
Phi Beta. Not many of them had shown up at our
meeting the week before, and without the right boys

we'd never get the right pledges, and then before we knew it S.L.T. would be going down; perhaps it was already slipping. As the last few sisters spoke, we shifted on our pastel skirts and plucked at our sweaters, combing our hair and checking our bras again, till finally, circle completed, we were back to the President.

"Before we adjourn," began Beverly, holding everyone back with her black eyes, "I have a few things to say myself." She turned directly to me. Smoothing the pleats of her skirt she rose on her knees and measured the distance between our eyeballs before going into her venomous trance.

I was ready. Our eyeballs met. *Now.*

"You don't seem to care who you step on to get a guy. You think you're pretty hot shit. But watch out. We're all on to you now. We know how you operate!"

I take off, slowly at first, then at increasing speeds, swimming through space.

I hear my mother shouting in comforting farewell from some vast distance, "Just you wait, someday they'll be sorry!" while "Liar! Schemer!" resounds in my ears.

Sitting on pastel clouds receding rapidly, the sisters glance at each other with assenting smiles. They are passing a long bubble pipe from cloud to cloud, all in cahoots. In their center a black-eyed medium sings out the prophecy, Katz's Curse. (Of course she is only a medium with acne and not responsible for what she says.) "You can't get away with this shit forever!" she shouts.

I am shocked. Can she know about the Bus Stop Game? My joy button? If not, what can she be talking about? Jimmy Brennan's thing? Iggy's phone calls?

"Glub, glub, glub," she mouths, diving under a circle of whitecaps and up through baby-blue waves.

At last I come to rest on my rock. Up she swims to my face inside a huge, expanding bubble. "You think that just because you're beautiful you can do anything you please and get away with it. But you can't! Someday it'll all catch up with you and then you'll pay! You'll pay for everything!"

The bubble bursts, drenching us all.

*Everything?* I wonder, as in the bubble's circular wake the prophecy echoes like a curse.

Though I decide it is a sane prophecy, the conclusions reasonable—no one should expect to get away with anything indefinitely—I nevertheless begin to tremble.

When the wave recedes, Beverly sits down again, being careful that the pleats in her skirt are smooth. She surveys the circle with triumphant eyes and everyone smiles back at her. I smile too, trying not to offend.

I remember something, but I don't know what. It is something strong and delicious, stuck between my teeth. Strong enough, I wonder, to sweeten the rue? I suck it out and roll it over my tongue, and then I realize: *Beverly Katz has called me beautiful, and not one word about nose or skin.*

She gets up to open the door. Out come the Cokes.

*Surely I must be beautiful if she hates me for it!* Well, let her hate me then, what do I care? Obviously this hatchery is not the world.

In come the boys. "Hi." "Hi." "Hi." "Hi, Sasha. Who got it tonight?" says, of all people, Iggy Friedman.

"I did," I say, surpassing protocol, and trying to master my pain by naming it. "From Beverly."

"Gee. That's too bad." Iggy looks down, slightly embarrassed. I shrug. Nat King Cole proposes that it's only a paper moon hanging over a cardboard sea.

"C'mon," says Iggy, touching my elbow. "I'll take you home tonight. We can go to Lenny's for a Lennyburger and you can tell me about it if you want to."

I taste sin. "Swell," I say. "Just let me get my sweater." For the first of what will be many times, I toss my head with a hint of defiance, like Veronica Lake. Beverly Katz may not see me, but she will hear.

I return in a moment with my sweater. "Ready," I say flashing my prettiest smile. And linking my arm in Iggy's I walk with him out the door.

What but destiny or extraordinary luck could have kept me apart from them, clinging to my rock? To have swum along with them once would have meant forever. I would make my way differently. With an eye at the end of each of my rays, I was better off a starfish. After having studied all the fairy tales and *Candide* and *Rasselas,* I knew there were some who crossed over the mountains and seas. At fourteen I believed that somewhere there must be a vast green ocean, deep and mysterious, with other currents more swift and powerful than those of this bay. There were some who escaped. Let my sisters curse me then, since their love was out of the question. Beautiful, I could try for the ocean.

♫♫

Music was spilling out of the cafeteria into the corridors of Baybury High. "Stardust," the S.L.T. theme song, announced that the annual S.L.T. Bunny Hop, celebrating spring and the big basketball game, was now under way.

I loved dances. But even before we arrived at the
dance, I was already giddy from the evening. In a
series of brilliant maneuvers beyond the hopes of
anyone in Baybury Heights, my own Joey Ross had
demolished snotty Shaker Heights and led Baybury to
victory by scoring one spectacular basket after another.
Of the eighty-one points scored by Baybury High
against Shaker High's bleak thirty-four, Joey, still a
sophomore, had made forty himself. After such a
dazzling performance, he would surely be made captain
of the team.

I floated out of the gym on Joey's arm, madly in
love. "Great game, Joey," called Rooney Rogoff on his
way to the locker room, snapping his towel at us.

"You too, stud," said Joey.

Hand in hand we mounted the stairs to the cafeteria.
On the landing Joey shot one hand to the wall to trap
me; then pressing his sinewy body flat against mine, he
kissed me hard. When his tongue glided into the
corners of my mouth I went limp like warm butter; I
could have melted right down the stairs. "Don't," I
managed to say. "They'll be judging us soon."

"So what?" said Joey, "you're gorgeous." But he
lowered his arm obligingly and in we went.

The darkened cafeteria was undulating with mute
couples grinding to a very slow instrumental. A canopy
of paper streamers hung overhead. "Great game, Joey,"
someone said as we walked through the door.

"How ya doin'?" Joey answered modestly.

"Great game," said my friend Eloise the ticket taker.
It was useless trying to hide my rapture.

At the opposite end of the large room Freddy and
Fink (*More sound than you think/With Freddy and
Fink*) had set up their amplifiers and turntables and

were playing records on request. Behind them the girls on the Dance Committee were putting last-minute decorations on the table that would serve as a platform for the coronation. Tonight a new Queen would be chosen. My stomach sank when once again I remembered the contest, but Joey grabbed me around the waist and pulled me onto the dance floor and made everything all right again. Pressing thighs, eyes closed, we melted together and swayed as one. Nearing the open window where the April breeze was puffing out the cafeteria curtains like parachutes, we floated slowly down to a standstill and kissed again. Oh Joey.

The music stopped. "Great game!" said Nat Karlan, one of Joey's Keystone brothers. They twined their arms over each other's shoulders and moved away. But not before I overheard Nat whisper to Joey, with an intimacy I never achieved, "If you don't get in tonight, friend, you never will!"

I was stung by the thought. Of course: those forty points overwhelmingly weighted the scales. Tonight Joey would have a powerful advantage. But even if I managed to resist again tonight, who would believe me?

In the five months I had been going with Joey he'd come closer to "getting in" than anyone else, but I had always managed to resist. What happened to the girls who gave in, and even to those only suspected of giving in, was an unthinkable nightmare. I had myself sat through the now-famous S.L.T. meeting in which Renee Thomas had been expelled for allegedly going all the way. Only a year had passed and already Renee's name was legend. Girls sneered at her, boys abused her, her name appeared in all the graffiti, freshmen gaped at her in disbelief. She would never marry in Baybury. She'd have been better off dead. If only she had heeded the warnings that one thing inevitably leads to another.

Between me and Joey already one thing had led to another—kissing had led to French kissing, French kissing to necking, necking to petting, petting to bare-titting, bare-titting to dry humping—but somehow, thank God, I had always managed to stop at that penultimate step. When the Sunday morning telephone wires buzzed with intimate questions ("What did he try?" "How far did he get?") I bluffed my way through them with respectable answers, always a few steps behind the truth. But how long, I wondered, could I be believed? And how long could I go on holding out?

I knew there was some Renee in me, as there probably was in each of us. Renee, too, it was said, had started out by falling madly in love. So precariously did I totter between yes and no—from the first delicious kiss that made my knees go limp, to the very brink—that this new possibility appalled me. *If you don't get in tonight, friend, you never will.*

Actually, I had grown to dread necking with Joey, it had come to be such a struggle. Whatever I did, he wanted more. It wasn't even safe to neck in my house any more, where my parents trusted me. Gone were those long, voluptuous hours of kissing on my living-room sofa or in the car at Shaker Lakes when I could abandon myself to Joey's sweet mouth, love his sinuous arms with my fingertips, and tickle my palms on his crew cut. The kissing and French kissing and petting I had so enjoyed had been reduced to a five-minute warm-up before the struggle, and I had been forced to trade abandon for vigilance.

"Please let me, Sasha."

"I can't, Joey."

"Please."

"No."

Now, after five kisses or ten, he'd slip his hand under my sweater or skirt and begin to tinker with me mechanically, then pin me under him on the back seat of his father's car and proceed to please himself. He was much too strong for me. In the beginning he used to lie on top of me so I could hardly move or breathe and rub his stiff clothed body against mine for a few minutes until a series of jerks let me know he was done and I could breathe again. I was bewildered by the shame and the thrill of it. Later he stopped short of the jerks, turned suddenly away, opened his pants, and came into his handkerchief. Once he secretly unzipped and rubbed his bare penis on my thigh without my knowing until, suddenly aware, I managed to push him off and make him finish by himself.

Though he never again forced me to touch it, he started taking it out and begging me to feel it with my hand or let him rub it on my leg, and he would whine when I refused. "Come on, Sasha, you're torturing me," he would say. But it was really he who was torturing me, squeezing me between two guilts. I cowered whenever a car approached. I felt that if anyone ever discovered what Joey did with me in that car, I would have to run away. Poor Mother. Poor Daddy. Poor, poor Sasha.

It disgusted me to see Joey close his eyes and groan in ecstasy, his handkerchief over his crotch. When I had melted from his kisses it had been for love of him. But he certainly couldn't be groaning for love of me, it was all for himself. It was a tossup which was worse: to be appreciated as a mechanical ejaculator with all the attendant risks, or to be despised as a prude.

I had become so anxious over our sex that though we were going together and were therefore permitted to neck, I tried my best to avoid it. Passionate as I was, I looked for excuses to go straight home from a date. When Joey invariably parked the car anyway, I kept my coat buttoned all the way up as an act of protest. But of course, my protests went unheeded. I didn't dare get Joey really angry for fear he'd spread things about me. The girls' axiom about the boys was true: *they always go as far as they can, and never backwards.* By fifteen I knew love was a dangerous emotion. It was dynamite. I knew it was safer to be a sex reject than a sex object, but it was already too late for me to choose.

Freddy and Fink put on a fast record. Joey stepped back with his arm around his buddy Nat, while a Deltan twirled me off into the crowd. Athlete Joey, like all Keystones, danced only slow; the articulate Deltans danced as fast and as smoothly as they talked. As girls were divided by their looks and permissiveness, boys were divided by their accomplishments. I would have been a Deltan if I'd been a boy; maybe that was why I fell in love with a Keystone.

Whirling and bobbing and double-stepping, I danced with one Deltan after another. Couple after couple dropped off the floor while I danced on. Around us the circle of spectators swelled until it seemed the whole school was there. Breathless, pulse throbbing, I kept on going, to record after record, until Fink stopped the music and Freddy announced a break. I felt my face flush burgundy. Everyone exploded in applause. An intoxicating evening.

Freddy and Fink moved the coronation platform and mike into the center of the floor. "One-two-three-testing, one-two-three-testing." Time for the contest.

While the judges arranged their chairs in front of the platform, I ran to the girls' room with the three other finalists to primp and calm ourselves. My God, I thought, looking down the long mirror at those beautiful older girls, I haven't a chance. They seemed so poised, while I was falling apart. Long eyelashes, a tiny nose, and glowing skin simply couldn't be enough. The one power I had developed to perfection, the power of my glance, I didn't dare use on the judges. There was not a single way to improve my chances: I could only stand up and be judged.

As soon as we walked back into the cafeteria, Fink played a few bars of "Stardust" through the amplifier to set the ceremonial mood. Freddy caressed the mike and announced the contestants' names and fraternal sponsors. When he called my name I stepped up on a chair, then out onto the platform. Somehow I managed a smile for the eight judges below, two from each fraternity. *Please let me be chosen,* I prayed, climbing down again and taking my place beside the other contestants before the judges. I felt helpless, like a passenger riding in a "chicken" race.

Fink put on a slow ballad and a few couples danced in the corners. The judges consulted with Freddy, then whispered gravely among themselves. Feeling foolish, we whispered together too, not daring to look out, plucking at our sweaters nervously, waiting. "Who wants to be Queen anyway?" we said, hating each other. I needed to go to the bathroom again.

Freddy ran up to us. "Would you mind walking back and forth across the cafeteria once, girls, so these guys can get a better look at you?" he said.

"Oh, no!" we squealed. Didn't they see us every day? But of course, one at a time, we paraded before the judges. I remember making a little deferential curtsey at the end to camouflage my trembling knees—and I remember to my shame hearing someone laugh.

An eternity passed before Freddy ran back up to the front and tenderly took the mike in his hand. Fink stopped the music. "Okay, folks," said Freddy, "your attention please." He frowned and tapped the microphone until it hummed. Then he began again, laying on the famous Deltan smooth.

"There's such a stack of pulchritude up for Queen tonight that our judges have had a hard time making up their minds between these four gorgeous glamour girls." Everyone moved in a little closer. "But I'm happy to announce that they've finally reached a verdict."

He nodded to Fink, who started "Stardust" over again from the beginning, a little louder this time. Everyone fell silent. All suckers for ceremony.

My hands began shaking so hard that I clasped them behind my back. I wondered about my blushing skin. I had to go to the bathroom desperately. I thought about how it would feel to be Chinese or to live on the West Side, and then snapped back to Baybury Heights. Though I knew the decision was already settled, so there was no longer any possibility of influencing it, abandoning all prudence, I offered up one last wish to the Blue Fairy: *Make me Queen and I'll never ask for anything more.*

"I have the pleasure," said Freddy like a professional, "to present to you the new Queen of the S.L.T. Bunny Hop—I might even say the Basketball Queen of Baybury Heights."

*Not me,* throbbed my temples. *Never me.*

"—that beautiful miss from Sigma Lambda Tau, the

Keystone's choice, the sweetest profile in Ohio, the Queen of the Bunny Hop, Sasha Davis!"

The music blared. Me! I couldn't believe it!

"That's you, Sasha," said Freddy, hugging me tightly and bending over to plant a loud kiss on my cheek. He pushed me up onto the platform. "Get up there now, honey, it's all yours!" I didn't dare take my eyes off him. "You're the Queen, Sasha," he yells up from below. "Smile!"

The others have disappeared. I'm all alone on the platform. The silver S.L.T. crown is on my head, and my arms enfold a huge bouquet of daffodils, tied with a blue satin ribbon on which are stitched in gold the letters S-L-T. In a circle below me everyone is singing out our song to the tune of "Stardust" and watching me. I smile till my gums show. I feel tears stream down my cheeks. Cameras are flashing. I feel so foolish and so happy. I am the Queen.

I confess, my coronation was such an undiluted triumph that I took it down in one long, sweet gulp that went straight to my head. Rashly I forgot that in the fall there would be another queen and the following spring another. Barely fifteen, that April night I reached such heady heights that the triumphs of the rest of my life were bound to seem anti-climactic.

Directly after my coronation I risked everything, celebrating with an act that wiped out months of restraint. Parked in our regular spot at Shaker Lakes, at last Joey got in. By allowing him to lie on me with his fly open, accepting his kisses with the delicious abandon of former days, I signaled that the struggle was over. It wasn't the forty points, or even Nat Karlan's prediction. It was simply that, being Queen, I

dared to believe I could get away with it. There was
something regal about going all the way.

I didn't get to remove my underpants, so eager was
Joey to cross my threshold. He stretched the elastic of
one leg and slipped his organ in; then with a little
moan of joy he began humping me the same as always,
plus in and out like an animal, wrinkling my skirt with
his belly.

*This is it!* I said to myself. *This is love! Enjoy it!* I
knew my daffodils were being crushed; nevertheless I
tried to enjoy it, at least to attend to this celebrated
moment in the most touted of acts.

It wasn't unpleasant with Joey inside me, but it
wasn't particularly pleasant either. It didn't even hurt. I
was surprised not to be feeling much, for Joey had
pushed his entire appendage, so much larger than a
finger, inside my opening. I couldn't imagine how it all
fit in. Watching him move up and down on me in the
darkness, I wondered: *is this all there is to it?* I had
loved Joey to the melting point, but now I resented
him. I received each thrust of his body like a doubt.
Really all? When it was over a few moments later and
Joey came groaning into his handkerchief as always, it
struck me as hardly different from our usual sex. The
only thing to recommend it was that it was ultimate.
But, really, kissing felt much nicer.

Joey sat up. "I love you, Sasha. You'll never be
sorry, I promise you."

He sounded so pious. I eyed him suspiciously. I
wondered if I had done it all correctly, and if so, if it
might not show or smell. Suppose some of the sperm
had gotten in? Suppose Joey wouldn't keep his mouth
shut? As I saw him wiping away the last traces of
sperm, looking proud and lavishing on his withered

organ more care than it deserved, I suddenly felt the enormity of my breach. I was utterly vulnerable.

I pulled down my skirt, hoping to become again inviolable. But there was clearly no going back.

If I get away with this, I consoled myself, I can probably get away with anything.

An hour later when Joey kissed me goodnight on my doorstep, I dutifully said "I love you," knowing Joey's new power to injure me. But for the first time, my knees did not go limp when he kissed me.

I was no longer simply "Joey's girl." I was a Queen myself with a life of my own.

<hr/>

I flush the toilet with sweaty palms, aware of the risk, and wait to face the consequences. At home and at school my Kotex disposal was down to an art. Even in public rest rooms there were almost always special containers, and if not—if I had to leave a soiled napkin rolled neatly in toilet paper on the edge of the sink or exposed unswallowed in a toilet bowl—I would not be around to take the blame.

Here at Joey's house I am trapped.

I'd stayed at the table as long as I could, hoping to get through the agonizing dinner and wear my napkin out of the house. But when I felt the sticky blood seep through my underwear onto my thigh I realized that however skillfully I shifted in the chair or crossed my legs, it was only a matter of moments before it would penetrate to my skirt and thence to Mrs. Ross's flowered cushion to disgrace me forever.

Now, locked inside the bathroom, I am impaled on my monthly dilemma: how to dispose of it? I can't walk into the kitchen past everyone at table, sheepishly carrying my dirty rag to the garbage can. I can't snoop around the bedrooms for a wastebasket or a bottom bureau drawer to bury it in, knowing that eventually they will sniff it out and despise me the more. No; there is only one thing to do, however risky: flush it down the toilet.

I send up a prayer and press down the lever. The water rises inexorably toward the rim of the bowl. I jiggle the handle, my pulse pounding. Past the normal water ring it rises, past the porcelain lip. Then just in time at the very brink the water crests, turned back by some Neptune of the sewer. It stands and waits, the Kotex caught in the toilet's hole, its tail protruding like a drowning cat's, and I draw breath.

But it is a false reprieve, for whatever the dangers, I will have to flush again.

Blocking my nose from the inside, I pull up the sopping Kotex by its tail. It is saturated. Slowly the water recedes: a blessing. With index fingers and thumbs I strip off the gauze and begin shredding the bloody pad; if the toilet won't swallow it whole, I will feed it bit by bit.

Another prayer, another tug on the lever, and at last the water whirls my clots and rags down the hole, letting me slip past one more month without facing disgrace.

I fasten a new napkin, wash my hands with soap, fix my smile before the mirror, and return demurely to the table.

School let out in June; after that we were doing it regularly every couple of weeks, except when I had my period or pretended to be having my period.

Joey would pick me up at the Baybury Pool on his way home from work at his uncle's shoe store. From the pool where I had spent the day developing a tan, we either went to the ball court at Eastwood Park, where Joey worked out shooting baskets while I watched admiringly with the other girls, or if he could get his father's car we'd drive up to Shaker Lakes, where he worked out on me.

Driving up the Lake Road giggling nervously over our destination, I received odd premonitions. I imagined the car crashing or the police stopping us for questioning.

"Surprise," said Joey one evening, opening the car door for me and tossing my swimming bag in the back seat. He seemed to be full of giggles himself for once.

"What's up?"

"A present for you."

"What is it?"

"You'll see." He turned onto the Lake Road.

"Tell me," I pleaded.

"Unh-unh. I've had it more than a week without telling you. You can wait a few minutes more."

As soon as he had parked the car at the shore of the lake and taken me into the back seat, Joey opened his wallet and took out a foil-wrapped Trojan condom. "Here," he said, presenting it to me as though it were an orchid.

I recoiled. I knew all about Trojans from dirty jokes, but I had never seen one. And here I was holding one. It was so unequivocal; what kind of a girl must he think me? There were two more in his wallet, leaving little ovals on the outside leather, dead giveaways.

"My God, Joey! If you carry them around in your wallet, everyone will *know!*" I dropped it in his lap,

offended. How stupid I had been to assume we
wouldn't get caught.

Joey stroked his so-precious prick a few times to
make it hard, then placing the rubber over the head of
it, rolled it carefully down the shank. "Don't worry,"
he said, "I just say they're for whores if anyone asks.
Or for Renee. Everyone carries them for whores."

I slipped my underpants off one leg, and Joey moved
on top of me. Being careful not to disturb the condom,
he pressed himself inside me.

Once in, it felt almost the same as without the
condom. But it gave me the jitters anyway. When I
heard a car pass on the road below, instead of just
holding my breath and crossing my fingers as I usually
did, I jerked so hard that Joey came out. "I'm sorry," I
whispered.

"Hey, take it easy!" said Joey pushing it back into
me with his fingers. He was annoyed. "If you jerk like
that it'll take twice as long." Then, gently, he added,
"There's nothing to worry about, baby. They can't see
us way back here."

He was right. Unless someone actually parked, came
up to the car, and caught us in the act, it didn't matter
what people merely suspected. As long as I was willing
to do it, Joey would be a fool to betray me, and
without Joey's testimony, no one could prove a thing.
We were unlikely to be caught because Joey always did
it very quickly and fully clothed, out of consideration
for me. Even his carrying condoms proved nothing. I
would deny everything if anyone accused me. Though I
was uneasy whenever I saw people whispering at the
pool, I realized it would take more than rumor to ruin
a Queen.

While half of me trembled at fugitive sounds, the
other half was proud of my daring and happy to be

done with the agony of anticipation. Fifteen, flat on my back with Captain Joey Ross pumping up a storm between my knees, I thought "Oh yeah?" to Beverly Katz and all the other S.L.T. girls. They dared not accuse the Keystone's choice, one half of a perfect couple. Let them try to make Renee of me!

But my feelings of triumph barely justified my nervousness or the plain discomfort of sex. The eleventh time we did it was more unpleasant that the first. I grew to dread it, but I could never come up with a good enough reason to get Joey to stop. "What's got into you, Sasha? We never got caught before," he would pout, and the record just kept on mounting. As the girls always said, *boys go as far as they can, and never backwards.* Watching Joey drop the sticky condoms into Shaker Lake, I was baffled that I could ever have thought I loved him. Oh, he was sweet in his way, and the biggest fish in Baybury, but he was my tormentor. Definitely not for me. As everyone said, it was never too early to think about marriage, and I had large inexpressible yearnings Joey could never satisfy. Whether or not he was the Captain, I was still the Queen. If only I could somehow escape from the back seat of Joey's father's car, I knew I could do much better.

*** 

"Marry for love," said my mother, "but remember, it's just as easy to love a rich man as a poor man." *Rich man, poor man, beggarman, thief*—if it was foolish for my brother to leave to chance which type he would be, it was foolish for me to leave to chance which type I would marry. My mother's advice to me was as sensible as her comparable advice to Ben: "study hard and be somebody." Both tips were perfectly suited to our possibilities.

More beautiful by far than other mothers, my mother deserved to be listened to. Her cheeks had a soft pink smell, a ripeness, which made me happy just to be sitting next to her. I overflowed with pride when she showed up at school or when her picture appeared in the Cleveland *Post* from time to time as chairman of one committee or president of another; who would not want to elect chairman or exhibit on the social page such a perfect face? Even more in matters of love and matrimony my mother's face, which could have enchanted any man, commanded respect. Having herself married well, she certainly knew what she was talking about. And in our own interminable adolescent discussions of whom to marry, no girl among us ever suggested that it would be better to marry poor, unless the alternative were not to marry at all. My mother was right. There was only one way for a girl to control her future: choose her man.

There weren't many things a girl could do to command the choice, but fortunately there were a few. First, she could make sure she did nothing to be kicked out of the market. Second, she could make herself available to the most eligible types. Third, and most important of all, whatever her natural endowment she could enhance her fine points to make herself as attractive as possible. It was no secret. Methods for achieving all three were spelled out for us in each new issue of *Seventeen* that arrived in the mail and in all the books, like *Boy Meets Girl, Junior Miss, Girl Alive!,* we were given for our birthdays. But the instructions were only the beginning. It was up to each girl on her own to make, as my mother called it, "the most of herself."

When summer ended and my junior year began, I had my first chance to branch out. Cookie Margolis of Elyria, Ohio, a premed student at Ohio State, invited me to the university's great Homecoming Weekend, and, Joey or no, I accepted.

I had met Cookie in August at Geneva-on-the-Lake, the decaying summer resort on Lake Erie's shore where the Baybury Heights sororities and fraternities rented cottages for two weeks every summer. With only one chaperone per cottage, and Joey stuck sorting shoes in Cleveland, I had found plenty of opportunity at Geneva to experiment with other kinds of Lake Erie fish. My sisters (virgins all, I believed) were so busy concentrating their efforts on our own Baybury boys that none of them noticed me searching the dance hall and the skating rink for odd species or wandering alone on the far end of the beach seeking adventure. Right there under their noses, if they had only troubled to look, they too might have found tall Cookie Margolis industriously cutting bait, his summer job. While they saw no further than their noses, I managed to bring off a hot romance, prudently remaining chaste in case they bothered to investigate.

It had not been easy, lying with Cookie on the cool sand under the stars hearing the wavelets lapping the shore like kittens' tongues, for Cookie's presurgical fingers melted me as easily as Joey's baskets ever had. But I had resisted, knowing better than to start doing it with two boys at once. I laughed tears for my poor lost virginity reading the relevant passages of *Girl Alive!*, realizing how recklessly I had upped the ante.

If you kiss Mike tonight, the next time you go out with him it will be natural to kiss him again. Each date with him you may go a little further in what will become a dangerous game, because you are releasing in him and in yourself emotions that you may not be able to control.

Meanwhile, you will go out with other boys and it's easy enough to slip into the same habits with them. In no time you have earned yourself the reputation of being a girl any boy can kiss. And if any boy can— well, . . . you will have saved nothing special for the man for whom you eventually feel genuine love.

What had I done? They were talking about kissing, and here I was applying it to . . . ! Fifteen years old! I was overcome by more than sufficient fear and remorse to enable me to resist Cookie. It was bad enough to be doing it regularly with one person; two was the road to nymphomania. I was too young, too young. Just as I knew for a fact that kissing led to French kissing, I knew that "sleeping around" at fifteen would lead to nymphomania at sixteen, and prostitution at seventeen, no matter how good my grades or my family or my intentions.

Once I reached Ohio State I saw it was worth all the pains I had taken getting my parents' permission to go. That brief first glimpse of the larger world was a revelation to me, whetting my appetite for the future as much as ten Little Leather Library books.

From the time I had read my first fairy tale I had tried to imagine what it would be like to live elsewhere and free. Even as a small child my pulse had quickened each time we drove over the Cuyahoga Bridge to Cleveland's West Side, past the huge Sherwin Williams Paints sign on which a can of neon paint spilled over a spinning globe bearing the legend *Cover the Earth*. There in that strange world west of Cleveland people had different kinds of names and houses and, I imagined, lives.

At Ohio State I saw it might be true. In Columbus girls lived in dormitories where, by signing in and out for each other and telling lies, they could come and go almost as freely as the boys, who of course had no curfews. No mother in her negligee, arms folded across her breast, to shout from the head of the stairs, "It's two o'clock in the morning! You were due home at midnight!" No father reading in the study, waiting in the bright lights (which would reveal one's shameful dishevelment) to embarrass one before one's friends by saying with excessive formality of anger controlled, "Young man, I cannot permit you to see my daughter again if you cannot get her home before one thirty A.M." Although in their talk the dorm girls were almost indistinguishable from the girls of Baybury—all sweaters and romance and marriage—their freedom seemed vast in comparison. How I envied them!

There was an even greater difference among the boys. At the football game on Saturday the college boys drank rye or gin out of pocket flasks. Besides cars and athletics they talked of life, mechanics, medicine, and the future. At the great Homecoming Dance on Saturday night, more than a dozen of them danced with me. Even the ugly ones seemed as accomplished and desirable as Cookie Margolis, more fascinating than any Keystone or Deltan I had ever known. From Columbus, Baybury Heights, where I was going to be stuck for two more years, looked like a puddle.

On my last night in Columbus, weakened by rye, I succumbed to Cookie in the attic of the fraternity house. He shamed me into bed, insinuating that any-thing less would be ingratitude, and took me as I was protesting. Of course, I alone was to blame; but, ignorant of college protocol and no virgin, I simply hadn't known how to say no. When I discovered a few weeks later that Cookie was in love with someone else, I knew I would have to keep up my grades so I could go to some other college than Ohio State. I couldn't afford to start out as a freshman with a reputation.

I was getting impatient with the whole problem of sex. Why did everyone consider it so important? Love was important, but sex was nothing but trouble. The philosophers I read didn't waste their time with it.

As long as I had to spend two more years in boring Baybury, I decided to use the time well. In a strange scientific book from my father's shelves, *Behaviorism*, by the famous Dr. John Watson, I had discovered certain indispensable facts. *"Personality,"* said Watson in italics, *"is but the end product of our habit systems. . . . The situation we are in dominates us always and releases one or another of these all powerful habit systems."*

If our situation dominates us, I would have to get out of my deadening situation. If personality is a result of habit, I would have to start forming the right habits. I would shun the rat race and prepare for college. I would practice raising an eyebrow, perfect my seductive glance, and cultivate a crooked smile. I would get top grades and harden myself.

Of course, I would let no one in on my plan. By some weird hypocrisy, it was considered as crass for a girl to improve herself by trying to get a better man as it was considered laudable for a boy to improve himself by trying to get a better job—even though everyone acknowledged that a girl's only purpose was to marry, her only hope to marry "well."

There was another, even more remarkable, passage in the book. "Between fifteen and eighteen," reported Dr. Watson, summarizing his vast scientific researches, a female changes from a child to a woman. At fifteen she is but the playmate of boys and girls of her own age. At eighteen she becomes a sex object to every man.

Every man! By all means, I must perfect my glance. But there was more:

After thirty, personality changes very slowly owing to the fact, as we brought out in our study of habit formation, that by that time most individuals, unless constantly stimulated by a new environment, are pretty well settled into a humdrum way of living. Habit patterns become set. If you have an adequate picture of the average individual at 30 you will have it with few changes for the rest of that individual's life—as most lives are lived. A quacking, gossiping, neighbor-spying, disaster-enjoying woman of 30 will be, unless a miracle happens, the same at 40 and still the same at 60.

I no longer believed in miracles. I would have to take matters in my own hands. How foolish the others were to expect that all they had to do was sit around and wait for their prince to come along, all the time developing God-knows-what ruinous habit patterns! I copied the entire passage into my notebook. "Don't believe everything you read," my father had warned, but I believed. The passage, with its time schedule, seemed to have been written expressly for me.

Watson's revelations tempered all I had discovered at Ohio State. There, the college girls, like the high school ones at home, were already planning to marry on graduation, if not before, and settle immediately into their ways. Their hopes were all pinned on it, their habit patterns already determined, their lives set. But it didn't have to be so. According to the learned Watson, if I played it right I still had fifteen years—as many

again as I had already lived—before my life would be
set. Precious years to use carefully. I would not, like
the others, become a "quacking, gossiping, neighbor-
spying, disaster-enjoying woman"! I would not be like
all those other women, so despicable to everyone, even
the lofty Dr. Watson. I would make myself the exception, refusing to let that habit system take hold. If I
could preserve my looks, I wouldn't even have to
marry until the last moment. I would fight and resist. I
would arm myself like the boys with psychology and
biology and a way to earn money. I would be somebody. I would be fastidious in my choice of "environment," vigilant in my cultivation of habits. Thanks to
my mother's looks and my father's books, I already
had a good start. But a start, I knew, was not enough.
It was the end that mattered. If, as the girls always
said, it's never too early to think about whom to marry,
then it could certainly not be too early to think about
who to be. Being somebody had to come first, because,
of course, somebody could get a much better husband
than nobody.

# T
# H
# R
# E
# E

It was the Zither player in Munich's Café am Dom who gave me the confidence I needed to leave. I was touched that he remembered me at all. I hadn't been to that café since before Spain, more than two months earlier. Yet, as soon as I walked through the door he started making a big fuss over me, smiling and playing his one American song, "Deep in the Heart of Texas." It was silly enough in English and on the guitar; it was preposterous in German on the zither.

Eating my *Florentiner* and sipping my coffee, I

laughed aloud instead of reading the mail I had picked
up across the street at American Express. "*Willkom-
men zurück, Fräulein,*" he said. Where had I been
these months? They had missed me. Had I perhaps
found another café? He twisted his mouth into a mock
pout, obviously unaware of all the changes I had seen
in Frau Werner's mirror; to him I was exactly the
same Sasha I had been two months before.

The very next day, armed with his admiration and
the assurances of a Munich gynecologist that I was not
pregnant, I made my move. I stuffed my suitcase with
a new batch of pink pills and a list of doctors to see in
Italy for injections to combat "insufficient ovulation";
an assortment of drip dries and a bottle of Joy; and
Henry James's Roman novel, *The Portrait of a Lady.*
Then I boarded a train heading into the Alps for Italy.
Free.

My first free act was to remove my wedding ring.
My second, vowing not to fall into bed with the first
man to come along as I had in Spain, was to select an
empty compartment. I would treat myself well and
share my bed with no one. Having forged for myself
that rare treasure, a second chance, I was determined
not to blow it.

"Okay, we'll call it a trial separation, if that will
really make you feel better," I had consented to Frank
as I packed my things. "Six months? Eight? Whatever
you say." Why deny him the comfort of his technicali-
ties, as long as he knew they meant nothing to me? I
would never go back. Not to Frank or any of the old
dead ends. I would go forward, wherever that might
lead. Take care of myself. Write a glorious play. Travel.
Practice discipline.

As we penetrated deeper and deeper into the Alps,
reaching the German-Austrian border, I was glad no

one but a border guard entered my compartment. I
wanted to be alone. Like Isabel Archer, whose long sad
story I began, I "held that a women ought to be able to
live to herself in the absence of exceptional flimsiness
and that it was perfectly possible to be happy without
the society of a more or less coarse-minded person of
another sex." My muscles were tired of smiling at
Germans.

When we stopped for the passport check at the first
border town in Italy, I leaned eagerly out the window.
The signs were written in a new language. *Bella.
Bellissima.* The Italian guards with cheerful smiles had
more brass on their uniforms than the Germans; their
very language had a certain lift. The officer who
checked my passport returned it with a *grazie* and a
flourish that raised my spirits. Outside the sun shone.
When he left my compartment and I opened my bag to
put away the papers, at last, unable to resist a moment
longer, I took out my compact and looked into my
mirror.

There was a small pimple on my chin, nothing
much; but at least the fuzz on my lip didn't show.
Probably no one would ever notice it indoors. If I remembered always to keep my back to the light—Sasha,
you worry too much. Though I knew it would vanish,
the pimple gave me a little pang. Through the years I
had learned to accept my imperfections and take them
in my stride. Yet it still took a while for me to get used
to every new one, however minor or temporary. It was
like wearing out a favorite pair of shoes—inevitable
and rectifiable, but sad all the same. And the new pair
would have to be broken in. Time was when I would
have stayed house-bound over a blemish, or at least not
given into it without a fight, but I had long since
learned. Life goes on. Does Queen Elizabeth cancel her

engagements when her skin erupts? Shortly after my own coronation I learned that, like everyone, I too would be growing older and uglier every day. Time was always running out, as Dr. Watson said. Only six years left till thirty. There was nothing to do but make the best of it.

❦

The first imperfection of my skin—the first beginnings of my slow, extended decline—had appeared the summer I turned sixteen on the night of a large family dinner party at our house. I admit I behaved badly.

That night my father's newest employee, a clerk fresh out of Harvard Law whom I was very eager to meet, had been invited to dinner. My summer vacation had already started, and while I was itchy to get into it, I hadn't yet formulated a plan. I knew I couldn't waste another summer hanging around the Baybury Pool where everyone thought I belonged to Joey. If I got some kind of a job or did volunteer work I'd meet new people, but they'd most likely all be girls. My parents had forbidden me to take a job away from home, so my father's hiring Alan Steiger, a young lawyer from out of town, was an omen. It might even be my answer.

We were already finished with cocktails. I had sipped a Mary Jane—lemonade laced ever so lightly with red wine—prepared by my mother. The family, seated around the dining table extended to its largest and covered with the best white damask cloth, had begun patiently watching my father struggle through the carving of some thick roast. Alan Steiger sat across the table not noticing me. In his mid-twenties, he seemed exactly what I wanted—if only he could overlook my being sixteen. I tried to show off for him silently, presenting my prize-winning *shiksa* profile as I watched my father carve.

I wondered if my father had spoken to him about me, and if so, whether he had mentioned my coronation. It seemed unlikely. My father was proud of my looks, but like my mother's, he accepted them as a mysterious gift he had been blessed with. Even if he had been able to forget his work long enough to promote my interests, he would have considered it immodest. His way of helping his women was as a critic.

"Why don't you tell your hairdresser to do your hair off your face, Laura? You look so much better with it off," he would say, brushing my mother's hair off her forehead with his hand, as she presented her newest coiffure. "Sasha, you have such a lovely neck, why don't you keep it clean?" "Your seams are crooked." "Aren't you going to fix your hair?" "Are you sure that dress is appropriate for the opera?"

He cared about us, but otherwise, the details of social and domestic life were a mystery to him which he would attend to only on the express insistence of my mother. If my mother's gentle reprimands didn't bring my brother or me around, my father might be called in to assist. If my mother was still dressing when guests arrived, my father might, with apologies, serve the hors d'oeuvres. It was my mother who planned vacations, purchased gifts (even for my father's clients), selected their friends, and arranged their social life. All domestic jobs—even such traditionally "masculine" jobs as barbecuing, fixing things, and tending bar—were so unpleasant to my father that he pleaded and practiced ineptitude, as now he was doing with the carving. Too aloof to trouble about sharpening the knives, even for company, he hacked away at the roast with more energy than skill. I was seated next to him, disgusted. A dinner party on a damask cloth, launched by a butcher! He had had this lawyer for weeks, and only now had he got around to bringing him home.

He leaned over and dropped the first hacked slice of meat onto my plate. Then, on his way back up, he began to scrutinize my nearby face. With more disapproval than curiosity he suddenly said, "What's that?"

"What's what?"

"That—on your cheek—there." He pointed at me with the carving knife.

I winced away. I knew perfectly well what he was talking about. What he had picked out publicly to confront me with was something that, after causing me no end of anguish that afternoon I had decided was simply a pimple—a round, brown, ephemeral blemish which I had clumsily tried to cover up with dabs of my mother's make-up snitched from the jars lined up on her crowded dressing table. But, a novice in such methods, I had succeeded only in altering its color. It was no disguise for my father's eagle eye, though it might easily have hidden the imperfection from Alan Steiger.

I could think of no response to the accusation but to deny the existence of the thing. "What are you talking about?" I said. "What's the matter with you?" To cover my fury I delivered my reply in a hoarse whisper, but my father would not let go of it. He reached over to me with an index finger on which he had deposited a generous dollop of spittle and started to rub, as though I were some child with chocolate smeared on my face.

"What in the world are you doing?" I screamed. I jumped up from the table and, throwing down my napkin, fled from the room and my father's inexcusable indignity.

"Sensitive Suzy," I heard him murmur behind me as he returned, I suppose, to butchering his meat. "It's a stage she's in. Next thing you know she'll be crying."

Upstairs in my room I boiled over. I was sixteen, no child. Furious, I hated my father for pointing. The presence of the ugly thing on my face seemed to me unquestionably his fault. He might produce another, and another. I had to get away.

Under my mother's fluorescent lamp I wiped off the make-up with cold cream and squeezed and sqeezed, to determine if my blemish were indeed a simple pimple. I was too red in the face to return to the dining room, even for dessert. I decided then and there to run away.

Joey's older brother Richard had said I could get a waitress job at some fancy hotel in Lake Placid, New York, where he had been tennis instructor the year before, just by mentioning his name. Because I was that pretty. "With my pull and your looks . . ." he had said, trying as usual to get at Joey. But why not? Wasn't I "that pretty"? I wouldn't ask my parents' permission.

Before my resolve could dissipate I got a suitcase from the back of my mother's closet, the one I had used for my weekend at Ohio State with Cookie. Into it I stuffed all the nylon underwear I could find, plus a shift, shorts, sandals, a bathing suit, my Emerson's *Essays* ("Trust thyself: every heart vibrates to that iron string . . ."), and my fairy tales. Counting my money, I figured I had enough either to buy a train ticket or uniforms, but not both. Well, I would just have to charge the uniforms at Halle's then, on my way to the station, and reimburse my father for them later, out of tips. I would be sure to keep a strict account. I absolutely refused to need anybody.

I dialed Joey's number to tell the news, then decided against it and hung up. Why tell anyone? Why not burst suddenly, dramatically, onto the scene, missing? Joey, Cookie Margolis, Alan Steiger—none of them were of any help to me now. I needed space, I needed to breathe and stretch. Had I spent those years developing my powers only to be thwarted and humiliated in the suburbs of Cleveland? Instead I dialed the railway station to check the schedule (I would be able to catch a sleeper the following afternoon), then settled down to compose a very righteous, very ironical farewell note to Daddy. If I mailed it from downtown, it would arrive in the following morning's mail just before my mother started upstairs to wake me. Finding me missing from my bed, she would probably reach impulsively for the telephone to notify the police when, suddenly, by her hand she would notice my letter and, ripping it open, read it with vast relief. How glad she would be! Better not to ruin the effect, I decided, by mentioning just yet about charging the uniforms. Since it was only the beginning of June, Halle's wouldn't be sending out the bill for nearly a month.

I woke early to find the train hurtling madly along a mountainside just as though it weren't clinging for dear life to a narrow ledge hewn in the side of a deep gorge. So close were we to grazing the rocks that if I had waggled my fingers out the window they would have been torn off at the knuckles. Out the window on the far side of the coach, deep-blue sky stretched as far down the precipice to the distant crags below as it stretched upward to the clouds. No flat cornfields here, among these colossal heights and depths! This was the world, this New York State. Here was no Ohio!

As the miles between me and Baybury Heights multiplied, I felt certain that if the train veered off the track, I could summon the Blue Fairy to come and carry us—engine, caboose, and all—on up into that endless blue.

I had been secretly grooming myself in my provincial court to confront this wide world for a long time. Taking brazen risks, I had developed my charms and cultivated my powers and finally claimed my rightful crown, all for this moment. "We must go alone," says Emerson; and "I must be myself. I cannot break myself any longer for you, or you." I was ready now to follow Candide across the seas, to climb like Rasselas over the mountain. Hereafter *I* would choose whom to love, how far to go, when to stop. Not this summer would I tremble at the sound of an approaching car, or worry over my reputation. I would neither submit to being dry-humped nor pretend to virginity. "Whoso would be a man must be a nonconformist. He who would gather immortal palms must not be hindered by the name of goodness, but must explore if it be goodness. Nothing is at last sacred but the integrity of your own mind. Absolve you to yourself, and you shall have the suffrage of the world." This summer, with Emerson to back me, love would be beautiful and I would be free.

The train passed Saranac Lake, moving from the mountain into ripe green hills, and approached the Lake Placid station. I had really escaped! As we slowed to a stop, I straddled my suitcase and studied my reflection in the window, frantically trying on pseudonyms. Emerging in a moment from the train's cloud of smoke I could be whoever I decided.

Boys in bright livery patrolled the platform, announcing their hotels. Capturing clients, they strode down the platform, packing as many as five suitcases under their arms while the customers they had managed to snag followed along behind them unencumbered. I, Alicia Alexander, admired how skillfully they worked, though none of them solicited me.

"Anyone here for the Belleview Palace?" I finally heard and answered, "I am," to a uniformed pimply-faced youth a year or two my senior.

He stopped and looked at me skeptically, without a glimmer of recognition. "Richard Ross sent me," I explained. "I've come to be a waitress."

"Oh," he said with an echo of disappointment. He made no move to take my bag. "Get in the back then," he said, steering me with a toss of his head to a waiting station wagon.

I climbed in and waited. If this kid were from Baybury he would have been happy to take my bag. In a few moments he was back empty-handed.

"There's hardly ever anyone on this early train during the week. For me it's a no-tip trip. But a first-class hotel like the Belleview Palace has to send a car down anyway. You're lucky—other hotels, you'd have to take a taxi." He started up the motor and off we drove straight into those luscious hills like nothing in Ohio.

As we rounded a bend and began climbing toward an imposing white structure rising out of the apex of one of the hills, bugles in my head played a fanfare. The Belleview Palace Hotel. Me. On a concrete gash through acres of lawn we drove to the stately entrance.

"Stay here," said the driver, jumping out of the car. "You're not allowed in the lobby." He disappeared into the revolving door, nodding to a portly doorman on his way, then reappeared in another moment.

"Come on, I'll take you back to Fritz," he said.

The driveway's flowered border turned to shrub as we turned onto a dirt road and headed for a low building in disrepair protruding from the elegant hotel like a tumor.

"This is the way you go in," said my driver pulling up beside the screen-door entrance to let me out. Fly-infested garbage cans surrounded the door. Just ask around for Fritz," he yelled, already driving off. "He's the maitre dee."

I looked around. Flies were everywhere and the garbage stank. I tried to peek through the screen but couldn't see in for the sun behind me. I picked up my suitcase and opened the door.

"Close that door! You can't let flies in a first-class kitchen!" shouted an old man in a chef's hat, peeling carrots.

This first-class kitchen looked as though it deserved flies. It was dark and dilapidated with here and there a stainless steel fixture to contrast with the wood of the rest. It was much hotter inside than out. Pots simmered and boiled on iron stoves; ovens baked and roasted; and in almost every corner of the room, someone stood shouting at someone.

"Fritz?" I inquired of the old man.

At the mention of Fritz several other people in chef's hats looked up at me warily from their peeling and pounding. The cooks were all men, but their looks didn't soften when they saw me.

"Fritz!" replied the old man. "Fritz doesn't come in the kitchen! Fritz stays in the dining room!" He indicated two giant swinging doors marked IN and OUT at the opposite end of the room. "Try there. And don't go out the IN door!"

I moved as quickly as I could across the hostile

room and pushed open the OUT door with my suitcase.
It was like going through the looking glass. On the flip
side of the door (miraculously changed from an OUT to
an IN), the sinister darkness of the kitchen gave way to
a shower of sunlight. Perhaps, I thought, on this side,
with the light to help, I would be better appreciated.

A sea of tables, laid with spotless white linen and
sparkling stemware, glistened before me. The empty
room stretched ahead to glass doors made up of little
leaded panes, dressed on the inside with crisp curtains
and on the outside with lilacs. How lovely it would be,
I thought, to dine here.

Two uniformed waitresses stood whispering together.
"Can you tell me where I can find Fritz?" I asked
them. We looked each other over, reserving judgment.

"He's there at his desk," whispered the prettier of
the two. "But he's doing the menu. You'd better wait."
As I turned I imagined their eyes beginning at my heels
and moving on up.

A small trim man in a tuxedo sat writing at a tiny
desk next to the dining room entrance. Fiftyish and
immaculate, as elegant as the tableware, he wore a
pince-nez on his nose and a golden corkscrew around
his neck.

"Fritz?" I asked.

"*Mister* Fritz," he said through clenched teeth without looking up. He went on writing. Through the
archway beside him I saw the Belleview Palace lobby
extravaganza, and again I thought I heard the bugles
blare.

At last Mister Fritz put down his pen, squinted his
pince-nez off his nose, and looked up at me. "Well?" he
said icily.

I started right in with enthusiasm. "I'm Alicia
Alexander. Richard Ross sent me. I've come to be a

waitress. The person who drove me over from the station said—"

Fritz closed his eyes and put the fingertips of one hand to his forehead. "*Who*," he cut in, pained, "is this . . .'Richard Ross'?" He managed to make the name sound like a dirty word.

"He was the tennis instructor last year," I began.

"*Tennis* instructor!" he said with contempt, and continued meditation. "Have you waited on tables before?"

I searched desperately for some story to enable me to answer *yes*. "No," I confessed.

He considered. "How old are you?"

This time I was prepared to lie. "Eighteen."

"Well, I'll try you out for a week, but don't expect to stay. I run a first-class continental dining room. Serving is more than simply hard work; it's an art. You'll have to learn to handle a heavy tray. I just lost one of my girls this week—otherwise I wouldn't bother to train you now. You're very lucky. You'll start at a back station; then I'll see."

"Thank you," I murmured, half terrifed, half ecstatic.

"You get seven dollars a week plus tips. And room and board. All right?" he snapped.

I nodded.

"Do your work and you'll learn I take good care of my girls. Angie!" he called to the prettier waitress. "Take this new girl here to the dorm and give her a rundown of the rules. Her name's—what did you say your name was?" he asked turning to me.

"Alicia Alexander," I repeated. I liked the name; I was beginning to feel at home in it.

"Her name's Alice," Fritz shouted, as though the measure of my worth were in syllables and he could

diminish me by two. Then, dismissing me coldly by
picking up his pen, he snapped his cuffs up into his
jacket sleeves with a flick of each wrist, placed his
lenses on his nose, and went back into his menu.

There were eleven waitresses in the dining room, girls
from all over, and I was at least as pretty as any of
them. The trouble was, none of them seemed aware of
it. Except for sprightly Angie, who after showing me
the ropes went on to teach me the angles, no one eyed
me oddly in the dormitory or tried to talk to me at
mealtime. Like the men in the kitchen that first day,
looking me over and passing me by, everyone went
about her business as though I were no threat at all.
After working through three exhausting meals a day—
each time setting up, serving, clearing off, and setting
up again—I would return to my Spartan room to read
my Emerson, alone. Only the fat cello player in Martin
Mercer's quintet, an artist of sorts, seemed to see in me
anything special. Hundreds of miles from home and
many hours from sympathy, here I was totally unap-
preciated. It was unsettling. I began to wonder if the
standards I had come to rely upon might not be simply
an Ohio quirk. Were the natural arches of my eyebrows
and the length of my lashes worth nothing in the
Adirondacks? And then it struck me that what my
father in his thoughtlessness had put his finger on
(which had still not disappeared) might be something
more than a pimple. Perhaps it was a hive, or a boil, or
a mole, or a pock. There was no decent mirror in the
dormitory, no adequate light to tell me if I was
blotching. Perspiring in my nylon uniforms, maybe I
smelled or was allergic. Hives at home could be accepted as a temporary aberration, but here no one would
know what I was *supposed* to look like. No one here

knew who, under normal conditions, I was. In fact—
and the possibility suddenly, devastatingly, loomed like
truth—in fact, if no one here found me beautiful, *then
perhaps I was not!* After all, how can skin glow
through a sunburn? Of what use is a gentile nose
among gentiles?

My service got better as the days passed—good
enough for Fritz to enlarge my station—but my state of
mind grew worse. I went from depressed to resigned.
In the Sky Lounge, where I served drinks on Saturday
night, the couples dancing to the music of Martin
Mercer and his Martinets danced differently from the
way we danced in Cleveland. Here in the Adirondacks
they did no double step at all (which I had studied to
perfection). While side-parted hair was *de rigueur* in
Baybury Heights, the ladies of the Belleview Palace
wore theirs in upsweeps, and some of the prettiest
waitresses had bangs. It made me insecure. In the
dining room I went unrecognized. The Bus Stop Game
didn't work on my gentlemen clients, who, catching me
at it while they sipped their soup, were likelier to spill
than respond. However stylishly I balanced my tray in
the air striding to my station, I earned tips no larger
than the next girl's. The customers complained if I
made mistakes, and Fritz threatened to fire me every
other day. In the kitchen Bo, the dishwasher, made me
scrape all my dishes; Jerry Jones, the vegetable chef,
allowed me no substitutes; Slim Hawley, the short-or-
der chef, wouldn't understand my orders; the head
chef, Tony Rosetti, yelled at me for carelessness and
for letting in the flies; and the meat chef, Jan Pulaski,
threatened me several times with a butcher knife. In
"The Zoo," where all the help, excluding Fritz, ate
together and carried on the insane battles between
kitchen, dining room, and bell service, my allegiance

was so seldom solicited that after a few days I began carrying a book in with me so Icould pretend I didn't care. At home I had sometimes worried about being loved for my nose instead of for myself; here the danger was not being loved at all. Looking down at the printed page while I ate stew or hamburger or hash, I knew my eyelashes were not one bit of use to me.

By my third week away from home I decided I would rather be a shark in the Baybury Bay than whitebait in Lake Placid. It might take longer for me to get to the ocean from Ohio, but once out there I had a better chance of surviving. Sneaking into the forbidden lobby late that night I got stationery and stamps with which to write to Joey. If beauty is in the eye of the beholder, I needed Joey to be focusing on me.

Dear Joey,

Surprise! First, don't tell *anyone* where I am except your brother since I used his name to get my job. All my parents know for sure is that I'm somewhere in New York. They probably also know by now that I'm a waitress (or else a maid or a nurse) since I charged a couple of uniforms to their Halle's account before I left and they've probably received the bill already.

You are most likely wondering why I left so suddenly. Well, as you may remember, the situation at home was getting intolerable, and the day I left it suddenly got worse. My father doesn't seem to realize that I'm not a baby any more and I can take care of myself! Anyway, that's the main reason I left, but also, I needed to be alone for a while to think things out —to find out what I really want and who I really am. I had to know for sure if I could manage by myself without *anyone*, not even you Joey.

I've pretty nearly found out. I know this much, I've got to be free! And that's why, though it may seem strange to you, I'll probably be coming back before fall. I want to find out what I have to do about college, because after college I really want to go to law school. I've decided never to marry.

Did I hurt you by leaving without saying goodbye? If so, I'm sorry. I knew you'd understand eventually. I just had to go without *anyone's* permission, not even yours. As Emerson says in an unbelievable essay called "Self-Reliance," "I must be myself. I cannot break myself any longer for you or you." Nothing personal, Joey. It's just that I wouldn't even know what self I was if there were anyone at all I *had* to say goodbye to.

What did everyone say when I turned up missing? It must have been funny! I wish I could have heard them!

As for this hotel—the work is exhausting but the mountains are unbelievably beautiful and I go for a long swim every afternoon. The people are generally nice. There's a cellist in the band who's giving me lessons. But the most interesting people are some of my customers. You wouldn't *believe* some of the stories, but you'll have to wait till I get home in September to hear them. (You'd love to see me marching around the dining room with a twenty pound tray balanced on one hand!)

There are a lot of pretty waitresses here, but they're all quite a bit older than me. One of them, named Angie, and I have a lot in common, even though she may be Catholic.

Say hello to everyone for me and remember what they say. Please call up my mother to tell her I'm all right. (Actually, I have one of my terrible sunburns and I'm peeling for the second time, but don't tell her *that*.)

You can write to me care of the kitchen at the above address, and then burn this letter.

Miss me and Love<br>
*Sasha*

X X X X

I wrote S.W.A.K. across the envelope and pressed the stamp on upside down. But however much I needed Joey, I would *not* come out and write "I love you."

One night when we were all lined up at the meat counter shouting in our orders for roast beef *au jus* before dashing off to serve the soup, Jan Pulaski leaned over the stainless steel counter and with an obscene grin on his beefy face whispered to me, "I'd like to fuck you, baby!"

I was beside myself. On the one hand, the remark terrified me: I had never heard that word used as a proper verb before. On the other hand, upon analysis, it was possibly flattering.

Jan Pulaski was the terror of the kitchen. I found him repulsive, though he was the only youngish chef on the staff. He was mean and enormous like a rhinoceros. Everyone in the kitchen teased the waitresses, but only Jan tormented them. "Say please," he would say before giving out the meat, and when the "please" came, he would brandish his carving knife and shout, "I thought I told you to say *please!*" I could not decide whether Jan Pulaski's attentions were a little better than no one's, or no one's were a little better than Jan's.

I moved quickly on to the vegetable table. Blushing and shaken, I ladled out of the two giant soup containers three small bowls of clear and two of thick. Into each I dropped the appropriate tablespoon of vegetables and barley, of beef bits, rice, or split peas. (Even in a first-class hotel, all soups, when strained, boil down to two: thick and thin. Only the menu is a work of art.) Nervous still, I pushed out the OUT door to deliver my soup, then back in IN with my empty tray, straight to the meat to wait.

"Number three, pick up, two rare one medium," shouted Jan Pulaski and slid the plates down along the stainless steel counter. I was not number three; I was number seven. But if the meat chef would like to f— me, wouldn't my number be coming up soon?

All the beefs were roasted very rare, or, as we called it, "blue." A "rare" order got washed in one spoonful of *jus,* a "medium" in two, a "well done" in three or four, and an "end cut" got run under the broiler. I looked on as Jan spooned *jus,* called out the orders, sharpened his knife, and carved again. No number seven.

As I waited, I watched him with a fascinated horror. His apron hung from under his flabby beer belly (which he sometimes punched proudly, bragging "muscle! muscle!"), and a naked woman danced on his hairy forearm every time he slapped down a slice of meat. He had acquired her in the navy, where, as he told everyone, he had learned to cook and make love. A profusion of tiny black curls crawled down the back of his neck and crept up his chest out of his shirt. He sweated over the roast beef.

At last, when some of the girls were already on their way back IN to put in their second and third orders, he placed my plate of beef on the stainless steel counter without releasing it and said, "meet me after work tonight."

"I can't," I said, reaching for the plate.

"Suit yourself." He took back my beef and began spooning *jus* over it.

"Hey, don't! I need it rare!" I cried.

"Oh do you?" he asked, spooning away. "Then you better meet me." His eyes narrowed craftily.

I couldn't believe he would really blackmail me. Trying to sound my sweetest, I said, "I'd really love to,

Jan, but I can't. I have another date." I batted my eyes the tiniest bit, hoping to assuage his anger.

"Tomorrow then." He inched the plate toward me temptingly.

"I have a date tomorrow too. Look Jan," I said, annoyed enough to pull my leveling line on him, "I'm afraid I really can't go out with you."

"No tickee no washee." His eyes turned mean, and he withdrew my plate for good. "Number ten, pick up two well. Goddammit! Where the fuck is number ten?"

On the nights roast beef was on the menu, almost no one ordered anything else. My customers had all long since finished their soup and were waiting impatiently for their main courses when I cornered Angie.

"Better say yes," said Angie when I told her what was going on.

"But I'm afraid of him," I said, close to tears.

"You've got to be tough to be a waitress. He's not as bad as he sounds. I know the girl he picked on last summer. If you don't go out with him now you might as well quit."

"Maybe I should tell Fritz. He wouldn't let this happen to his first-class dining room."

"Don't kid yourself, honey. If this was really a first-class place we wouldn't even be working here. In a first-rate hotel they've got waiters, not us; the only females they hire are the chambermaids. You won't get a better job than this one. You better go with him." And off she went with her salads.

I returned to the meat counter. "Well?" said Jan smiling over at me.

"Day after tomorrow. Now give me my beef!" I hated him.

"Number seven, pick up two rare and a blue," he said smiling.

Luckily it was a slow night in the dining room. At my five-table station of three "deuces" and two "squares," which took fourteen diners at a time on a Saturday night, only five customers had shown up so far for dinner. Fritz, hissing "Hurry up!" through his clenched teeth when he saw my customers' places empty, had told me to expect a party of four transients later on. At the moment, however, only two deuces and a single were waiting for their roast beef.

I expected the deuces to be perturbed, but not the single, Mr. Winograd. He was a tiny, barely audible millionaire in his sixties, constantly oppressed by the entourage of doctors and nurses with whom he traveled. The day I arrived he had taken me into his confidence because, on a strict diet excluding fat, salt, and sugar, he needed my collaboration to cheat. I loved him for it. He took all the meals he could alone, out of sight of his nurses, except for Saturday night dinners and Sunday brunches when he would entertain friends from New York City. They were all Jewish refugees from Amsterdam like him; he would maintain our intimacy by talking to me in English and to them in Dutch or German. Though regular customers tipped by the week, Mr. Winograd always left a few extra dollars on the table for me on a Saturday night as well. When he ate alone he frequently ordered extra food for me to hide away under a napkin to eat in secret after the dining room closed. In exchange for a shrimp cocktail, or an eclair he'd order with his fruit compote, I'd help him to a teaspoon of sugar in his Sanka, or a side of hollandaise, or a bowl of vichyssoise.

"You won't tell on me now, will you?" he'd ask, twinkling through his accent.

"I won't tell on you if you don't tell on me," I would twinkle back.

Angie and I had stealing food down to an art. Since the staff ate only leftovers at The Zoo amid all that culinary opulence, we figured whatever we could steal was coming to us. To keep us supplied I had my angel, Mr. Winograd. Angie instead had daring. At 8:25, just before the kitchen officially accepted its last order, Angie would call in a steak (rare), or pick up a few extra desserts to hide at her station. While the customers were finishing up we'd slip the evening's stash under the largest empty table in our stations. There it would wait until, after helping each other clear away and set up our stations for the morning meal, we would join the food under the table. Whatever we managed to take we shared fifty-fifty, except for leftover wine, which only Angie liked. (She never tired of admiring Mr. Winograd's taste.) While the other girls were still cleaning up, Angie and I would wolf down shrimps, steak, and baba au rhum, safely concealed from Fritz's roving eye by the tablecloth. We spoke to each other only with our eyes and eyebrows, suppressing all our giggles as, above us, Fritz shamed the slower girls by praising us. When we were certain that everyone had gone home for the night, we'd hide our dirty dishes at our stations and sneak out through the French doors.

The story around the hotel had it that Mr. Winograd's wife and children had been slaughtered before his eyes by the Nazis, after which he had fled to America with his diamonds, Old Masters, and cash. Now he wallowed in misery among his riches in some Westchester mansion, except in winter when he went to Florida and in summer when he came to the mountains. Hounded by fortune hunters and medics, he sought respite at my station.

That the story was seriously flawed seemed to me

obvious; nevertheless I accepted it at mealtime. For me, sorrow enhanced Mr. Winograd, and I fancied I reminded him of some dead beloved daughter. Out of mischief and love I played the accomplice, sneaking him out of the dining room after breakfast so that he might make it out to the golf links undetected, or swearing to his nurse that two eggs Benedict had really been one four-minute-boiled. Though his was invariably my best tip, I loved him for himself.

"Sorry the roast beef took so long tonight, Mr. Winograd. I had a little trouble with one of the chefs," I apologized.

"It's okay," he said frowning. He tucked his napkin back under his collar and added, "but please I hope you don't let this happen again."

It was the first time he had shown displeasure, and I took it badly. I had come to the mountains to test my powers, thinking I could name the game and pick my partner, and maybe even set the stakes. But if Mr. Winograd or Fritz or the kitchen staff didn't want me here, I wouldn't even get to play. It was all very fine for Emerson to insist that "nothing can bring you peace but the triumph of principles"; but I could clearly see that if I wanted to keep my job I would really have to go out with Jan Pulaski.

Two nights later right on schedule I was sitting nervously beside Jan in his two-tone blue hard-top convertible careening down a mountain toward Mirror Lake. How would I ever get out of this?

The instant Jan had appeared behind The Zoo with his muscular neck confined in finery, a silk handkerchief protruding from his jacket pocket, and his untamable curls slicked down, I saw the whole scenario.

Though the wolf had donned sheep's clothing, he didn't fool me for an instant. He simply intended to have me as a last course instead of as a first.

"Cigarette?" said Jan. He pushed in the car lighter and snapped open a cigarette case.

"Thank you," I accepted. "Where are we going?"

"Oh, a little spot I know."

I could tell by the pride in his voice that the "little spot" was either going to be very expensive or very romantic or perhaps a place where Jan knew the head waiter. I saw the whole evening stretching before me like one of Fritz's five-course dinners, with me the *pièce de résistance*. First the little spot where I would be expected to drink and be impressed; then somewhere for a bite to eat; then a feeler to see if I was ready yet, and if not (and I wouldn't be!), then a nightcap at another little spot; and finally, no matter what I'd say, off to park the car at some natural wonder to admire the view and devour me. There wasn't a thing I could do to prevent it, for, having got himself up in this necktie and pomade, Jan was far too uncomfortable and ridiculous to risk not having his way. He would be spending too much and trying too hard to be willing to go away hungry.

"Where you from, Alice? How did you wind up at the Belleview Palace?" He was trying to match his conversation to his getup, pretending our exchange in the kitchen had never taken place.

"I'm from Cleveland. Richard Ross told me about the job. He was the tennis instructor here last year."

"Richard Ross. Yeah, college boy," said Jan nodding contemplatively. He ran a finger around the inside of his awkward collar and stepped on the gas.

I read his meaning. Already I was being wronged.

Just because I would be going to college the following year while Jan would never, he was going to think me a snob for turning him down. As one had thought me cold, and another had thought me stuck-up, and another had thought me chicken. It was so unfair. It was as impossible to refuse as it was to submit without being maligned; damned if you do and damned if you don't. "If there's one kind of girl I really can't stand," Cookie had thrown at me after making such sweet love to my lips, "it's a C.T. Cock Teaser!" and devastated, I had lain back and opened my legs for him. Maybe, I thought, I ought to open them for Jan too, to prove my devotion to democracy. But when I looked over and saw the smug grin on his beefy face, all my hate came rushing back. What did I care what he thought of me? Snob or no, I'd refuse. *I cannot break myself any longer for you, or you.*

"How old are you, Alice?"

"Eighteen."

He looked at me carefully. "Eighteen. You're a sweet kid." It was the same phrase Cookie had used to disarm me.

The sweet kid leaned back captive and regarded the mountain.

SCENE 1:
*The Blue Room of the Grand Adirondack.*

"Well! Jan Pulaski! Whatta ya say?"

"How's it goin', Mike? You're looking great. Got something up front near the floor for us?"

"It's pretty tight tonight, but for you, Jan, I've always got something. There'll just be a little wait. Why dontcha order at the bar while I set you up? The show doesn't start for another twenty minutes. (He looks at me.) You're looking great, Jan, really great."

Jan steers me by the elbow to the darkened bar where the musicians are tanking up for the next show. He orders our drinks and then squeezes my elbow and smiles down at me. With someone else I'd drink rye and ginger, but with Jan I ask for a Mary Jane. It's a hard choice; hating the taste of rye I can nurse one a long time, while Mary Janes tend to slip down easily; but in absolute terms, Mary Janes are less potent. Hoping I will never again have to screw out of charity or prudence, I choose to exercise self-control with Mary Janes. With Cookie, rye had been my undoing.

The floor show starts. Ethnic comedians make ethnic jokes. A sad lady, bleached and buxom, sings badly songs of love and joy. Jan sits back in his chair expansively, proud to have got us our table. He is attentive to the show except when he fingers the card that states the cover charge or when he lights a cigar. Bored but polite, I trace patterns on the table in melted ice with a swizzle stick. When the show is over Jan reaches across the table and squeezes my hand. I smile a minimal smile.

"Let's dance."

We dance.

"I'm afraid we don't dance this way in Cleveland," I say, overcome by embarrassment. "Let's sit down, okay?"

We go. Jan tips the waiter ostentatiously, lights a cigar for the road, and on the way out slaps the captain on the back. "Thanks, buddy," he says in a low growl, and then to me, "Jesus I'm hungry! How about something to eat?"

## SCENE 2:
### The Snack Shop of the
### View Haven Swiss Chalet.

I gobble a jumbo shrimp cocktail. When I finish the shrimps I start on the lettuce, dipping it into the cocktail sauce. Jan, sitting across from me in the booth, eats an openface steak sandwich and french fries, the whole drenched in catsup. He tears huge bites of steak and bread with his knife and fork, then pitches them into his mouth left-handed, using his palate as a backboard. I watch in amazement.

"Want another shrimp cocktail?" Whenever he addresses me his eyes narrow and his thick face grins a little; I wonder if it is a tic.

"No thanks." I sip at my coffee. "How's the steak?"

"Okay. A little tough. This hotel ain't what it used to be." He makes a set shot and masticates. "How'd you like the Adirondack floor show?" he says with a mouthful.

"Nice."

Now comes THE FEELER:

"I think it's too bad to spend a night watching a show inside when there's such a great show going on outside. I mean like Ausable Chasm or Mirror Lake or even just the Milky Way. Natural beauty like that is better than any entertainers up from New York City, don't you think? Ever seen the face on Whiteface Mountain?"

"Mmmmm hmmmmm." I hum it so cynically that Jan, taken aback, decides to retain SCENE 3 and deftly sets the stage, saying:

"I know a place on the road to Whiteface Mountain where you can look out and practically see up the old man's nostrils. C'mon, I'll show you. You've been a good girl so I'll take you up there for a nightcap. Let's get out of this joint." He pays the check, takes a toothpick, and starts picking and sucking at his teeth.

"I've had so much to eat and drink already, Jan, I'd rather just go home now if you don't mind. I've got a headache too."

"C'mon. A drink'll do you good. It'll clear your head. Brandy and soda for a headache. You listen to your old Uncle Jan." As his eyes narrow ever so slightly I see behind them the faint flicker of carving knives.

SCENE 3:
*The White Face Tavern.*

"There now. Isn't that better?"
"I'm afraid it's worse. I really want to go home now Jan. Please."

SCENE 4:
*The top of Whiteface Mountain (4,870 feet),
renowned for its view.*

Since it is night time, it's almost impossible to admire the view; instead we start admiring stars. I wish quickly on the first one, but I know it won't work. The headache hasn't worked. Sulking hasn't worked. Not even a miracle is going to get me home free from a twenty-dollar date, even (especially) one I never wanted. If a man can't collect on his investments he must admit to being a fool. The only question is: How cheaply can I buy out? What will I have to pay him to let me go?

I identify the Big Dipper, the Little Dipper, the Five Sisters, Cassiopeia, and the North Star, hoping my erudition about the night sky will preclude getting romantic.

"You mean that one, *there?*" says Jan, pointing at the North Star from around my far shoulder. Once over, he keeps his arm around me. I move close to my door, but the arm moves after me and then the man. I try to remember some other constellations, but they have all deserted me.

I ask for a cigarette. After it is presented and lit, back comes the arm. I try the radio. That too he manages to use against me. "You are too beauuuuu-tiful for one man alone," he croons and exerting pressure on my captive right shoulder attempts to probe me with an opening kiss.

Disgusting! "You *are* too beautiful," he moons, coming up for breath (true or not, it doesn't matter), then presses his thick lips down on me for another. Our teeth touch.

Enough. I start out straightforwardly, pushing against his chest with my hands to let him know how I feel and to give him the opportunity to withdraw nicely. It's like pushing a mountain: he doesn't budge. I pull my head back at the neck. (To pull back lower down, from the shoulders or back, would permit him almost effortlessly to flatten and mount me.) He presses in after.

He lets the fingers of his right hand slowly down onto my breast, like a date at the movies, at the same time that he begins blowing into my ear. After taking the precaution of crossing my legs I reach up toward my breast and grab his fingers. But he must think I simply want to hold hands, for instead of pitching the

battle over the breast, he slips his other hand up my
skirt, carried away, I guess, by his vision of his
irresistible charms. When he finds the passage blocked,
he tries to open it by stroking my thigh, inching higher
and higher. My earlobe receives a vicious nip ("baby,
baby!"). Abandoning my breast to his right-hand flank,
I bring in my remaining limbs to assist my legs.

He's not a rhinoceros but a squid! Somehow he has
got both my hands, which had been pulling at his
probing arm, off the field, and with one of his extra
limbs has pushed me down prone on the car seat.
Oh-oh. With a single hard thrust of his knee he can
now break my defenses, wedge my thighs open, and
make for the opening.

"Stop!" I cry.

"Oh baby, baby!" he replies, sucking on my ear and
trying to slip his fingers inside my underpants. He
thinks that a finger inside me will make me desire him;
they all read the same bad books.

Assessing my position I see that this man doesn't
care in the least that I reject him. He won't hear of it. I
must submit or outwit him; he cares only for cunt.
How discouraging to have come these three hundred
miles only to wind up struggling in yet another parked
car. In flat Ohio they drive you fifteen miles out into
the country; in the Adirondacks they take you up four
thousand feet. In either case, once they turn off their
motors and the lights it is very hard for you to get back
home. "Scorn appearances," says old Emerson, and
here I am, hundreds of miles from my reputation just
dying to scorn appearances, yet as terrified of this meat
chef as of anyone in Baybury Heights. What is the
difference? Having come this great distance to be
myself and make love freely, must I still try all the old

tricks to avoid being raped? What is going on? If Candide had been born a girl, would he too in this best of worlds have wound up being ravished on a mountaintop?

Now I know time's up. No matter how tightly I squeeze my legs, if I don't get Jan out of there *right now* I haven't a chance. "Power ceases in the instant of repose," says Emerson. I can't waste another instant using the wrong tactics. Anger is out. If I scream or slap this man he'll slap me back and unzip. Pleas and flattery are useless too. He has long since faced his needs and dismissed mine with a simple *there's only one way to handle a woman—take her!* No, I have only one resource with which to move him from his investment; only one trick in my arsenal stands a chance of working. If he isn't to be paid off in sex for his trouble and expense he will have to be paid off in tears. It works on fathers, doctors, and teachers; maybe it will work on Jan Pulaski, making him, too, feel powerful and benevolent. If it doesn't, I might as well save my dress and cooperate: I am vanquished anyway.

I make myself cry, sobbing and sniffling.

"What's the matter?"

"Nothing (sob). May I have your handkerchief?"

Awkwardly he gets his silk hanky out of his pocket with his free hand and gives it to me. "Here." More awkwardly still, from under him, I dab at my eyes.

"Thanks."

"What's the matter?"

I bawl away, no longer faking. "It's just that— ohhhhh, I can't tell you. Ohhhhh." My face will be blotching up from all the tears.

"Hey, now. What is it, kid?" He sits up. "Does something hurt you?"

"I don't know. I'm so embarrassed. You see, I'm not what you think I am. I'm a . . . a virgin." He removes his hand from under my skirt and I go to town. "I've never been touched. Alice isn't my real name. And I'm not eighteen either. I'm not even seventeen yet. I lied to you, about everything. Oh, take me home. Ohhhhh."

"Okay, okay."

It is working. I press on. "Take me home Jan. Please. You've just gotta take me home right now. Ohhhhhhh."

"Okay, kid, okay, I'll take you home. We're going right back to the Belleview Palace. Just try to stop crying a little, will ya?" He turns on the motor. "Just leave everything to your old Uncle Jan."

"My father's a judge," I throw in to scare him. "He'll be so mad!"

All the way down the mountain I cried real tears. The virginity I defended was imaginary, but the innocence I mourned was not. I knew I might as well go back home.

I finished out the month of July at the hotel so Fritz could find a replacement for me and I could announce my departure and collect my tips. Then, once again packing up my Emerson, I left the mountains for good.

Back in Cleveland everyone treated me as though I were daring, accomplished, and beautiful: Queen of the Bunny Hop returning home in triumphal splendor. I alone knew I had really come back in defeat.

I spent August in retreat, listening to Beethoven and studying the college catalogues, adjusting myself to my reduced circumstances while pretending to everyone that I had had an enviable and expanding experience. I so beguiled Alan Steiger with stories of my mountain adventures, and I so beguiled Angie through the mails with stories of my homecoming, that I actually began to believe in them. When I finished peeling completely and my skin began to glow again, I felt as though it had never stopped. My parents were as sweet and soft as applesauce. And the ugly blemish I had worried over in June had by September become a tiny brown mole, a permanent "beauty mark," which eventually I came to accept, like something I had been born with.

Every year until he died Mr. Winograd sent me an engraved New Year's card at Christmas time accompanied by a short note which I always answered at length. He was my one remaining channel to the ocean. He made me very happy until, after I moved to New York four years later, he invited me to visit him in Westchester and I accepted.

His butler picked me up at the station and delivered me to the Winograd mansion. I was shocked to see how wizened the old man had become. He had no voice left at all, and he stopped to rest every few steps. We dined alone under a magnificent crystal chandelier, laughing over old times. A mad Van Gogh watched us from the wall as we ate our elegant meal. For dessert we had a tall *Baum Kuchen* drenched in brandy, and throughout dinner we whispered little jokes about the service of the butler and the maid. After coffee, Mr. Winograd took me on a short tour of his priceless collection. Whenever he stopped to rest, I, towering over him, stopped too. When we returned to the living room, in a little burst of energy, sparkling and twinkling, Mr. Winograd presented me with a small eighteenth-century sepia drawing of a nude in a garden. He sat down—the better to watch my reaction, I thought. As I gaped in amazement, stuttering my thanks, he pulled me onto his lap.

Now, looking back, I'm not surprised. Why else than for sex would a failing millionaire refugee be interested in a teenaged waitress? But at the time sex never entered my mind. I loved the old man and had thought he loved me a little too. I extricated myself as quickly as possible from his wispy embrace, and, begging to be taken to the station, left his drawing discreetly behind me.

One morning about a year later, as I was pouring out the breakfast coffee for my new husband, Frank came across Mr. Winograd's obituary in the *New York Times.*

"Say, Sasha, what was the name of your millionaire? Winograd? He just died, and listen to this."

It turned out that the story that had circulated about him at the Belleview Palace was all true—Nazis, diamonds, everything. His will divided his fortune among several nephews and a faithful nurse, and gave his paintings to the Metropolitan. I was not mentioned.

"I'd have thought from the way you talked about him that he'd have left you at least one painting," teased Frank in that smug way of his I could never answer. "You must have loved him more than he loved you," he twitted.

From the *Times*'s list of his maladies, it seemed that Mr. Winograd had died of everything. He was sixty-seven years old, and I had just turned twenty.

# FOUR

Beneath the Pincio a pale mannequin bends
Under the leaden burden of green eyelids,
Proposes poses patiently and spends
Her last lire on a pack of gum.
Atop the dum-dee-dum Janiculum—

It was no use. I had been working on the poem for
three mornings and I had only got through the easiest
of Rome's hills. Even if I managed to do the Janiculum
today, there would still be the Palatine, the Capitoline,
the Esquiline, the Quirinal, the Viminal—impossible.
An opening paragraph of a short story, one stanza of
one poem, and the setting for a play. Not enough. If

only I knew how they were supposed to end; if only I knew what I wanted to say. I was a failure.

I snapped closed my notebook and looked across the piazza at the vivacious fountain. Young men in lean trousers and pointed shoes sat on the rim smoking while children played in the street. At least an hour more before I could begin picking a trattoria for lunch; too late to do a museum. Another morning shot trying to write, trying to be somebody. I might as well have gone to Pompeii with Frank's Academy friends the Ericksons or stayed in Spain. The days were passing me by and I was closer to broke than to a solution. As I washed down my pink pill with my espresso, I wondered if I should see another doctor. Was the fuzz on my face spreading? I felt it with my finger. *Insufficient ovulation*—when would my treacherous body stop playing tricks on me?

I finished my espresso, left a tip on the table, and put out my cigarette before crossing the piazza to the shady side. In Italy nice women don't smoke in the street. In Spain I had ignored the customs, laughing when Manolo warned me I could be arrested for kissing in the street. But I had had a man to protect me then; now I was no longer up to it. My nerves were in such a state that I needed all my energy just to survive the ordinary indignities of walking alone; I wasn't going to ask for trouble over a lousy cigarette. When in Rome ... But of course it wasn't just Rome; it was everywhere. Everywhere, harassed by day, afraid by night. Why? Eyes to the ground, I passed the young men smoking on the fountain's rim and followed the ancient paving stones back to my hotel, self-conscious of every step. I stuck out all over.

I knew it was supposed to be flattering to be hissed at, but it was not. At best—when I felt good about myself—it was annoying, like the aggressive solicitations of derelicts; there was no way to ignore it and every response was wrong. At worst—when I felt bad about myself, which was most of the time these days—it was a humiliating assault. A woman needed an excuse for walking the streets alone. Like blacks in white neighborhoods back home, we had to walk with our eyes to the ground. In fact, the only sure way to walk the streets unharassed was to be with a man.

The obvious excuses—a guidebook, a novel—seldom worked. They didn't even enable one to sit reading in the park. "Good book?" a man would ask, sitting down beside me on the bench in New York or Rome, and I would either have to insult him, jolly him, or get up and move on. Easier not to sit in the park. Once, back in New York, in the subway station late at night a drunk had started pawing a woman down the platform. I went to find a transit cop. When I returned with one, the drunk had disappeared, and the cop graced us with his wisdom instead. "You're lucky this time, girls, but it should be a lesson," he said. "You girls should know better than to wander around alone at two A.M. You should be home."

It was always the same story, in subways or suburbs. From my beginnings in Baybury Heights, a nice neighborhood where we moved because it was "safe," it was always the girl who was kept in the house after school if a boy molested her, never the boy. Ostensibly she was kept in for protection, but how was it different from punishment if she couldn't even play on the street? Since boys would be boys, they might be scolded, but no one ever kept them indoors; they could take care of themselves. No one ever said "girls will be girls"; for girls were expected to be ladies. Every Baybury girl was early taught her place through the ritual rape called "pantsing." My own occurred one muddy March day in the third grade.

My best friend Jackie was staying after school to practice on the bars that day, so I stayed too. We were practicing a new trick: over-and-over-two-legged. It was a hard trick, but I mastered it. On the bars practicing was what counted; lithe and limber, I practiced and was good. Over and over we went, skirts and hair flying down and then up, the skin behind our knees smarting from the friction with the steel, until the pain finally forced us to stop. We gathered up our trading cards and were just heading through the Victory Gardens for the road when Jackie remembered she wasn't going home after all, she was going to wait for her mother at her cousin's house down the street from school.

My stomach flopped over as though I were still on the bars. Without Jackie, I would have to walk unprotected past all the vacant lots on Auburn Hill. I looked back anxiously for someone else to walk with, but there wasn't a soul in the playground.

Jackie and I started walking slowly down Cranberry Road. It was still wet enough from the previous night's rain for a few worms to remain on the sidewalk, and we walked slowly to avoid them. I hated the sidewalk worms. Besides, the skin behind our knees smarted if we went quickly. But no matter how slowly we walked, I knew the moment was coming when we would have to separate.

Finally we reached Jackie's cousin's house. With no visible regrets, Jackie turned into the drive, kicked at the gravel, and said goodbye.

"See you tomorrow," I managed to answer, as though it were any other day. And then, proceeding by myself to the end of the block where I turned reluctantly into Auburn, I began my lone descent of the hill.

Dawdling as I walked, I pretended nothing could happen. What was there to be afraid of? Didn't I know all the boys in my class? Not even they, I told myself, would want to hide in the weeds among worms. When I saw the grasses moving on the flat of the hill just before the descent, I began to think the whole walk home was a dream, that the sidewalk worms were really snakes moving the grasses. *Please get me home,* I begged of nobody I knew under my breath. Tensely I gripped my trading cards. I quickened my step as I neared the spot where the grasses moved, then marched past, eyes ahead, heart pounding, fingers crossed, not daring to look around.

Just as I was ready to break into a gallop for the final stretch home, a red bandanna descended over my eyes, and I was dragged backwards off the sidewalk into the wet field.

"Get her down!"

"Get her ankles!"

"Quick! Sit on her!"

It was happening, then. I was going to be pantsed.

"Somebody sit on her," I heard again.

"I can't breathe! I can't breathe!" I cried, thinking I would suffocate under the blindfold.

Someone pulled my arms over my head and pinned them down at the wrists, others took my legs, squeezing at the ankles, holding them from kicking until someone else sat on them.

"Let me go!" I kept crying until my words melted into tears. I felt humiliated by my tears (cry baby! cry baby!), though I cried as much from rage as from fear.

When I was finally able to catch my breath I began to fight, kicking and biting, as though there were some possibility of fighting free. But of course there was none.

They gripped my legs at last and, raising me from the buttocks, ripped off my underpants. Then they forced my legs apart at the knees and held them open for one endless moment, staring deep into my secret. No one touched, no one spoke; they *saw,* their eyes burning me like dry ice.

It wasn't shame I felt then, only hot, inexpressible fury. You, Melvyn Weeks! You, Bobby Barr! You, Richie Englehart! You, Nazi Richard Conroy! But in the end I was stripped even of my wrath. For the project of my pantsing, once completed, seemed to lose all its appeal to its perpetrators. Stripping me had been only a gesture, an afternoon diversion for a lazy day. Maybe the third-grade boys of Baybury Heights Elementary School already felt *seen one, seen them all,* or maybe they were only interested in power. For, a moment later, they pulled me shaking to my feet and pushed me back on the sidewalk as though they were my friends. They threw my pants and my trading cards after me, and ordered me on pain of "getting it" never to tell anyone what had happened. Then they ripped off the blindfold, gave me a shove, and diving quickly back to their hiding places in the wet field, finally set me free.

***

Grown men didn't do things like that to us—not in broad daylight, not without an excuse. They kept us in place with veiled threats and insinuations; and they only undressed us mentally, an indignity it was hard to prove. But walking alone was still a problem. In Spain, where no one had felt qualified to interpret my motives, my celebrity had kept me immune from judgment. In Munich I had been justified by having a husband. But here, as a single woman assumed to be in the running, I was subject to all the abuse the Romans could dish out. It is not always, as Mae West says, "better to be looked over than overlooked." All those dashing Italians I had fallen for in my first enchantment with Rome—Giuliano, the guard at the Colosseum; Angelo, the guide; Mario and the other cowboys on the Piazza di Spagna who followed American women to the cafés of the Via Veneto and whispered extravagant phrases in their ears between sips of Cinzano-soda—those romancing Italians were so full of mocking adulation that they could barely conceal their contempt. I gave them up when I realized that for them I was interchangeable with every other presentable American of a certain age, even the poor starlets who hung around the Via Veneto. Romans collected Americans as Americans collected Romans: parasites all. I felt better now, knowing I could refuse them, but I still had to face them in the restaurants and cafés, at parties and on the street.

I walked into my hotel, too weary for midmorning. I was way off schedule. I would have to face the world twice today.

"Any messages?" I asked at the desk.

"No messages, signora."

I walked up the three flights to my room.

Stockings and underwear were strung across the room on a portable clothesline. They stretched from bedpost to light fixture to doorknob, cutting off access to the chair. So much dirty laundry. I made for the bed. Why shouldn't I take a siesta like the Italians? So what if I took mine before midday? I knew I ought to be giving myself a pep talk, studying the guidebook to regain my enthusiasm, picking out my afternoon excursion. But little puddles were forming under each piece of laundry dripping onto the discolored marble floor of my room, and I wasn't up to tourism.

So much had changed since I had first arrived in the Eternal City full of energy and resolve. On my husband-less high, I had slid into my new life with wide eyes and a loose schedule, taking Rome slowly like old wine. One sight a day, preceded by plenty of home-work. Like James's lady, Isabel Archer herself, I had gone about Rome in a "repressed ecstasy" over the "rugged ruins" and "mossy marbles," wandering among ruins that had once been emperors' palaces. I had sat in cafés behind dark glasses watching the crowds, or, tiptoeing through naves and apses, been dazzled by medieval mosaics and Renaissance paintings. To be taken for more than a superficial tourist while I wrote my play was all I'd wanted. "I'll be living in Rome for a while," I had written everyone at home, giving a genuine street address, not merely American Express.

Now, after only a few months, I had apparently succeeded. Even when I conspicuously carried a guide-book, no one took me for a tourist any more. I was becoming a fixture at this café and that *tabac*. But far from being fulfilled by my permanent status, I had become exposed. The only purpose I could produce had vanished. *If I wasn't a tourist, then what was I doing here?*

People had various justifications for being in Rome. Frank's old friends the Ericksons up at the American Academy were here on a prestigious grant—that is, Paul Erickson was. There were painters here, business-men, and plenty of genuine tourists too, distinguishable by having departure dates. Some had eccentric pur-poses, like the twenty-one-year-old Oklahoman I met at the Vatican who, passing for a tourist, briefly attached himself to me, even courting me by the guidebooks. After a week of Alfredo's for fettuccini Alfredo, Sistine Chapel for Michelangelo, Via Condotti for neckties, he finally confessed what he was up to. (Too bad; I had enjoyed being with such a seeming innocent in that sly old city, a tourist again myself.) We were exploring a recess of the catacombs together one Sunday, searching out ancient Christian bones with flashlights, when suddenly he touched my arm gingerly and threw himself on my mercy. His father, he said, had sent him abroad to get laid.

No shit! I tried to imagine my father sending me to Europe to get laid. There was a smell of old martyrs in the tomb. I felt old and jaded.

Now, he said, it was almost time for him to return to the States and he still hadn't made it. Wouldn't I help him out? I, married, with nothing to lose, an older woman, a Jewess, worldly, understanding—

"You're a sweet boy, George, but I'm off sex." He probably didn't even find me pretty.

"I didn't think you would. I just thought—I mean, I hoped—"

"I'm really sorry, George."

"Oh well. It's been very nice knowing you anyway, Sasha. I liked you."

*If I wasn't a tourist, then what was I doing here?* The streets answered for me: Manhunting. Like secretaries on a cruise; like "career girls" in Washington; like college girls, nurses, entertainers, stewardesses, actresses, moldels—like all unclaimed women: looking for a man. No answer I could give was half as good as Nancy Erickson's "my husband is at the Academy," though what Academy wives actually did was of interest to no one. They kept house, visited the ruins,

studied Italian or Italian cooking. Some took special
courses arranged by the Academy for Academy wives.
Even so, in some ways poor Nancy Erickson was better
off than the starlets and models on the Via Veneto who
all had that recognizable haunted look, as though they
were being spooked. I couldn't take my eyes off them.
They were pure parsley, nothing but garnish—worthless without a man to adorn. If they sat alone in a
café they kept looking nervously at their watches,
pretending they were waiting for someone in particular.
I knew that syndrome. *Mannequin* was the perfect
word for them: somewhere they had given away their
souls and now they had only bodies, lovely bodies, left
to show.

My program was different from theirs, but in form
only. Mornings writing in some café: lunch; Roman
culture in the afternoon; dinner. And always my book
to read. They looked at their watches pretending they
had a man; I looked at my book pretending I didn't
want one. But we were all waiting. As I observed the
models from behind my book, I wondered if they knew
all about me, too.

"What are you doing in Rome?" "Studying Roman
culture"; "gathering material for a play." However
sincerely I gave my answers, they all sounded as flimsy
as "I'm an actress, temporarily unemployed." The
moment we appeared on the streets available, we were
all tossed into the same salad, consumed fresh or
deposited in the crisper to wait. It was impossible to
make oneself out an exception. And so, as the weeks
slipped by, I found myself spending more and more
time like this, just lying around in my room avoiding
the streets, watching the puddles under the laundry
enlarging drop by drop into days and weeks, waiting.

Waiting for messages; waiting for inspiration; waiting for my money to run out.

The buzzer, like a shot of adrenalin, startled me off the bed.

"*Pronto, pronto*"—my best Italian word.

"*Telefono, signora; signore Leonardo Bucatelli.*"

"I'll be right down."

Quickly I inspected my face and ran a comb through my hair (impossible to leave the room without); then, avoiding the puddles on the floor, I picked my way to the door and dashed down the stairs to the lobby to answer the phone.

I had met Leonardo in the American restaurant I sometimes went to for a hamburger with catsup and french fries or a chocolate milkshake. Reading *The Portrait of a Lady* while I ate, I had noticed out of the corner of my eye one of the lean-trousered Italians eyeing me through dark glasses from across the room. While my eyes stayed on the book, I tracked him with my antennae, getting ready to rebuff him if he sat with me. But when I peeked up, I saw him walking to my table with Gregory, the restaurant owner, for a proper introduction.

As soon as we were introduced, Leonardo picked up my book, turned it over, and said in English but with the lilt of Italian, "Ah, Henry James."

"You know Henry James?" I asked surprised.

"Leonardo's half American and his wife is American," said Gregory, as though that were explanation enough.

"My *former* wife," said Leonardo. He asked if he could sit with me, then ordered American coffee.

I was impressed that he did not start in whispering sibilants in my ear. In the course of the conversation he mentioned he was leaving the following evening for Sicily.

"Sicily! How lucky you are!" I said.

"Why don't you come along? I'll be back in less than a week."

"Are you serious?"

"Sure. I have some work to do, but it will be nice to have company the rest of the time. Gregory can vouch for me."

For the first time in months I did not feel, sitting with a man, as though I were parading before the judges.

Speeding down the famous coast into the fragrance of lemon trees and the soothing breezes of the Mediterranean, Leonardo told me his story. His father was Italian, his mother American. He had grown up rich in Italy, then gone to college in Florida. There he had taken a full-blooded American wife, transplanted her to Rome, and given her "everything." He would never understand how she could, only months before, have left him for Miami. "Isn't it a woman's duty," he cried, throwing his arms dangerously in the air on one of that shoreline's spectacular curves, "to live where her husband lives?" When his hands returned to earth, one of them made for the steering wheel, and one of them made for me.

I suppose it was foolish of me not to have made my position absolutely clear before setting one foot inside Leonardo's white Alfa Romeo. I ought to have declared straight out: No fucking; I want to see scenery, not bed sheets. But as it was, the blue miles were speeding by and my explanation was still only an unconfirmed hypothesis. It could not, as I had hoped, go without saying.

Finally I cleared my throat and began. (It's always so hard to explain oneself.) "It's not that I'm against sex on principle," I heard myself saying. "It's just that it usually makes for unpleasant complications." When I looked over, Leonardo was eyeing me suspiciously.

It did sound prudish—shades of *Girl Alive!*—it was not what I meant.

I tried again. "I mean, in principle I believe in free love. But in practice, I try to avoid it."

His look was getting worse—as though I were some sort of proselytizing religious creep. I still wasn't saying it right. The sea breeze, free and capricious, mocked my failing efforts at precision.

"What I mean is," I tried one last time, shouting now to cover my uncertainty, "I like you very much and I'm sure we'll have a fine time together in Sicily, but I never intended that we'd sleep together. I mean, can't we take separate rooms and split the expenses?"

It sounded absurd, like something out of a B movie or a teen-age novel. Listening to myself, with the voluptuous smell of lemon trees enfolding us and now and then the rush of the sea, I was ashamed to find myself sitting inside a rather unpleasant American prude. I knew she was a fraud: there were times when she fucked like a bunny, yet now she was acting like a Midwestern schoolteacher, sounding positively dowdy. No wonder the poor driver looked uncomfortable. I wanted to expose her, but I knew I couldn't say a word without becoming implicated. Well, she would just have to explain herself; I had all I could do to watch the speedometer and the treacherous road, on which Leonardo, finding himself a captive, was driving faster and faster in a futile effort to escape.

Part way down the coast we stopped for the night in Sorrento, where I rejoiced to see my first unpotted

palms. The air was lush as the song. I stood awkwardly
aside as Leonardo spoke to the desk clerk in Italian;
more awkwardly still when he informed me that there
were no single rooms left, only double rooms at fifteen
dollars apiece. "Do you really want a separate room?"
He seemed almost as embarrassed as I. And what could
the desk clerk be thinking?

My position was untenable. "I guess we can share a
room," I said.

In the room, we were both surprised to find only one
(double) bed. "I'll sleep in the chair," offered Leonardo.

It was insulting. Did I impress him as really so
inflexible that I would insist he spend the night sitting
upright in a chair? "That's all right," I threw back,
moving off to the bathroom with my toothbrush and
robe. "We can share the bed."

Lying next to Leonardo in the dark, sensing the hot
breath in his lungs and the blood in his veins, I felt
miserably misunderstood. How had I managed, despite
such care, to wind up once again in this predicament?
My life looked like a repeating decimal. Lying apart on
my side of the bed was tantamount to declaring myself
frigid. That silly prude in the car had contaminated me
with her dowdiness, and now I needed a good cleansing.

"Goodnight," said Leonardo politely.

"Goodnight," I said. But longing to merge with my
antithesis into a clean, new creature, I made some
slight sign for Leonardo to approach me.

Our encounter in romantic Sorrento was quick and
gentle, of little moment in itself; but as we fell apart to
sleep I felt it take on a special significance. For, as
unwittingly as a Typhoid Mary or the lucky one-mil-
lionth depositor in the Bank of America, uncircumsized

Leonardo Bucatelli obligingly becoming my twenty-fifth lover, had boosted my lifetime average up over one a year. Another first.

The next day we drove down to Messina where there was a car ferry to Sicily. On the way, Leonardo inquired into my views. He listened thoughtfully as I denounced the double standard, sexual hypocrisy, and lechery. I used the largest words I knew to defend my position. He nodded gravely now and then, treating me with all the respect due a woman who not only fucks but insists on paying her own way. Mine, he said, was a rare and liberal doctrine. "I have always preferred intelligent, liberated women to the beautiful sluts on the Via Veneto." Though he noted my words as pure philosophy, appreciating that he had stumbled onto a good thing, he had no idea what to make of me.

Sicily meant Taormina, the pride of the travel folders, with perfume added. In the mornings in Sicily we took our breakfast together on the terrace of our hotel overlooking the sea, and after gobbling those rich native pastries that are made so poorly by comparison in Rome, we went separate ways, coming together again at suppertime. Enchanted by the Sicilian seaside I, who had never before seen free-growing cactus, steeped myself in the surprise of cactus fruit sparkling like garnets in the sunlight and the magenta profusion of bougainvillaea. Leonardo set off in the mornings in a business suit to act out PR Man for a prestigious American firm, and spent the afternoons in bermuda shorts marching through the streets of the picturesque village with his camera glued to his eye like any American, snapping his own native hibiscus. Nothing but sex ever passed between us.

In order to avoid the stigma of being a whore, I

posed as an intellectual, abandoning all pretensions to voluptuousness. It was scary to find myself in sensuous Sicily disarmed of my best weapon. Instead I used my second best. "Don't you go anywhere without your notebook?" asked Leonardo. Oh, I was hooked on my book. "You know," he said, joining me for an hour on the beach, appraising me coolly in that hot sun, "you ought to get yourself a bikini. Your body is really very nice. You should show it off a bit."

Discovered by some foreign connoisseur, like the Greek ruins of Sicily! Leonardo's invidious compliments only provoked more of my bookish rhetoric, so inappropriate in that tropical setting. I turned my back to the sun to hide my mustache (if any) and took refuge in the warm waters Ulysses himself was said to have sailed.

Floating on the surface, I communicated with the outer world through a snorkel and studied the stylish fishes who swam up to my mask enticing me after them, only to wriggle effortlessly out of my reach after prizes of their own. Though my back burned, that warm water was my element and those fishes my paradigm. It was they whom I missed when the time came to ferry back through Scylla and Charybdis and drive on up the coast to Rome.

I could tell by Leonardo's manner as soon as I picked up the phone in the Alberto lobby that there was something wrong. I hadn't heard from him once since we had returned to Rome, and now all of a sudden he had to talk to me about something "very serious."

"Is there something the matter, Leonardo?"

"Yes. We'll talk about it later. Do you want to meet me at the Ristorante Navona in an hour?"

"An hour's fine," I said. "I hope it's nothing terrible."

"We'll talk about it at lunch," he said ominously.

Anyway, lunch. Whatever he wanted to discuss, at least today I wouldn't have to brave a restaurant alone. "*Ciao*," I said and returned to my room to fix myself up.

Perhaps, I thought, slipping my feet into Italian shoes, I'd give the poem another try tomorrow after all; maybe the play would come too if I could loosen up.

Leonardo, suntanned and manicured, sat chewing a toothpick and girl-watching behind his dark glasses. It was a little past noon—the most revealing hour under the cruel Roman sun. The café glittered elegantly in its finely wrought Piazza Navona setting. As I fluffed my hair and walked to his table, Leonardo popped up to pull out a chair for me. "Let's sit inside," I said, shading my face.

Inside, I had the good sense to keep talking all the way through the pasta, so that we were well into the meat course before Leonardo came to the point. Even during the small talk he had revealed his mean intentions by sprinkling the conversation with sarcasm like so much grated cheese. Now, despite visible efforts, he was barely able to keep the fury out of his voice.

He wiped his mouth and put down his napkin. Was I aware, he asked at last, of being ill?

Yes, I was.

Then why, he demanded, had I not warned him about my disease before assaulting him in bed? Why had I not at least allowed him to take precautions? However the same stunt may have been pulled on me, there was no excuse for me to pull it on him, who had been nothing if not kind to me.

I put down my fork, rising to the attack. "Wait a minute, Leonardo. *Who* assaulted *who?*" Vindication rose in my throat. "I told you as soon as I got into your car that I had no intention of sleeping with you."

"Yes, you told me your intentions. You and your highminded theories. I was fool enough to fall for them."

"What are you talking about?"

He gripped the table and pushed a reddening face toward me. "Your disease. I've caught it."

I relaxed, relieved. "But that's impossible, Leonardo," I said kindly, resuming the meal. "In the first place, what I have isn't catching. And in the second place, even if it were, *you* couldn't get it. It's a female disease."

He looked at me with contempt. "Look, Sasha. You might as well face it. What I've got is gonorrhea, and I got it from you. Now, if you have any concern at all for the people of Italy, you will come quietly to my physician and take the cure."

*The people of Italy!* I took a long, stalling swig of my wine to let it sink in: *The clap.* Souvenir of Spain? As I reached for the carafe to fill my glass again, Leonardo mounted his assault.

The words go whizzing by my ears, but I am barely able to catch them. Leonardo has abandoned the polite formality with which he usually speaks his mother's English for the passionate gesticulation of his father's countrymen.

I duck as he calls me *una donna pericolosa* (a dangerous woman!), but at last the accusation "carrier" catches me square in the ear.

I—a carrier! Quickly I compute: from the time I left Spain until I was led astray by this PR man I've slept with no one but my husband, who doesn't count.

Though I can as easily have caught it from Leonardo as he from me, I note he's the one doing all the shouting. His voice rises and my lofty persona dissolves. I see I had better behave. Even if they've done no other damage yet, the insidious bacteria have already destroyed my image.

Yes, I must have a cure. A V.D. victim needs all the help she can get. The embassy won't bail me out of this, the Ericksons would snicker if they knew, and all those foreign doctors with their shots and pills have likely been operating on a false diagnosis. I'm afraid it's Leonardo's help or no one's: I'm utterly alone.

Over dessert we reconciled. With the magnanimity of a gentleman, Leonardo asssured me that the cure would involve nothing more than a routine series of penicillin shots which we could take together. At least, I consoled myself, it would be a good reason to get up and out in the morning. Sipping our coffee we were thick as conspirators, and when we finally left the restaurant for the doctor's office, it was arm in arm.

"*Eccola!*" exclaimed the doctor excitedly, as Leonardo, gazing into the microscope's eyepiece, scrutinized a tiny precious part of me smeared on a slide. I bared my buttock and received the needle.

During our cure, Leonardo and I grew closer than we had been in Sicily. We met for breakfast each morning at a café near the doctor's, unless I had spent the preceding night at his place. We stretched out our single bond like taffy. There was nothing aphrodisiacal in the antibiotic; it was just that, sinners together, we suddenly had more and worse in common than with anyone else.

The tourists were swarming to Italy and we were just over our cure when some rich friends of Leonardo's came to Rome on an extended homeymoon. Nice Americans. Jumping to the usual conclusions, they assumed I was in love with Leonardo. They were so solicitous I could tell they felt sorry for me. It was unbearable.

"I understand you're separated from your husband," said the wife sympathetically, wandering with me among the ruins. Up ahead her husband and Leonardo had stopped to study the map of the Forum. "Is your husband in Italy too?"

"We were living in Munich when we separated. He's probably gone back to the States by now."

There was an awkward silence. "And how long do you plan to stay in Rome?" she asked politely.

I had used up all my answers. "Till my money runs out I suppose; after that I just don't know." The very words that had once proclaimed my daring now rang of defeat.

We caught up with the men following the tourist map through the Forum—the Forum where Vestal Virgins had once guarded the sacred fires with the power of their chastity; the same Forum where Isabel Archer had turned away the most eligible suitors on the continent. I hung back while the others talked over old times until the sun set and it was time to choose a restaurant. Spaghetti alla Carbonara? Zuppa di Pesce alla Romana? Carciofi alla Giudia? Let the newlyweds choose among the specialties of a Rome I had already tasted.

In the back of my mind I was deciding I really mustn't see Leonardo any more.

No question my nerves were shattered. I was oversensitive and touchy. My excursions had become a sham: I found myself leaving the maps in my room and turning

corners at random to avoid the street people. All the
ruins started to look alike. My writing was a failure,
and I abandoned it. Each foray into a restaurant was
an assault, with everyone seeing I was eating alone.
*What is she doing here*? I could see them wonder;
*Doesn't she have a man*? Isabel Archer had finally
married, and just as her story promised to be resolved
it turned out it was only beginning.

And mine? Was twenty-four old or young? Was I
ugly or beautiful?

The frightened face in the mirror had the haunted
look of the mannequins. Just under the surface I sensed
a fine network of ugliness which might begin showing
through any moment. Too late to start a career; too late
even to go back to school. I, who had always prided
myself on being the youngest in the class, couldn't now
join those chain-smoking women who "went back to
school" after having their children. I remembered them
shyly attending our classes wearing either sensible shoes
or clothes embarrassingly young for them, trying to
speak an alien slang. I had cringed for them as the
young men, suppressing sneers, momentarily suspended
debate while they asked their female questions. I knew
I would never be able to survive that.

On my twenty-fifth birthday, alone in my room, I
received a cable from New York. It was from Frank.
HAPPY BIRTHDAY. TIME TO COME HOME. The next day
on an impulse I put my wedding ring on again, and
after that it was much easier to walk the streets. I even
wore it to a farewell party up at the Academy the
Ericksons threw before they sailed for home. They
invited everyone they knew, including a genuine Italian
princess. All the Americans, drinking sparkling *lam-
brusca* as though they would never taste it again, kept
singing "Arrividerce Roma" louder and sloppier the

drunker they got. In the days following, most of them left Italy for another academic year.

The tourists were leaving too. It became possible once again to view the Sistine ceiling without stepping on someone's toes. The Roman pines stayed green, but the days had already perceptibly shortened; the sugar maples would be turning on Connecticut's Merritt Parkway. Maybe Frank was right; maybe it was time to go home.

# F
# I
# V
# E

The ink had not yet dried on my high school diploma when I rushed off to begin my future at Eliza Baxter College of New England University in western Massachusetts. I was in a big hurry. With a time schedule based on Dr. John Watson and not a minute to waste, I was all set to do the four years of college in three so I could enter law school at nineteen and pass the bar at twenty-one. I had the whole thing mapped out.

But somewhere during my sophomore year my fine resolutions turned to dreams as I fell hopelessly in love with philosophy.

The romance started innocently enough. Like any lover I can recall intimations of the affair long before it began in earnest—a lingering glance, a chance meeting in the library, a greeting withheld. I still smile remembering an even earlier time when I wouldn't have looked twice at philosophy, it so smacked of religion.

I had had my fill of that discipline in the Sunday school (that met on Saturday) my parents had enrolled me in as a child to learn "about my origins." I wasn't having any of it. I was willing to accept as "literature" the Bible stories presented in literature class; I might even have learned to recite them in Hebrew as we were expected to do in Hebrew class; but when they filed into the history class dressed as real events that had once taken place, God and I parted company. If there was ever a possibility that I might have fallen for stories like Genesis or Moses and the Ten Commandments, it was destroyed by the ridiculous title of the textbook we used: *When the Jewish People Was Young.* An author capable of such a travesty had about as much authority to convince me of God as my Grandfather Charlie, who, despite the presence of several respected MD's in the family, shamed us all by taking himself to the local apothecary to be treated with leeches whenever he had the sniffles. And my father warning me every Saturday, "You mustn't believe everything you hear," didn't boost the temple's credibility. I sat through the weekly compulsory religious service following History class with a skeptical heart.

The God of Abraham forfeited every challenge I threw him. Either He had no dignity or He didn't exist. He didn't even strike me down for standing among the mourners and weeping during that most holy portion of the religious service, the Prayer for the Dead. After I whispered the forbidden name of God and still nothing happened to me, I knew I had flushed him out. If He existed at all, He was chicken shit—certainly not worthy of worship.

My love for philosophy took an opposite course: whatever challenge I came up with, philosophy always had an answer. I never once got the last word. My little skepticism was like dusting powder next to the cosmic doubt of a skeptic like Hume. I watched heavies like Descartes and Leibniz or Plato and Aristotle slug it out together, perfectly matched champions. Who knew who would win? They were all incomparable performers, each with a style of his own.

Though it was several terms before my infatuation became a passion, I can trace the affair back to a vision I had during final exam week in my freshman year.

It was probably because of the No-Doz pills I'd been using to cram and the high level of tension around the dorm, for it was more than an ordinary insight. It was a genuine vision, complete with flashing lights and sirens in the background. Suddenly all the little rooms in my mind popped open at once, and the vision flashed through them like a comet. *Every event in life can be ordered on a single continuum.* All the diverse chronologies that had been complacently resting in the various rooms of my mind for years suddenly got up and started rearranging themselves. Until the vision, in one room there had been cavemen (who really came first), followed by Indians, Pilgrims, African slaves, and the Presidents. In another room had been the Egyptians (who came first), followed by Queen Elizabeth, the Renaissance, and Napoleon. And in yet another room had been first Beowulf, then the Middle Ages, then Biblical Times (including the Arabian Nights), and ancient Greece and Rome—all mostly mythical. Not until after the No-Doz vision did it occur to me that they could all fit cozily on a single continuum together. Eureka! The American Indians and the ancient Egyptians on the same line not only wind up nowhere near each other, but the Indians do not necessarily come first!

Even when exams were over and I went off No-Doz, I fought to keep hold of my vision. It was too large to assimilate all at once. I believed it intellectually but it took a long time before I felt it in my gut; it required a habit of faith too new to serve me daily, and again and again I would come up short as I was struck with fact upon astonishing fact:

There were slaves in America (slaves!) less than a hundred years ago!

Beowulf was composed after Deuteronomy; King Lear before the Declaration of Independence!

Before long I noticed vast stretches of my line with nothing filled in. They made me uneasy. What happened between Ancient Rome and the Middle Ages? between Voltaire and Victoria? I wanted to fill it all in so I could see the line whole. I knew it would require diligent application over a very long time, but theoretically at least, it was possible. If one took the longest view, holding that simple Time Line clearly in mind, one could eventually fill in all the details and know everything.

For someone starting, like me, from scratch, it was a breathtaking thought. Everything. So far I knew nothing; I believe I hadn't yet even registered for the second semester. But spending my time in pre-law when instead I could be on my way to learning everything seemed a tragic waste. Perhaps I ought not even bother becoming a lawyer. People were always saying how silly it was—all that work, when I'd wind up getting married anyway. Whereas, knowing every-thing could always come in handy.

Not that I had any choice in my program. The freshman courses were all requirements anyway—no electives at Baxter until sophomore year. But I started applying myself to my studies with a special ardor. Any course was a good starting place.

*Western Civ.*: Instead of examining cultures as discrete units, as the teachers taught, I examined them as moments on a continuum and ignored the details. Though I scribbled down furiously the same notes as everyone else, coughing them back up on exams, to me the Renaissance was not a series of Italian names and dates constituting what-happened-in-Italy; it was a Time with a Character. Why, Elizabethan was Renais-sance! I hoped that someday I would be able to stand back far enough to see all Western Civ. itself as a Time with a Character.

*Survey of English Lit. I.*: English Literature was a parochial flourish on a segment of my line. Beauty was Truth.

*French Grammar* (otherwise loathsome): a blue chalk for coloring bits of my line.

*Intro. to Psych.*: a sharp pencil for detail work.

Classic, Romantic, Economic, Social, Cause, Struc-ture—indispensable iridescent hues. I knew that only when all the colors blended together would I achieve that pure white blinding beacon that would show me All.

Getting the feel of my line, by semester three I found I could run quickly through it and pull out a little something from every epoch or a little more from just a few to make a neat subline, good for a term paper. I crammed for final exams by squeezing onto a single sheet of notebook paper, in perfect subdivided outline, every fact I had learned in the course: if I couldn't comprehend the whole course in one glance, it was of no use to me. Since I had to list something, I chose history as my major, but wars and rulers, like conjugations, minor poets, and other particulars, were profoundly boring unless I could view them as reflections of something larger and more abstract. It was impossible for a notion to be too abstract for me. Abstraction was the key to seeing everything at a glance.

It was in the second semester of my sophomore year that I accidentally stumbled onto that abstraction of abstractions, History of Ideas, which opened my mind to philosophy and closed it to such comparatively trivial needs as food and rest. Offered for history credit by the Philosophy Department, the odd course was taught by one Professor Donald Alport, a hulking philosopher with strange intonations, a grey mustache, and thinning hair, who must once have had my very vision, so learned was he. My French verbs went unconjugated, the War of the Roses went unexplained, as under Alport's tutelage I contemplated the Great Chain of Being and the Idea of Progress.

Too late for history or law, I was smitten. History itself was but an idea occurring in a mind: like Number, like Justice, like Truth.

By the next semester, taking the ultimate abstraction, Logic, and both Philosophy of History and Professor Alport's History of Philosophy, with each class I fell more desperately in love. A hopeless case. I didn't even care that I was reading myself right out of the marriage market but gave myself wholly up to my new passion. I could hardly drag myself out of the library back to the dorm at night. Before long I began to see my onetime dream of knowing everything as foolishly naïve. Socrates was right: the more one knew, the more one must recognize one's own ignorance. But he was also right that the unexamined life was not worth living.

I plunged in, pursuing the ideas deep into ancient texts, losing myself among subtle distinctions. Nothing else mattered. I analyzed with Aristotle and flunked my French midterm. I synthesized with Augustine and stopped going to chapel or gym and eventually stopped eating everything but Cheezits and black coffee. Discovering with Spinoza the connectedness of things, exploring with Kant the mind that thinks so, I stopped going to chapel or gym and eventually stopped sleeping at night. My brain was in a constant state of intoxication. With Schopenhauer I saw the world as pure will, until, with Bishop Berkeley, I saw it as pure idea. The more I studied, the less sure I was of anything—even of what I had sworn by the week before. My letters home grew enigmatic, alarming my mother. When I wrote that I planned to stay at school during Christmas vacation so I could study, she called up long distance begging me to come home.

"What's the matter Sasha? Are you in trouble? Are you falling behind?"

"No, I'm not behind. I just want to read, that's all."

"Can't you read at home? Is it really something else you want to stay for, darling?"

"There's nothing else."

"Your father and I have been counting the days until Christmas. Everyone's been asking after you. If you don't want to come home we can't make you, but we're worried about you, dear. Your letters have been so ... so ... strange. Won't you at least tell us what's wrong?"

She was right: something was wrong. Without gym or chapel or French I wouldn't graduate, yet I had wiped gym and chapel and French out of my life. The official notices and warnings I had received from the Dean of Women were stuck away in the corner of my room among a mounting pile of empty Cheezit boxes, unanswered letters, incomplete law school applications, and No-Doz pills.

"Nothing's the matter, Mom, really. I just need to spend some time thinking. But I'll see, maybe I will come home." I had a week left to decide.

That night I dreamed I wrote all my finals in a mysterious secret code, the more brilliant the matter, the harder to decipher. I had much to say, but I couldn't make myself understood. Helplessly I watched my potential A's dissolve to F's. Waking in a panic, I spent the rest of the night reading Saint Augustine, and the next day, in desperation, I went to the infirmary to see the psychologist. It was an extreme measure for a former believer in the Behaviorism of Dr. John Watson.

The nurse looked up at me curiously, then handed me a pink paper. "Fill out this form and take a seat," she said.

"Does it go on my record?"

"Of course."

I sat down with the form. Name. Date. School. Year. Age: 18. Class: Junior. Major: Philosophy. Minor: Philosophy. Religion: Philosophy. Complaint:—

"What does this question mean, nurse?"

She looked at the form. "Put down what your problem is."

I hesitated. "I don't know what my problem is. That's why I'm here—to find out."

"Doctor has to know what kind of a case you are. Now go write a sentence stating your problem."

I couldn't name my problem. How can we know that we know? What is Truth? What is the meaning of

Problem? If there were any answers, they were all in an indecipherable code. I put the pink form back on the nurse's desk and walked out. There was no help for me here.

I returned to the dorm and flung myself on my bed. Around my room at eye level I had run a strip of masking tape representing Time. It started at the door with prehistory and stretched, densely crowded with tiny writing, all the way around to my bed. There wasn't room on it for one more entry, but I didn't care. What I yearned to know could not be fit between a *then* and a *now*. It could not be numbered. It was simple and yet hugely complex, like a perfect circle and the *Grosse Fuge*. It existed outside of Time. If I were lucky it would come to me in another vision that would be so stunning as to obliterate forever the triviality of unlearned French and the pettiness of chapel.

A junior from Cleveland's West Side called to offer me a ride home in exchange for a tankful of gas and some of the tolls. I accepted. In the car, three Ohioans in N.E.U. sweatshirts and dungarees sang hillbilly songs and Christmas carols with the radio all the way across the Pennsylvania Turnpike. I slumped in the corner pretending to sleep. Not that I disliked the music; I loved to sing and would even have tried to harmonize if it hadn't been for another tune buzzing in my ears. The farther west we drove the harder I strained to hear it. With my nerves taut as harp strings and my brain cells poised to replay every tantalizing signal, nothing could shake my conviction that I was listening to the Music of the Spheres.

\* \* \*

At home I cowered through Christmas, avoiding

"Jingle Bells" and relatives. Only the books I had brought from school and baroque music could soothe me. I read deep into every night that vacation. In the daytime I slipped off to the quiet garden of the Cleveland Museum of Art where, thrilling to Bach on the organ, I could contemplate with Spinoza the vanity of all human wishes save one. I followed each idea to the next, finding one subsumed under another, itself subsumed under yet another, soaring after that single axiom or thought or word that would somehow sum up everything.

"Sasha, you've hardly eaten a bite the entire holiday. Don't you think you're studying too hard, darling?" asked my poor mother. But the only nourishment I took was for my mind; for my body I couldn't care less. Like Descartes's, my mind and my body led separate lives, but unlike Descartes, I found no satisfactory way to connect them.

I had always despised my body. Slowly my contempt spread to all things material. For the only time in my life, I didn't care how I looked. Neither Leibniz, nor Spinoza, nor Newton, nor Locke, nor Berkeley, nor Descartes's God Himself could bridge for me the growing gap between mind and matter.

My second day home I had gone to an engagement shower for an old high school friend. It turned out so unhappily that I didn't want to see another Baybury soul.

"Sasha! We never thought you'd come," said the hostess. "We thought you wouldn't want to associate with us anymore since you got into that fancy college."

Fancy college! Just because it wasn't Ohio State! "Baxter's not fancy at all," I said. "It's just far away."

"Well," said the hostess, "nobody ever hears from you."

"Come on, admit it," said another friend. "You have to be a Brain to get into those Eastern colleges. But then, Sasha always was a Brain."

"That's not true—" I began excitedly. It was the dream again. How should I begin to explain myself?

"Calm down, now. You're probably both right."

"You must be meeting a lot of interesting people there."

"We were sure you'd be engaged by now. Things turn out so funny. The three girls from our group that are left are the ones we all thought would go first."

"She always said she wasn't going to get married right away."

"Yeah, she said she was going to be a lady lawyer. Maybe she really will."

Being spoken to in the third person didn't make me feel any more comfortable. After the shower I decided to spend my evenings in the house.

"If it's for me, say I'm not home," I hollered whenever the phone rang, and retreated to my room. (Actually, it was now only nominally my room. Since I had gone away to school, it had been converted into an upstairs den. My bed was still there, and my things were still in the closet, but my pictures had been taken down, the room had been painted blue, and a large TV set had been installed on my desk in place of my phonograph and records.) I refused all Christmas parties and phone calls. "You always have to be different, don't you?" asked my father, shaking his head.

I decided that would be my last vacation at home. When it was over I took a Greyhound bus back to school rather than accept a ride from some frivolous student. I couldn't bear to be distracted by human chatter. Professors alone, pure mind, didn't stink of humanity.

❧

"Sasha Davis?"

"Yes." I stood in the doorway of my narrow room peering at a tall blond girl in a school blazer. Her hair was cropped short at the neck like Joan of Arc's—not like all the other Baxter girls with smooth pageboys or feather cuts like mine.

"I've seen you in the dining room, but I never knew your name. I thought you might be missing this."

I let out a gasp as delicate fingers held out the small black notebook to which I committed certain of my profoundest thoughts. I had not yet missed it.

"It seemed too private to turn in at the Dean's office, so I found out your room number. I'm Roxanne du Bois. I write too."

She dropped her voice and eyes so modestly on the last sentence that I wanted to take her hand. She couldn't have read my notebook, or she would have known that, as a matter of fact, I didn't "write." But I didn't tell her.

"I guess that makes us both creeps," I laughed warming with gratitude. "Thank you. Do you want to come in for a few minutes?"

She smiled and walked into my sanctuary, sitting on my unmade bed. It was one of the rare times I had invited anyone into my room. I had chosen Baxter College in the first place because I knew no one there, and I wanted to keep it that way. But this tall, pale girl with the soft voice and delicate hands seemed as separate as I, and fragile besides. "I'll make us some coffee," I offered.

As I plugged in the coffee pot to boil the water, I felt

her take in my black walls, my Time Line, my cases of books, and the bulletin board on which I mounted pictures of me at college, me at several dances with dates, me with my family, and our Baybury house.

"Black walls. What a great idea," she said. "It really gets the feel of this place. I'm surprised your roommate lets you have black walls. My roommate put some flowered horror in our room, but since she paid for it all I can't complain. It's better than the prosiac green we moved into."

"I don't have a roommate," I said, handing her a cup of instant coffee and sitting down on the foot of the bed. "I'd rather have stayed home than have to give up my privacy." As soon as it was out of my mouth I was sorry I'd said it, Roxanne looked so fragile and distant.

"Not me," she said. "I'd gladly have ten roommates to get away from Richmond (home), Virginia." Embarrassed, she reached out for the book lying on my night table. She picked it up, then looked from it to me. "You like Eliot? I love Eliot," she said. "I think I'd rather have written *Prufrock* than any other poem in the English language. '*Then how should I begin to spit out all the butt-ends of my days and ways*?' "

" '*I should have been a pair of ragged claws scuttling across the floors of silent seas*,' " I answered her. A silence passed between us, a rest note in a soft duet, as we sipped our coffee.

"Are you majoring in English too?" she asked.

"No. Philosophy." I braced myself against the awful next question, What is your Philosophy of Life? But that sensible girl didn't ask it.

"Philosophy! I'd probably flunk it if I ever took it. I'm flunking all my subjects except English. But I don't care," she said, growing distant again. "Unless I flunk out. I'd hate that. I'd have to go *home*." There was a trace of mockery in the exaggerated Southern way she said "home," in two syllables. "How come you're majoring in philosophy?"

I stirred my coffee, stalling. How could I tell her why I chose philosophy? I couldn't tell anyone, it sounded crazy. I shrugged my shoulders, but she wasn't watching. She had put down her coffee and begun examining my books, all tidily arranged on the bookshelves in perfect logical order.

Delight suddenly lit up Roxanne's face as she discovered the tiny volumes of my Little Leather Library. "What dear little books," she squealed, turning them over one at a time. She was okay, I thought. She handled them so reverently that I offered to lend them to her.

"Maybe they'll help you out," I said. "They've always helped me."

It was an odd thing to say, but Roxanne seemed to understand what I meant. "I have a few books you might like to look at too. Nothing like this. ... My room's on the first floor in the West Wing. Room 108. My roommate Dandy is away every weekend, but I'm always here. I don't have anywhere to go. Drop in some time if you feel like it." She walked to the door. She was evidently too refined to mention the Time Line. Definitely okay.

"Thanks for the books," she added. "I'll be careful with them."

"Thank *you* for my notebook," I replied.

Roxanne hesitated on the threshold. Then, dropping her eyes shyly again, she said, "I want you to know I didn't read anything in it, except your name."

"I know you didn't," I said.

She was clearly the exception to prove the rule. A girl I could trust.

Two loners together are different from a pair of ordinary friends. They have more respect for one another.

Roxanne and I quietly became friends; so quietly that people began to mistake us for each other. She was right about having books I would love. She introduced me to Gerard Manley Hopkins and Franz Kafka, as I had opened her eyes to Voltaire and Mencken and Russell. My own reading improved when I began underlining with Roxanne in mind, seeing the world through four eyes instead of two.

Our compulsions and fears complemented one another's. I sat with her in the dining room since she was afraid to eat alone. She hid me in her room during gym and chapel. She listened compassionately as I struggled with the mind-body problem or the problem of free will, and I sat rapt as she read me her poems. After I taught her chess, as my father had taught me, we played by mail, dropping our moves in each other's postal boxes between classes. Together we went to the movies, or avoided the Smoker and the Student Union. We traded clothes, and lent each other money when we needed it.

On weekends we sometimes went to Boston together, sitting apart from the other Baxter girls on the train. They went to Harvard or Boylston Street or Filene's, while we wandered in the old bookstores or took in a concert. Occasionally Roxanne called up a friend she dated at M.I.T., and if his roommate was free they'd join us at Symphony Hall for a matinee or meet us for dinner at Durgin Park.

Roxanne's friend Dave wasn't bad, but his roommate Gary was so unpleasant I kept forgetting his name. I was temporarily off boys, and would certainly never have gone out with him except for Roxanne. Nevertheless, it was at one of those Symphony Hall matinees that I got my first inkling of a possible solution to the mind-body problem.

We were looking around for someone to light our cigarettes during intermission, when I found myself standing next to Professor Donald Alport. He was alone, standing a full head taller than everyone else, gazing over the crowd distractedly. I was thrilled to see out of context this mind that knew everything. His was the only mind I had ever known that had probably seen my vision, and here it was walking around Boston on long legs, winding up in exactly the same auditorium, and at precisely the same moment, as mine.

"Dr. Alport," I said.

"Hello there." He slowly focused on my eyes. "Are you enjoying the concert?"

"Oh, yes! The Eroica's my favorite symphony. Are you?"

He didn't answer, just looked at me. Suppose he had hated the concert? To cover up, I changed the subject. "Professor Alport, this is Roxanne du Bois, and her friend Dave Merritt, and . . . and . . . and . . ."

My mind blacked out. I couldn't remember Gary's name. Dr. Alport was looking at my face severely now—so severely that I wanted to disappear. I tried to remember the name again, but I couldn't. If only someone else would say something; if only Dr. Alport would stop staring at me.

I was still searching for Gary's name when it occurred to me that Dr. Alport wasn't waiting for me to produce the name of my date at all. He was concentrating his gaze too deeply into my eyes for that to be it. Inexplicably, I felt the flow of adrenalin. My eyes began to waver under the stern gaze, and I was filled with self-loathing at the defeat. It's the defeat of the Bus Stop Game!—I may not touch it tonight.

I feel myself turning crimson. Now I know what is happening. I have an itch for this hulking man whose power has forced my eyes, unworthy to look at him, into humiliating retreat. This itch that has been such a long time coming—years and years!—this itch spreads little waves from my joy button to my scalp and fingertips. I know I am deep purple by now, and still I can't raise my eyes.

"Yes, how do you do?" he is saying, ignoring that I have still not introduced my date by name. He has let me off the hook.

And then I understand that the penetrating gaze was only Dr. Alport's own attempt to remember my name, which he has now given up. It is he who wants off the hook. He does not know quite everything. Outside the classroom he doesn't even recognize me.

He moves off. Everyone forgets my gaffe. The gong is sounding for us to return to our seats and I move with the others down the aisle. In my head I hear a distressing discord, more than the sound of the orchestra tuning up. I prepare to hear the music. But the staggering itch remains.

♥

"Miss Davis."

"Yes?"

"I found your paper on Nietzsche extremely interesting. Did anyone help you with it?"

"No, Professor Alport. No one." Although I had patently adored Dr. Alport for over a month, unable to take breath without hearing his voice, this was our first private conference. Between last week, when he had called it, and today I had walked around in a mist of anticipation, rehearsing for this moment, taking now my part to Roxanne's Alport, now Alport's to Roxanne's me. But facing him in person, flesh to flesh, I forgot all my lines.

"It's a very good paper." He put a pencil to his lips and scrutinized me. Though my pulse quickened, I was paralyzed.

"Has anyone ever told you you have an interesting turn of mind?"

"Not really. Thank you," I managed, reddening beyond endurance.

"Particularly for an undergraduate. You might want to consider doing some special work." He was biting deeply into the pencil, making the end disappear under his dense grey mustache, indistinguishable in color from his eyes.

I had slaved over the Nietzsche paper, agonizing over each word, exhausting the library and the unabridged, listening to Wagner, all toward this particular A. But never did I expect anything more. *O my soul, I gave thee the right to say Nay like the storm and to say Yea as the Open heaven saith Yea. . . . Thus spake Zarathustra.* Nietzsche's own daring had inspired me, and the Liebestod, soaring higher and higher in my head provoked such desire that now, watching Dr. Alport's pink lips move caressingly over the yellow cylinder of wood, I was struggling against the liquefaction of my spine, urging myself: *do it!*

"A remarkable grasp. If you think you might be interested, I could give you a special reading list. No need for *you* to stick to the textbook selections."

Too much. He had remarked my acumen and erudition, and I could never begin to repay him. If only I were worthy of him, he could have me as soup for lunch. *O my soul, I washed the petty shame and the*

*by-place virtue from thee and persuaded thee to stand
naked before the eyes of the sun.* ... *Thus spake
Zarathustra.*

"How're your Saturdays, Miss Davis?" (*O my soul
... Who knowest as thou knowest the voluptuousness
of the future?*) "Saturday morning I'll have time for a
good long chat. We could meet at the library or"—he
took the pencil out of his mouth and leaned forward
over the desk—"or here in my office if you prefer."

*I heard a laughter which was no human laughter—
and now gnaweth a thirst at me, a longing that is never
allayed. My longing for that laughter gnaweth at me, o,
how can I still endure to live? Thus spake Zarathustra.*

"Dr. Alport?" My eyes had locked in their old
daring glance, somehow managing not to falter.

"Yes?"

"I wanted to ask you something."

"What is it?"

"Dr. Alport?" He waited, his grey eyes as unflinching
as mine, till I blurted out: "Are you seducible?"

I felt faint. I had had crushes before, starting as an
orthodox bobby-soxer in Baybury Heights with the
hots for Frank Sinatra, but never a crush like this. This
huge ungainly man destroying a pencil between his
jaws personified all that I valued and nothing I
scorned. I worshiped him. What did I care that he was
twice my age and probably married? I did not believe in
youth or marriage. He was so far above the petty
concerns that corrupted every shallow young man I
knew that I didn't care if he was forty or one hundred
and forty. I loved him for his mind that knew everything—a provocative mind whose experienced eye could
penetrate through layers of mask, clothes, skin, muscle,
and bone, straight to the center of me where my own

untutored mind, now a quivering mass of jelly, lay
waiting to be given form and life.

He unknitted his brow and sat back. "I think that
can be arranged, Miss Davis."

Indeed, I led a charmed life. Things went too much
my way to be all accident. The Blue Fairy of my
childhood had evidently given way to a genie of rare
skill. How else explain that this remarkable Professor
Alport, of whose mere attention I was so unworthy,
should say yes? He barely knew me. And yet he, with
his hundreds of students, had recognized buried in my
term papers and among the pages of my B-plus bluebooks the one quality I treasured in myself. Not my
nose or my skin; not my eyelashes or my ass—but my
"interesting turn of mind," as he dubbed it. My authen-
tic preciousness. Oh, it was his.


Saturday morning came slowly and ceremoniously, like
a virgin's wedding day. From his office where he was
already waiting when I arrived at nine, Dr. Alport led
me to an old brick building just off campus. At the
entrance to a third-floor apartment he fumbled with
lock and keys until the door finally yielded; then,
lifting me effortlessly in his lanky arms, he carried me
to the dark inside and lay me gently on someone's
unmade bed.

Did it really happen? With sure fingers he unbut-
toned my sweater, reached under me to unhook my
bra, and lay both garments on the floor without moving
his eyes from my already heaving chest. Slowly he bent
his head and placed one long kiss on each breast,
unkissed before.

"So beautiful, so perfect," he murmured, removing
my dungarees and sox with the same deft touch. And
suddenly I lay exposed and quivering under his gaze.

Shame almost turned me over; but I so longed to please this generous man who had brought me here that I forced myself to stay on my back, exposed.

He stood up and removed his own clothes, then lay down beside me. I closed my eyes. I no longer thought to please, I was so captivated by the thrill of toes on toes, his somewhat convex belly on my concave one, his prick on my thigh. Lying naked in a bed with a man for the first time in my life might explain a little, but not the joy of my untutored head fitting perfectly on the shoulder of one who knows everything; not the rapture when at last he kissed my waiting mouth while his practiced fingers continued to stroke me. My back, my neck, my thighs—I had never been touched or kissed before, and now suddenly, out of a large generosity of spirit, this gifted teacher would give me in one day a supply of caresses to make up for years. Beginning at my fingertips, he kissed one finger at a time down into the webs and up the next and moved slowly over every inch of me with his generous lips and tongue. He lingered over each freckle, each beauty mark, as I lay back, eyes still closed, incredulous. I, who had nothing to give him but gratitude and adoration, was being kissed, despite my smells, in the armpits, on the nipples, the navel. Gently he spread my thighs and moved his mustached mouth down one, then the other, until, after an eternity, he zeroed in on my very center, so many times invaded but never once kissed.

Happy me, to be kissed and covered like this at last, to be inexplicably noticed and loved. Starting like a pebble plunging deep into a pool, my gratitude stirred under those tingling kisses and spread through my body in little concentric circles, little shock waves, warming me, fanning out to my fingertips, my nerve endings, touching my glands and ducts until tears overflowed my eyes, and from somewhere deep inside me rose a strange little whimper of joy.

So this was what my joy-life meant! So this was the point of it!

His tongue lingered for a last caress, and then he entered my body with a single welcome thrust. My knees and lips guided him into me, greasing the way for him. I clasped my legs around his massive trunk to merge my own self in his. Like a quarter's worth of nightcrawlers we undulated in unison until everything we knew came together.

Suddenly he jerked himself out, and pulling my head abruptly to his lap, came in my mouth. I considered it an honor. We smoked one cigarette without a word, and then we started all over again.

Alport was married, with a wife, a house, several small children, and an unfinished research project—all more deserving of his time than I. Though I hadn't expected to see him again outside of class, I was grateful for the occasional Saturday morning he gave me, and I treasured the veiled messages he wrote on my bluebooks and the A's I wasn't sure I deserved. Unable to speak in his presence, instead I spilled my feelings to Roxanne or held passionate conversations with him when I was alone in my room.

When summer came, Roxanne went home, but I stayed at Baxter. I registered for both of the summer courses Alport taught, Ethics and Metaphysics, expecting no more of him than any ordinary student, but wanting to make myself available just in case. It was my genie, I'm sure, who arranged that we would spend the free time between the two classes having coffee together.

I never believed I could be so happy as I was from nine till one every day that summer. We sat in the darkest corner of a certain coffeeshop, straining toward each other across a small table, barely able to keep from touching. I could see that he had the same trouble as I. We began building elegant metaphysical fugues on some theme arising out of a class discussion or a line of text, embellishing and complicating together. Our music grew rich as, little by little, I opened up. Soon there was no more room for my shyness. Willingly, I sat at Alport's feet. I did all the tasks and read all the books he assigned me. My mind never worked better. Even when he corrected me it was with such care that I emerged unharmed. I played Héloïse to his generous Abélard. One compliment from him on a question I asked set me up for a week, and under his direction I composed charming pieces of my own. He responded with such open delight that I began to believe he loved me a little, too.

We made love every Saturday morning—not nearly enough. I wanted to spend my life with him. Before the fall term of my senior year, I decided to take a room off campus so we could be more together. I had managed the ordeal of getting a diaphragm for Alport, why not a room as well? My dream was to spend one whole night with him, curled up in the curve of his body, waking up beside him in the morning.

I had five hundred dollars' worth of war bonds I could cash if my parents wouldn't pay the rent. I wrote Roxanne about my plan (she would have to masquerade as my roommate) and made up a good pitch for my parents. Fearing Alport's veto, I didn't say a word to him. Then I got the room.

Black walls, my books and phonograph, and a bed were all I started with. I was crazy to keep everything pure, like my love. I didn't even put up the Time Line or my pictures.

"Wait here," I said when the room was ready. Quickly I ran inside to start the *Grosse Fuge* on the phonograph while Alport waited. Then I went back outside for him and led him in with his eyes closed.

"Promise not to open them until I tell you to?"

"I promise."

In we went. "You can look now," I said, watching his face. He opened his eyes. "Do you like it?" I squealed. "It's ours."

He just carried me to the bed for an answer.


When Roxanne came back to school after the summer, she was more distant than usual. Her roommate Dandy had married and dropped out of school; I thought maybe it was my leaving the dorm too that depressed her. Maybe she thought I had used her, or abandoned her. I begged her to move in with me.

"I can't."

"Why not?"

"My mother would pull me out of school if she found out I was living with *the Jewess*."

"How would she find out?"

"She'd find out."

She grew glummer and glummer until, finally, she told me what was the matter.

"I think I'm pregnant."

"Pregnant! My God! Have you missed your period?"

"No, not yet, but I'm sure I will."

"How can you be sure?"

"My luck."

She was already sick, vomiting in the mornings and unable to eat. She didn't dare go to the infirmary, since pregnancy meant automatic expulsion from Baxter.

When she missed her first period, I begged her to get a pregnancy test, but she wouldn't. "Why bother with a test? I know I'm pregnant." She smiled an ironic I-told-you-so smile. I knew she wouldn't take the test out of the same defeatism that kept her from taking the zoology exams: she simply wasn't prepared to deal with the result.

She had been knocked up by a West Point cadet friends had thrust on her late in the summer. So eager was he to make out that he had hardly pulled off her pants and lay on top of her before he'd come all over her legs. It had been their third, and, she had determined, their last date. It was a freaky impregnation, but, as they say in the hygiene books, all it takes is one sperm and one egg.

When she missed her second period she finally consented to have a test. We searched among the doctors in the Boston Yellow Pages for a sympathetic-sounding obstetrician. There were only a few names left after we eliminated all those sounding Catholic (O'Brien), expensive (Van Aken), or Puritanical (Goodwin). We finally picked out a Dr. Brodsky ("Pick a Jewish name," said Roxanne; "at least he won't·be Catholic") on Flint Street, and the following Saturday, while Roxanne waited in a diner across the street, I took him a sample of her urine in an instant-coffee jar. It was I who put on the dime-store wedding ring and walked into the doctor's office because, should the police be called, unpregnant I could deny everything. We used a pseudonym with my true address.

The result came a week later. Positive—Roxanne's luck. We couldn't go back to the same doctor, because now it was Roxanne who had to be examined, not I. She wanted an abortion, but she had neither money nor an abortionist. I offered her all my money, but she had no one to spend it on. Tucked away in western Massachusetts, we knew no one to go to for help. Absolutely forbidding me to discuss it with Alport, Roxanne decided to go to Boston and tell Dave, her M.I.T. friend. Maybe he could find the name of an abortionist.

"What did he say?" I asked eagerly when she returned.

"We had such a nice weekend I couldn't tell him."

"You mean you wasted the whole trip?"

"I knew he'd think I was trying to pin it on him if I told him. Anyway, it wasn't all wasted. We had a good dinner and we read *King Lear* together. I played the women, and he played the men."

"Roxanne, you don't have any time to play around. *I'm* going to tell him if you won't. Or else I'm going to get in touch with the father."

"No you won't," she said firmly.

"Well, what are you going to do, then?"

"I don't know."

It was already almost too lote. Roxanne spent precious hours in front of the mirror trying to see if the pregnancy showed instead of getting rid of it. To torture herself she put on her tightest clothes and examined her profile.

"Don't you think it shows?" she asked hysterically, and changed her clothes again. She stopped attending classes and began to withdraw, spending more and more time in bed. She refused the food I brought to her room, saying, "I'm going to starve it out."

She looked terrible. "I am going to notify the father, that bastard. Let him find a doctor. It's his fault," I said.

But Roxanne wouldn't hear of it. "He's got his own problems. Anyway, I can't stand him."

When she missed her third period and it was too late to do anything else, Roxanne went home to her mother. "Don't worry," she said, preparing to leave. "She'll find me a nice home for wayward girls and maybe I'll finally get some sleep. I'd never graduate anyway, since I'm flunking zoology and history. Maybe I'll get a degree from a correspondence school."

She planned, after she gave away the baby, to get a job in New York City and write poetry. "I'd rather take Martha Foley's writing workshop at Columbia than stay here worrying about zygotes. At least," she said with her ironical smile, "by then I'll have lots to write about." The more cheerful she tried to sound, the more desperate I knew she was.

"Take the Little Leather books with you for good luck," I said, thrusting several at her.

"Good idea," said Roxanne. "If the nuns enforce lights-out after evening prayers, I can read Voltaire under the covers by flashlight. *Till human voices wake us and we drown*—or till we have to get up and change a diaper." She smiled her distant smile. "Well, so long. You'll be hearing from me. I hope everything works out with you and your dreamboat. Be careful not to let the old man knock you up."

Alport came to my room for occasional quickies in the evening, or between certain classes, and on Saturdays, but we never did get to spend a whole night together. The best we managed was a whole Saturday, from nine until six, with a long delicious nap in the middle. I was grateful for whatever I could get.

There were no more courses of his left for me to take, so I stopped being his student. Still, we managed to see each other almost every day, if only for coffee,

whether or not there was time to touch, whether or not
I was having my period.

In all my classes but French, I began to feel like a
pro. My dream was coming true; finally I saw the
entire history of ideas, at least in outline, at a glance.
Every new text fit so neatly into place that I was able
at last to concentrate on details. I may not have had
the answers, but I felt familiar with the standard
questions. I could recognize and catalogue them as
readily as Beethoven's quartets.

I got out of gym with a fake heart-murmur letter
from one of the family MD's and officially protested
chapel on philosophical grounds. It was a good ploy to
submit my junior honors paper (on the Refutation of
Anselm's Proofs of the Existence of God) in support of
my position. The Dean of Women, afraid of contro-
versy and aware that I was born Jewish, allowed me to
skip chapel if I agreed to give some alternative service
instead—tutoring poor town children in math, for example. I agreed. Alport insisted that I learn my French
giving me Descartes's little *Discours de la méthode* to
study from. Since he expected me to pass, I did,
preparing to cheat on the final if necessary. Nothing
would prevent my graduating.

The wife? Alport refused to discuss her, and I tried
not to think about her. She was simply one of the limits
within which I was forced to operate like the Kantian
categories. She was the invisible context. Though the
thought of her filled me with pain, I wasn't jealous, for
she had preceded me and would survive me in her
claims on Alport. To understand that was, as Spinoza
taught, to accept it. My only claim on Alport was my
love.

Alport helped me fill out applications for graduate

school. Despite the mediocre reputation of its graduate philosophy department, I applied to New England University to be near him, as well as to the University of Chicago and Columbia. To all three Alport wrote me glowing recommendations.

"Let me see what you wrote." I grabbed for the letter.

"It's highly irregular," said Alport in his deepest voice, raising the paper out of my reach.

"I don't care. Let me see." I leaped up and snatched it from him, then read it with my heart in my throat. It took no more than one sentence to remind me of my irrepressible itch. "Do you really believe this stuff you wrote? Is that person really me?"

"Yes, I really believe the 'stuff' I wrote. Yes, that person's really you."

There was only one way I knew to express my graditude. And even that was sadly inadequate.

It was a long time before I heard from Roxanne. I was so worried about her I called her house in Virginia. But her mother refused to tell me where she was, and I had no other leads.

Finally in April I got a letter. It was from an army base in Dallas, from a Mrs. Whitney Boyd Jr.— "housewife, mother, and camp follower." It was heartbreaking.

Roxanne's mother had "convinced" her to marry the cadet instead of bearing the baby out of wedlock. With herself as the living proof, Mrs. Du Bois had said: "You can always get a divorce; it's better than being used merchandise." And for Whitney Boyd, Jr., it was evidently better than sacrificing a commission. Roxanne said she was naming the baby after me if I didn't object—"unless it's a mongoloid." Luckily my name was good for either sex.

She described her domestic life with an elaborate military metaphor, matching detail for detail. The talent Martha Foley would be losing! She ended the letter bitterly: marriage was "not much better than home." "Write me anything you like," she said in closing, her distant smile rising from the page. "My husband is functionally illiterate."

♌♌

Something was wrong. Even before I opened the door to let Alport in, I sensed it. He was late, and wasn't the knock different?

Inside, everything was arranged the Saturday way: coffee in the pot, our two mugs set up on the floor, a Rasumovsky quartet playing on the phonograph; and I, hair freshly washed, legs and underarms newly shaved, diaphragm in place, had bathed and dressed again in my one sheer nightie.

Yet something was not quite right. I undid the bolt and opened the door.

A woman. She didn't have to say a word for me to know who she was. Alport's wife.

She looked me over through my nightie, burning my skin with her eyes. Nowhere to hide.

"I think it's time you and I had a talk, don't you?" she said, planting herself inside the room. She bolted the door and placed her back firmly against it, folding her arms across her bosom. I backed slowly toward a dark corner, imperceptibly diminishing.

"Well? Aren't you going to invite me to sit down?"

"Please. Sit down," I managed. I didn't care. I had

already slipped out the window leaving only a sticky shell of me behind in the room to manage the charade of offering coffee and maybe saying a word or two.

She sat down on the bed. "No thank you, no coffee. But I'll wait while you put some clothes on, if you like." She took a cigarette out of her bag and leaned back on the bed against the wall while I obediently pulled on a heavy wool work shirt—my bathrobe. She lit her cigarette and, exhaling, spread her presence through the room.

"Ashtray, please?"

I brought her an ashtray.

"That's better. You may sit down too."

My shell sat at the end of the bed. Even seated, she dominated me from an imposing height. She was a large, beautiful woman of forty, say, or thirty, big-boned, big-bosomed, big-hipped. Lush. Her proud face with its fine toothy smile and piercing eyes emanated a sureness that made mush of me. She had my mother's pink smell—the same face powder?—but none of my mother's softness. No, there was nothing soft in this one, nothing to play on.

"What's your name?"

"Sasha."

"How old are you, Sasha?"

"Nineteen."

"Nineteen. Why, Donald's old enough to be your father."

A strange thrill flickered through me. *Donald*. To me it was just a name in the college catalogue. I never called him anything, and thought of him only as Alport. She called him Donald.

"Do you know how old Donald is, Sasha?"

"Forty-three?"

"Yes. Forty-three. With a son of his own only a few

years younger than you. And two little girls. And, of course, a wife." She paused, respecting the magnitude of the pronouncement. "Tell me," she said, covering my hand with hers, "aren't you ashamed of yourself?"

I was indeed terrified, but hardly ashamed. "For what?" I asked.

"For trying to take a married man from his children and his wife. For jeopardizing his job. For putting everything he cares about in jeopardy."

It had never crossed my mind that I might be taking Alport from anything. He did the taking. I was just there, available for him to take. "That's his choice," I said. "I can't make him see me. Maybe he cares about me too."

She got up, walked to the phonograph, and took the needle off the record. "Do you mind?" she said. I shook my head. "It's very hard to try to compete with Beethoven." She smiled down on me, crushing my shell into the mattress.

"Now, Sasha, I'm going to ask you to do something for me. It may be difficult for you, because I'm sure Donald has charmed you out of your senses, but I'm going to ask you anyway. For your own sake and his sake, as well as mine. I'm going to ask you not to see Donald again."

But of course.

"He's been in this sort of trouble before," she continued. "You're not by any means his first little ... friend. But if he gets in trouble again, that will quite simply be the end of his teaching career. He has three young children totally dependent on him for support. Do you understand what that means? He has an enormous obligation to meet." Her fine nostrils flared out as, again, she exhaled her will over me, and crushed out the cigarette.

"Why don't you ask *him?*" said my shell. From outside the window I admired how coolly my shell answered her back.

"Oh, I shall, don't worry. But I wanted to meet you first."

She suddenly smiled at me so warmly that I wanted to trust everything to her. She seemed fully competent to manage things and unscramble us.

"Tell me," she said with concern, "do you love Donald very much?"

I nodded. Why waste on words the little strength I had left?

She nodded too, sympathetically. "I know. Luckily, you're very young. You'll love again. But it's not everything. You'll see that one day." She raised her perfectly arched eyebrows and asked, "Where are your parents? Do they know about this affair?"

I shook my head. I saw that my hands were trembling, though I didn't feel it. I hid them under me.

"I do hope it won't be necessary for your parents to be told, Sasha," said Mrs. Alport. She put her cigarettes back in her bag and walked to the door. "I hope I haven't upset your Saturday too terribly. But when you start this sort of thing, I suppose you really ought to be prepared for the consequences."

She looked at her watch and unbolted the door. "You'll understand if I say I hope we won't have to meet again. Goodbye, Sasha."

I saw him three times more. The first time, that very day, he was enraged to learn that his wife had been to see me. "It's none of her business. *I'll* decide whom I see and how I spend my time!" But he had arrived late, and had to leave early, and when we made love I didn't come.

The second time he stayed longer. I brewed us jasmine tea. Just before he left he told me he was going away during exam week to use some documents in the library of another university.

"Is your wife going with you?" I asked.

"Yes, she'll probably come along," he said. I had never before felt the right to ask such a question. But with her presence still dominating the room, it just slipped out.

Exam week, between cramming and listening to the late quartets, I gazed out through my crumbling defenses to see there was really no room for me in Alport's life except in the crevices. Philosophy, I consoled myself, had been my first love anyway. Why study here when I could go to a place like Columbia? The music was so poignant that I found myself bursting into tears, especially during the fugal passages. Perhaps it was because of all the No-Doz pills I took cramming for exams. I even cried in the middle of one exam, writing an essay on Aristotle's thesis that it's love that makes the world go round. Fancy crying, when I knew I was writing bullshit!

The third time I saw him was after he came back. Over coffee I told him I was pretty sure I was going to Columbia.

He said nothing for a while, just sat on the floor and sipped his coffee. Then, stretching his long legs out before him, he said, "You know I hoped you would stay here with me. I wanted that more than anything. But I can't blame you for wanting to go to Columbia. It's got the best department in the country. You'll go there, and you'll get married, and I can't blame you at all."

"I'll never get married!" I cried. "I don't believe in marriage! Or in having babies or changing diapers or wearing aprons or owning anyone or being owned, either!"

He smiled a superior, knowing smile that made me want to kill him.

"Why don't you leave now?" I screamed. "Why don't you just go on home right now?"

He shrugged his shoulders. "As you wish," he said softly, and walked out of my life.

# S
# I
# X

Nothing like seven days on the high seas for thinking things over. I boarded the *Benvenuto Cellini* at Genoa to the music of a little brass band and a hundred weeping families. After checking my cabin (no roommate: a good omen), I went directly to the Tourist Class dining room, where a sailing party was under way—champagne for everyone.

I entered expectantly. A whole shipload of new people; an international atmosphere. I sat at a table with only one other woman, old and evidently married. She nodded to me, then spent her time engaging a soft-spoken engineer from Brooklyn on her right and a Milanese exchange student on her left. There was something reminiscent of an old movie farce as we made our own introductions and nibbled at plattersful of French hors d'oeuvres.

"You have been in Italy long, signora?" asked the student from Milan, noticing my ring. He was on his way to Bowdoin College.

"Only a few months, I'm afraid. Not nearly long enough."

"Perhaps someday you will come back," he said, raising his glass. He had those deep, long-lashed Italian eyes.

"Oh, yes," I smiled, already pained to be going home, "I'll drink to that." In that tinkly atmosphere, all Italians were once again charming.

An hour later I finished off a last glass of champagne and went to the Purser's Desk to sign up for second sitting. I wanted my meals to be long and leisurely. With a weekful of parties in every public room, and me the best-looking female passenger I had seen so far, I knew it would likely be a pleasant crossing. But I wanted more than that. Since this brief ocean voyage would be my last taste of freedom before I surrendered in New York a second time to a loveless marriage, I wanted one last dose of love.

♥

By the time I married, I had been in love up to my chin. For a whole year I'd wallowed in it, waking up and licking it off my fingers like a child gorging itself after Hallowe'en. But even without Mrs. Alport to tell me, I knew it wasn't nourishing enough to live on, and I didn't choose it for my daily diet. As the philosophers implied, love was the frosting that made life delicious, not the stuff of sustenance. I made a "sensible" marriage instead.

I hadn't really wanted to marry at all. I wanted to make something of myself, not just give it away. But I knew if I didn't marry I would be sorry. Only freaks didn't. I knew I had to do it quickly, too, while there was still a decent selection of men to choose from. Dr. Watson might be right about personality not hardening until thirty, but old maids started forming at twenty-one. I was twenty. The heavy pressure was on. In years I was still safe, but in distance I was borderline. I had finished college and started graduate school. The best catches were being picked off while I was educating myself right out of the running.

I had altered my ambitions once for love; I didn't dare do it again. My first love, philosophy, still claimed me. Now I had to choose a mate who would share me with it. That ruled out Prince Charming.

After a lot of careful thought I chose Frank. Not that he was perfect—no one is. But I was fond of him, none of his parts were missing, and unlike all the other eligibles I knew, he seemed willing and able to make a little room in his future for mine.

Franklin Raybel was in the History Department at Columbia, studying Modern European History. He had a perfect name for a title page and a graduate fellowship, which meant he probably had a good future. It was an important point for me, because if we were both going to be teaching, my husband would have to be able to get a job at a university large enough to accommodate me, too.

Like me, Frank was a Midwesterner sufficiently threatened by New York to need fortification. From Gary, Indiana, and twenty-seven, he had come farther and further than I. I would have preferred someone from the Philosophy Department, but my Columbia classmates all treated me either as an interloper or an anomaly. "So you're the dish I heard about; I was hoping I'd get into a class with you," they said. In my seminars no one ever listened to a single word I said without grinning, and then as soon as I had finished they'd all return to their heated disputes as though I had never spoken. They treated me a little better than they treated the older women in the department, at least acknowledging (after class) that I existed. But it was still a terrible comedown after Baxter College, where my classmates had listened to what I had to say and Alport had encouraged me.

Those Columbia classes were all the more disheartening because in them were held the headiest discussions I had ever been privileged to sit in on. Theses and antitheses, arguments and counterarguments, premises and conclusions ricocheted off the walls and exploded midair above the mahogany conference table in brilliant illuminations. After only a couple of weeks of classes, however, I felt so intimidated, and then stupid, that I didn't dare participate. I just did my reading and tried to look as though I considered all that disputation beneath me. I chose obscure minor figures to write my papers on, hoping no one in the seminars would know enough about my subjects to ridicule me. And on weekends when the philosophers invited me to their parties, instead of sitting dumb and pretty through their snappy talk, I helped their girlfriends from other departments (English, Teacher's College, Barnard) serve the food and coffee that kept them going at each other till two A.M.

"How come *you're* studying philosophy?" my colleagues would ask me over beer with bemused smiles. "Do you really want to get a Ph.D? Do you really expect to teach?" The way they asked their questions, I knew better than to answer yes. I quickly learned that there was only a handful of teaching jobs in philosophy in the country—all coveted, all for them.

"I just like philosophy, that's all," I'd answer. "I don't know what I'll do with my Ph.D. Maybe I can work for a philosophical journal. Maybe I can teach in a finishing school."

Franklin Raybel spared me such questions. He talked too little to talk down. Sitting in Riverside Park of an autumn Sunday afternoon, we read the poetry of Yeats or Donne together, equally moved. As philosophy was considered a "harder" subject than history, Frank allowed that I might be serious, even awarding me a certain respect. He once listened to my explanations of Leibniz which, he later told me, he was able to repeat to advantage in his own department. He was gentle and noncommittal, permitting me to select our movies and set the time for our meetings; he gave me his favorite books to read and picked me the last buttercups along the Hudson where warm Sundays found us walking.

"Loves me, loves me not, loves me, loves me not, loves me," he said self-consciously, stripping a buttercup of all five petals.

"No, silly," I laughed. "Buttercups will *always* come out 'loves me.' You can only get the truth from daisies. Buttercups tell you something else."

"They do?" he asked surprised. "What?"

"Whether or not you like butter."

He looked dubious.

"Really," I assured him. "Hold them under my chin. Closer." I thrust out my chin invitingly and closed my eyes. "Now—is my chin yellow or not?"

He tipped my jaw up with his index finger and kissed my mouth. "Yes," he whispered.

"That means I like butter. Now let me do it to you."

I took the bouquet from his hand and held it under his chin, brushing shamelessly against him. His only trouble, I decided, was shyness.

"Well?" he asked, his eyes half-closed.

I shook my head. "I'm afraid you definitely don't like butter. That means we're probably incompatible," I concluded with a pout.

"Flowers can lie," said Frank, and daring to push them to one side, kissed me again.

To find out the truth of it (and because I had a paper due and would not go home to Baybury) we spent Christmas vacation in an off-campus room of a friend of his. Compatible? Let me say we were not incompatible. I craved appreciation. The better I fucked the more he liked me, inspiring me to put on an ever better show. I could see from how cheerfully he brought in Chinese food for us to eat in the room and how eagerly he introduced me to several of his friends that he was pleased to spend the time with me. I was pleased too: there were worse sensations than being wanted. But I didn't expect him to come out and "love" me. We had hardly ever spoken personally.

"How can you say you love me? You hardly know me," I said, turning down the phonograph to hear his first shy declaration. I was quite surprised. Even in Baybury, where strangers had not uncommonly declared their love in mash notes or anonymous phone calls, I was always surprised.

He told me quite plainly how. "You're the first girl I've ever known who was smart *and* beautiful," he said. "The pretty girls I've gone out with have always turned out dumb, and the ones with brains have never been more than good friends. I can't help it," he confessed, "but I know I'll never love a girl who doesn't have both."

So! He considered me exceptional, appreciating my best aspects, and at the same time revealed himself innocent and honest—good qualities in a husband. If, as the poet says, only God can love one for oneself, at least Frank didn't try to play God. A true liberal, he would likely respect his wife and treat her well.

I investigated. "What are you thinking about? Truth, now."

"You really want the truth? I happened to be thinking about your resemblance to a certain painting by Boucher of Mlle. Morphy, who was a favorite of Louis XV. ... Don't misunderstand," he added, "I mean your looks, not your character."

He knew I'd been no virgin—knew, in fact, I'd had an unfortunate affair with a married man—but he liked to think of me as an innocent led astray. As to my professed belief in free love, it was fine if I were involved with someone like him, but dangerous if I were involved with someone as unscrupulous as Alport. He overlooked it as he overlooked my dashing across the street against every traffic light: antics of impetuous youth.

Between Christmas and intersession I examined him closely. If there were ten good reasons to marry him, why then I would do it! On Ash Wednesday, while people in churches repented, I stayed in my dorm and made a list.

Ten good reasons, and besides, it was time. We'd each be getting what we wanted.

"If you really love me so much," I sprang on him over spring vacation, "then why don't you want to marry me?" A sl question, worthy of my fellow philosophers.

He reached for his cigarettes, stalling. But he fell for it.

"What makes you think I don't?"

"Well, do you?"

"Yes."

"Then let's get married."

"Well . . ." He hesitated, but I knew I had him. "Okay."

I waited while he nervously lit a cigarette; then, handing him an ashtray and blowing out his match, I said softly, "How about tomorrow?"

"Tomorrow! We can't tomorrow! It takes time to get the license and everything."

Oh, he was squirming.

"As soon as we can get the license, then."

"In the middle of a semester? Why not wait till summer? What's the big rush?"

"No *rush* exactly," I said. "Just, if we're going to do it ever, we might as well do it now. There's no reason *not* to. When in doubt, *do it!*"

"But what about our families? This is crazy. I've never even mentioned you to my parents."

"Is it their life?" I asked contemptuously. "It's ours! Would you let your parents influence you? They should be happy to be notified."

He could certainly have said no if he'd wanted to. I couldn't force him to say yes. He could have composed his own list of pros and cons.

"Look," I said, with a hint of impatience. "It's not as though we were planning to have a family. We'll ask for cash instead of wedding presents and live on that, and we can both work summers till we get our degrees. If it doesn't work out, we can always get a divorce."

How could he dispute my logic without seeming small-minded? Magnanimously, he succumbed.

"Okay. Everyone will probably think we're mad, but if you want to, we'll do it."

We kissed. I was positively high.

"You crazy adorable little girl," he said, warming to the notion. "Shall we call our parents now?"

"Remember," I warned, "once we tell them, there's no going back." (If he says yes three times, it must be true.)

"I know."

We go to the phone booths at the back of the dorm lobby to call. He calls first. I listen to him tell his mother (my mother-in-law!), smiling wrinkles into the corners of his eyes. He hands me the phone. "How do you do, Mrs. Raybel, this is Sasha. . . . We really just decided this very minute. You're the first person we told. . . . We'll let you know just as soon as we know. Mother."

Then I put in a call to Baybury Heights.

"Mom? Guess what? I'm getting married." I can just imagine her face! "To Franklin Raybel. A graduate student in history from Indiana. . . . This coming week-end at City Hall, if we can manage it. . . . No, darling, of course not. Really, nothing like that. I'm getting married 'cause I want to. . . . Yes, really-really. . . . Oh, mother, you're so silly. . . . You'll meet him and see for yourself."

I cover the mouthpiece and lean out of the booth to kiss Frank. What a nice gentle husband I'm getting.

"Well, Mom, aren't you going to wish me luck?"

Dear Sasha,

Just a note to offer my personal congratulations on the completion of what was obviously your thesis. The incorporation of outside intelligences is what this family needs badly, and my personal feeling is that you have likely done well. Lots of luck, and my best to your husband.

Affectionately,

*Uncle Bob*

Dear Sasha,

I knew all that talk about never getting married was just a cover. However crazy you behave sometimes, underneath you're a sensible girl. And why not? You come from a sensible family. I look forward to welcoming Franklin into our family. It will be nice to have a brother, and maybe someday a nephew.

Love,
*Ben*

Almost immediately, the habits of matrimony took over. I had used my dime-store wedding ring for the City Hall ceremony, but when it began to tarnish and itch, I gave in and bought a gold ring, the cheapest we could find. We stayed in our respective dorms for about a week, then moved into a rooming house together off Riverside Drive. To avoid confusion, I changed my name on my graduate records to Mrs. Franklin Raybel. Did I only imagine the philosophers treating me with a new respect?

Except on weekends when we went out for Chinese food or heated Chef Boyardee spaghetti dinners in the communal kitchen (our room came with "kitchen privileges"), I continued to eat in the dorm where, with no refund forthcoming, my meals were paid for. But we studied together evenings, taking a break to walk down

Broadway holding hands and returning to sleep in the
same bed. No more sneaking around; no more blind
dates; no more wasted hours on the telephone; no more
lonely Sundays. I brewed us real coffee for breakfast,
using the coffee grinder someone had sent us for a
wedding present. We drank it in our room with dough-
nuts from the A&P, and on Sundays we'd spend half
the day in bed reading the *New York Times* together.
It was a pleasure to snuggle up at night to another
body; it was a pleasure to be married.

One day, not long after we had moved in together, a
large envelope arrived in the mail from my mother. In
it were a few late congratulations that had been sent on
from Indiana, and two copies of a clipping from the
Cleveland *Post*. The Women's Page announcement of
my marriage. The copy, though embarrassing, was the
usual so-and-so, daughter of so-and-so, marries so-and-
so, son of so-and-so; the couple will reside in New York
City. The shocker was the large reproduction of my
high school graduation picture which accompanied the
article. The reporter must either have remembered me
or have checked back into old Baybury yearbooks; for
there under the picture, in boldface type, was the
caption: SASHA DAVIS, FORMER BAYBURY HEIGHTS PROM
QUEEN, WEDS GRADUATE AT COLUMBIA.

I was overcome with shame. Frank had never seen a
picture of my other self. Even I hardly recognized her
with those shiny cheeks and that eager smile, those long
thick lashes and carefully tousled hair. Had she said
"cheese"? Was that Joey Ross's Keystone pin on her
sweater?

She was someone else, not me. The picture was a
gross distortion, at once too lovely and too crude.
Studio pose, magazine lighting, years past. I tore it into
tiny pieces and flushed them down the hall toilet,

grateful Alport would not see it, grateful Frank was not home. ("Gee, Sasha," Frank would say, focusing from the clipping to me, "You mean I'm married to a Queen of a Bunny Hop?") But when I went back to our room and saw the second copy mocking me from the table, for some reason, instead of tearing it up, I folded it carefully into a square and deposited it with the rest of my past (my scholastic aptitude scores, my list of lovers in a secret code, my childhood poems) in a manila envelope I kept hidden among my sweaters. There was really no decent hiding place in my new life; I would have to rent a post office box for mailing things to myself.

A little later Frank returned from his class. "Any mail?" he asked.

"Nothing much," I said, pouring us each a cup of freshly brewed coffee. "Just some more greeting cards from your relatives." I wondered if the lie showed. My mother always said she could tell when I was lying. Something I did unconsciously gave it away. Like Pinocchio's nose suddenly growing.

"What do you mean, *my* relatives?"

"Your Indiana relatives."

"Then what's this big envelope from Cleveland doing here?" he asked.

On our wedding day I had promised Frank grudgingly that I would not sleep with anyone besides him, though I'd made it clear that the promise was against my principle of free love. Now, hoping to throw him off the track, I exploded with a terrible precedent.

"What is this, an inquisition? Can't I even get a letter from my own mother without your thinking I'm having an affair? That envelope is what the cards came in."

Frank said nothing. Instead, he punished my outburst with a withering look and a perfectly pronounced French couplet the meaning of which I didn't understand.

"What does *that* mean?" I snapped.

"Oh, never mind," he said, satisfied to have made me ask. And with a sigh he picked up his book and withdrew.

It was our first quarrel. It set a pattern for all that would follow, and of course there would be others.

When we went to bed that night, Frank said, as calm as an afterthought, "Sasha, you'd better understand right now, if I ever find out you've been unfaithful to me, I'll divorce you on the spot."

Though I wanted to be a good wife, from the beginning I found it impossible to subdue my desires. I was in fierce competition with my husband, though Frank, completely absorbed in his own studies, was probably unaware of it. He believed he had married an impulsive girl, even a supergirl, but not a separate, feeling woman. He was years ahead of me at Columbia, and though I read faster and studied better than he, I had too far to go to catch up. He was the darling of his department; I was nothing in mine. Though we had agreed to study like fury till our money ran out and then take turns getting jobs, at bottom we both knew it would be he who would get the degrees and I who would get the jobs.

After the summer we took a cheap one-and-a-half-room apartment on West 108th Street. Together we built bookshelves of raw boards and stolen bricks, and slept on a Hide-a-Bed we bought at the Salvation Army Store. But once we were settled into our appropriate young-married quarters, Frank withdrew behind his glasses into his studies, and that whole year we never had one genuine conversation. Though Frank was a live-in husband, we were more like roommates than man and wife, and I had never wanted a roommate. Even during supper when we might have talked, Frank turned on the evening news, reserving his words for the young men in his department, with whom on weekends he never tired of discussing department politics.

I began clipping recipes from the Sunday *Times*. I cooked Mrs. Fielding's Texas Chili, Boeuf Bourguignon (I & II), Creole Jambalaya, Coq au Vin—all in quantity, as Frank let his single friends know they were welcome for dinner on weekends. We always had a wide range of homemade whiskey, too, since a friend who worked in a Bronx hospital gave us 200-proof lab alcohol by the gallon. We diluted it by half, flavored it with a shot of name-brand booze, poured it into reclaimed bottles, and defied anyone to tell it from the real thing.

I enjoyed those Saturday nights. Frank took visible pride in me then, showing me off and openly admiring my cooking. Not one of those tyrannical husbands to criticize his wife before his friends, he called me endearing names in baby talk and sat beside me on the sofa stroking my neck or my knee over coffee. Even after they fell into shop talk, while I cleared away the dinner dishes, he would send me affectionate glances for everyone to see. Sometimes his aroused affection carried over into bed on Saturday night when, after all the ashtrays were emptied and the paper cups thrown away, after his spectacles were deposited on the night table and my diaphragm retrieved from the drawer, he would roll on top of me to make love and tell me how happy he was to have me for a wife.

### Franklin Raybel's
### Chicken Suprême Tarragon

Stuff chicken breasts (skinned, boned, and halved) with
tarragon, salt, pepper, parsley, lump of butter; secure
with toothpicks; dredge with flour. Brown in butter on
both sides. Add chopped shallot or a slice of onion, a
whole clove garlic, tarragon, white wine, chicken
stock, a soaked dried mushroom. Cover. Cook forty-
five minutes, turning once. Remove breasts to a hot
platter and keep warm. Reduce sauce and add two
tablespoons heavy cream; cook to proper consistency.
Add bits of butter at the end. Spoon sauce over breasts,
dust with parsley. Serve with green salad and rice.

### Cucumbers in Lime Dressing

Marinate an hour or so: sliced (or diced) cucumber in:
juice of one lime, sugar, seasonings, diced (or grated)
onion. Chill. Serve cold with curries.

My first job after the wedding money gave out was as a
bookkeeping machine operator in a Wall Street bank at
sixty dollars a week. As Frank forbade me to be a
waitress, and I dreaded being a salesgirl, there was little
else for a twenty-one-year-old nontypist to do. Without
typing I was chronically "overqualified." Without
typing I couldn't even wangle interviews for the jobs
listed in the *Help Wanted Female* section under *College
Grad*, nor could I apply for the nontyping researcher,
editor, or "trainee" jobs for which I supposed I was
suited, listed under *Help Wanted Male*.

My bookkeeping machine (Burroughs F212) was
formidable. I named her Trixie. The work was taxing,

but I liked the precision of it and, eager to master her, found a certain excitement in striking my balance at the end of each day. Until our debits and credits balanced exactly, until every decimal error had been discovered and rooted out, Mr. Calley, the department supervisor, would not permit his girls to go home. After my last deposit had been entered and the last check deducted, I would extract the subtotals, totals, and grand totals the machine had been storing up all day, push certain magic buttons, let the circuits run, and with suspended breath wait for Trixie to end her calculations and reveal in a small window on her face and printed on the record on her back two numbers which, if I had posted everything correctly all day long, would exactly, digit for digit, match. Even my disappointment when the numbers differed was exhilarating.

At first I was slow in balancing, never passing a day without error. Sometimes it was seven o'clock before I descended into the West Side IRT subway station with my book in hand, and almost eight before I surfaced again near Columbia. But by attending to Trixie, setting myself records to beat and techniques to master, I gradually improved my performance until I was as good on my Burroughs as anyone. And as though the suspense were not intoxicating enough, the clattering of fifty cumbersome calculators all totaling at once in a single room provided me with a sense of solidarity against disaster I had never before felt in New York City.

It was broken only by a fifteen-minute morning coffee break, when I made eyes at New York out the window, and a precious solitary hour for lunch. At lunchtime I explored the caverns of Wall Street, thrilled that I, Ohio-born and twenty-one, was living among skyscrapers and traditions. I saw where the Stock

Exchange had been scarred in the twenties by anarchist bombs; I ate hamburgers with college educations. I heard actors rehearsing in lofts, saw pushcart markets, tasted Indian curries and baklava, listened to choruses singing Bach in Trinity Church at noon. When the weather was fine, I took a sandwich to Battery Park, on the very tip of Manhattan Island. There, watching the ferries and tugs and cruise ships passing in the harbor, I fancied myself a boy joining one of the crews sailing off to Jamaica or Barbados or even the distant source of all mental and sensual goodies, Europe. When the weather was foul, I sat in the lounge and read my book, still hopeful of one day knowing everything. Only at night when I returned to Frank who, having polished off yet another tome toward his degree, was ready to help me out cooking our dinner in time for the news—only then did I know that neither would happen.

Not that Frank was to blame. Hardly. I had no doubt he felt almost as bad as I that I was no longer a student. Hadn't he married me half for my brains? No, I alone was to blame for being too tired to study at night and too distractable to read anything but fiction on the subway in the morning. And when I wanted to go to the movies in the evening or walk in Central Park on a weekend afternoon, Frank was too much the gentleman to allude to my lapsed ambitions. He intended no invidious comparisons as he said, "Look, I'd really rather stay home and work. I've got too much reading to do. But why don't you go on without me? You'll relax, and I'll be able to use the time." I felt guilty even asking him to interrupt his work, and didn't blame him for wishing me out of the way. My restlessness was not the easiest thing for a scholar to live with.

So I went off with a neighbor, or a friend from work who lived in the Village and introduced me to pot, or alone. And sometimes, in the huge Grant's Cafeteria on Broadway, or in the back section of the Thalia Theater, where I sat watching foreign films—sometimes I looked for Prince Charming, just in case he too happened to be out alone catching a breath of air or taking in a movie.

"Miss Raybel? Or is it Mrs. Raybel?"

"Mrs. Raybel."

"Mrs. Raybel, it has come to our attention that you are a college graduate," said the personnel manager, an elderly gentleman dressed by Brooks Brothers.

What could he want? Mr. Calley, the bookkeeping department supervisor, patting me kindly on the rear, had assured me, sending me down here, that I was not to be fired.

"In that case, we are going to offer you a promotion. We are prepared to transfer you to the Foreign Department at a starting salary of seventy-five dollars a week," he beamed.

"Doing what?" I asked.

"Translating."

I swallowed my surprise. French, my only foreign language, had always been my worst subject. "Translating what?" I asked.

"Letters, documents, letters of credit."

I knew I couldn't manage it, but the raise was substantial. "What languages?" I asked.

"You'll translate from all the languages into English. French, Spanish, German, Italian. Not Chinese," he smiled.

I nodded. What difference did it make whether I was unable to translate from one language or many? "My German may need a bit of brushing up," I offered.

"Oh, don't worry. You're a college graduate. You'll

pick it up," he said. "We have some real foreigners up there to help you out. How's your typing?"

Real foreigners. Spanish sailors with bearded lips; Italians; German philosopher-refugees. "Pretty good," I lied, praying to be spared the humiliation of a typing test.

"Fine. You can start on Monday, then. Report to me first thing Monday morning, and I'll take you up to Foreign and introduce you around."

"Thank you."

"Good day."

We shook hands, and I returned to Bookkeeping to say goodbye to the women in the department and try one last time for perfect on Trixie.

At a party over the weekend I became acutely sensitive to the ubiquitous married *we:*

"*We* love Indian music."

"*We* were shocked to hear about Artie."

"*We* thought from the review *we* would love the new production of *Whim*, but *we* walked out at intermission, *we* found it so bad."

When Frank used it about me, I shouted before everyone, "Speak for yourself!"

It puzzled him, because the statement in which the offending word occurred was unobjectionable; in fact, true. But I felt misrepresented by it anyway. Trapped, suffocating in that abysmal *we.*

I lasted less than a month in the Foreign Department. A flirtation begun with the man at the next desk (a Wharton graduate on the Executive Training Squad whose assistant I was) ended abruptly when he was transferred to another branch. Once he was gone, I was ashamed of ever having taken up with him, even for a lunchtime diversion.

Nothing was working out. Frank had bought me a five-language commercial dictionary at the University Bookstore, and I studied German by listening to the *Threepenny Opera* sung in the original German. The singer, Lotte Lenya, the composer's extraordinary wife, became my new inspiration. I bought all her records. Most of her songs were about a prostitute, Jenny, who refused to be trampled on. *"Wenn einer tritt, dann bin ich es"*—"if somebody's to do the stepping, it'll be me." After work and the dinner dishes, I would sit listening to her songs, following the record jacket translation of the lyrics, memorizing Lenya's strange inflections. Sometimes I was moved to tears singing along with her, sometimes to fury. Even Frank peered suspiciously over his glasses when Lenya and I sang the one in which Jenny gets to decide who in the city shall be spared and who shall be killed (a fantasy twice removed, and doubly safe). *Kill them all,* says Jenny— *alle!* And when the heads roll, she says *Hoppla!*

But it was the wrong German for the bank, and even the dictionary was of little use. The job turned out to be a typing job after all, and they were bound to discover I couldn't type. I wondered if they would fire me before I quit, or if I would just stop going to work one day. The prospect of being fired was depressing, but there was unemployment to collect if I stuck it out. I didn't care; it was time to start exploring another section of the city anyway.

When Frank learned that he was to receive the coveted Haversham Ellis History Fellowship for the following year, he broke precedent and called me at the office.

"Hey, that's great, Frankilee!" I said, using his mother's diminutive.

"How about celebrating?" he said. "I'll meet you downtown after work."

It was an assistantship, far too prestigious for him to turn down. But it hardly paid enough to live on. Come September it would be his turn to work and mine to study according to our master plan, but that was obviously out of the question now.

I maintained a firm silence through both martinis, concentrating on the bartender's art. For me to be anything but supportive was perverse. I could certainly not be so selfish as to act out my "neurosis" and sabotage what was going to be an exceptional career. Self-destructive, too, since Frank's success would carry me up with him. If I could not be content with his success, the least I could do was wait, or state my terms. After all, I was still young. (Young!) My turn was coming. There were many dissertation widows at Columbia: none of them complained.

I tried to be gracious as we moved to a booth to map out our future. Publications and professorships, sabbaticals and grants to study abroad. The gates were open. Applying for the right grants with care would get us anywhere Frank chose to go.

"I hope you realize," I said at last, for the record, "I'm not moving out of New York City for any professorship, except maybe to Europe." I chastised myself for my failure of enthusiasm, but I no longer cared what Frank thought of me. Bitch? Okay. I could just see myself pouring tea at, say, New England University. Sasha Raybel, faculty wife.

"Don't worry," said Frank with his wry condemning smile, "no one would dream of asking *you* to make any sacrifices."

Job hunting was the same as the year before, only I was a year older. In the employment agencies where I took typing tests and hopefully filled out forms, there were more pretty girls than I had remembered. Too many; New York, so glamorous and promising, was a tough city.

Every night, returning home jobless, I brushed my hair one hundred strokes and took long hot baths to soak the filth out of my pores. I thought I would never soak clean.

"Face cream?" taunted Frank. "What kind of a job are you looking for?"

I didn't know what kind. My singular assets were worthless without experience behind them. Besides, they were already slipping. I needed my looks. What was Russell's Paradox again? What was Plato's doctrine of the soul? I drifted off into sleep each night trying to remember, except when Frank, claiming his due, left his own books early to join me in bed. If I could, I pretended to be already asleep when he came in, but more often I received his odd hurried thrusts, matching his rhythm and milking him quickly with affected groans and sighs so he would turn over the sooner and let me dream in peace.

☆

"Guess who."

It was a voice from the dead. "Roxanne!"

"Right. Glad to see you're still passing tests."

"Where are you?"

"At Penn Station. We've moved to Fort Dix in New Jersey, and I'm just in for the day. Want some company?"

"Do I! How are you? Do you know how to get here?"

Frank looked up from his book, keeping his finger on the spot of the page where he had left off reading, while I explained who it was.

"Very nice," he said. "I'll go to the library after she comes and leave you two girls alone. You probably won't want me around anyway."

I ran around emptying ashtrays and straightening up. I wanted it nice for Roxanne. I was ashamed to introduce Frank to her, who had known Alport.

"I brought you some poems from the sticks," said Roxanne in the doorway as though it hadn't been years since we'd seen each other. She looked strong and beautiful. She hadn't aged a day, not even with childbirth. We had both let our hair grow long and abandoned lipstick. I wanted to hug and kiss her, but we didn't touch.

"Come in. This is Frank."

She handed me a long envelope and gave a shy hello to Frank. "I'm glad to meet you," she said. "You probably won't like my poems, but you're welcome to read them too."

"I'd be glad to read them for you. Sasha has spoken of you often. I'm due at the library now, but I'll be back later. Please excuse me."

I couldn't wait till he was out the door, he embarrassed me so. Due at the library!—like an important book.

"Quick. Tell me. Have you left your husband?" I asked Roxanne as soon as he'd left.

"Not yet," she said, "but I'm preparing my escape." Her hair fell delicately over her pale cheeks. I couldn't take my eyes off her. "Once my Sasha starts nursery school I'm going to look for a job. Meanwhile, I've made up a résumé and I commit at least one act of attrition a day."

"Attrition?"

"Sabotage."

"What kind of sabotage?" I asked, pouring us some coffee. Roxanne smiled her old inward smile that spoke of a certain pain.

"All kinds. There's no end to what you can do if you just attend to it."

"What do you mean?"

"First there are the dailies: mismating the socks, scorching the favorite shirt, not hearing him when he talks to me, over-Accenting the scrambled eggs. You wouldn't believe what a mere first lieutenant can demand to be served for his breakfast, and every course presents a new challenge to the ingenious homemaker."

She was in marvelous form, though I didn't believe a word she said. Frank would have called her "shrill."

"But besides the dailies, there are the specials," she went on, dissolving sugar in her cup. "Sometimes I read him recipes out loud when the ball game's on, rub his nose in it. I used to leave dirty diapers in selected spots. And once," she said, her eyes lighting up, "once when he and his buddies were going fishing, I put a raw egg in his lunchbox instead of a hard-boiled one."

She spoke with such glee that I began to suspect it was true. "What happened?"

"To me? Nothing. I played innocent. But you should have seen Whit when he came home."

Later, after lunch, she showed me snapshots of my namesake, a curly-haired blond with Roxanne's faraway look.

"Why are you still living with him?" I ventured.

"No money," she said plainly. "Can't leave till I can come here and get a job. Can't get a job till I can do something with Sasha. If I left now, I know I'd wind up in Virginia with mother. But don't worry, I'm preparing. I don't intend to spend my life stuck on some foul army base. No," she leaned back on the sofa and looked around our drab quarters, "this is where I want to be. New York. Columbia. Free."

I felt sorry for her, imagining her alone and divorced. In her shoes, I thought, I would have made do. That was the main reason I intended to have no children. But to have no husband either? Perhaps she could get another husband. It seemed unlikely with a child to raise—what man would put up with someone else's child? It was a wonder how strong Roxanne was, given her handicaps. I wished I had the guts for such risks. I admired her more than I pitied her.

At last I opened my own old wound, telling her about Alport's wife and how I happened to get married.

"At least you have a husband you can respect," said Roxanne. "I don't think he likes me much, but then he didn't marry me."

I knew what she meant. Everyone had the same response. "You have to forgive Frank for being so formal," I said. "It's just his style. People usually think he's judging them, but really he's just shy. Even with me. He hardly ever opens up."

But by then I knew Frank's silence wasn't shyness at all. He simply had nothing to say to me. Roxanne saw in five minutes what it took me almost a year to discern: he disapproved. Of her, and of me too. I had long since stopped being exceptional. When he did speak it was usually with a smug wit that put one instantly on the defensive or else in affectionate mindless baby talk. His silences themselves were accusations. He came across like one's father, making one want never to hang up one's pajamas or clean up one's room.

"Well," said Roxanne, with a pensive smile, "it's probably better to have a husband who never opens up than to be stuck with one who never shuts up."

ॐ

After several weeks I finally landed a receptionist job in a trading-stamp company on the East Side where I was supposed to sit alone in a large plush room on the executive floor and screen out undesirables without offending. Desirables were to be entertained. By memorizing a rogue's gallery of executive photographs, I was to distinguish the faces of the million-dollar customers from the mere thousand-dollar ones and know whom to serve coffee or a highball, and whom to get rid of. The job required tact and paid eighty dollars a week. The executive assistant who hired me said, "I like you. You've got class written all over your face." I was not permitted to read on the job ("it doesn't look nice"), but on the other hand, no one ever asked me if I could type.

I spent the long hours between customers picking my cuticle and daydreaming. I played games with myself, guessing what sort of man would walk in next. When the elevator opened and a customer came in, it was a little event. I liked some of them; I felt awkward with others. But with each one, million-dollar, thousand-dollar, or just messenger boy, I was obsessed to know if he thought me desirable. I began to devise little tests for finding out. But no matter how clever the tests, I never could be sure. I kept outsmarting myself with my subtle criteria.

In a desperate attempt to defy my limitations and know the unknowable, I made an ultimate test. Was it diabolical or just an extension of my job? I went to bed with a customer.

He was a heavy-set, middle-aged highball-drinking customer from my own Midwest who, out of admiration or inattention, took me for a New Yorker. He came into the office late one morning, leafed through several *Time* magazines and *Fortunes*, and was still waiting to see my boss at lunchtime.

"Have lunch with me?" he asked.

"Why not?" I answered. He reminded me a little of Mr. Winograd. Both had hair growing out of their ears and both were millionaires.

We went to his hotel, only two blocks away. No one broke the Muzak as we rode up the elevator. I looked straight ahead at the light moving behind the floor numbers. 12. 14. 15. 16. So this is how it's done, I thought. I wondered how he had known I was willing to go to his room.

He put the DO NOT DISTURB sign on the door handle and turned the key in the lock. Then he gave me a big smile.

"Do you have a contraceptive?" I asked, embarrassed. I thought: I'll have to get a diaphragm for the office.

"Sure thing," he said, grinning. " 'Always be prepared,' is my motto." He took a condom out of his wallet and held it up. "See?"

We undressed, fucked, and dressed again. "I hope you'll excuse me," I said, checking my face in the mirror. "I've got to get back to work now." I was sorry there'd be no one to tell.

"What about your lunch?" he asked.

"Don't worry about that. I never eat lunch."

"That's not good," he said, shaking his head with paternal concern and tucking a bill in my coat pocket. "You should eat."

I didn't peek at the bill until I got back to the office. The mere thought of it lying there in my pocket was exhilarating enough. All the way back, my heart pounding in time with the clicking of my heels on the pavement, I kept thinking: *if he thinks I'm beautiful it will be twenty dollars at least*. Twenty struck me as a very large amount. But of course, with my enormous capacity to trick myself, I might actually have been setting what I knew to be a low price just to save my ego. Like the excuses I had given myself for my mistakes on Trixie. I was never able to devise a thoroughly unambiguous test.

It was a fifty-dollar bill. I was jubilant. I looked in the mirror. I *am* beautiful, I thought.

But when my customer came back from his lunch a couple of hours later and acted as though he didn't know me, I was quite as uncertain of how I looked as I had been in the morning. There was really no way to tell.

❖

"How do you do? I'm Dr. Webber. Please sit down."

I sank into a deep leather chair opposite his large desk. The room was soothingly dark, but even so, I couldn't look at the doctor. Or at the motel-modern pictures on the wall, or at the family photos in a silver frame, or out the shaded window. I focused on the telephone.

"Perhaps you would like to tell me what made you seek help?"

With those pictures and that voice how could he possibly help me? But having an answer ready, I decided to use it. "I think I'm frigid," I said. It came out softly, as though I were on the verge of tears. Nevertheless, I forced myself to look at him as I said the word.

He was grey and slim, with a goatee. Younger than he sounded. I had an urge to curl up on his lap.

"I see," he said. He matched the fingertips of his left hand with those of his right, leaned back in his own leather chair, and contemplated the digital connections. Looking down his nose that way made him seem cross-eyed. "How old are you Miss Raybel? Or is it Mrs. Raybel?"

"Twenty-three. Misses."

"Oh, that's fine," smiled the doctor. "You're very young. I can think of no reason that you can't be helped."

"Really?" I could think of several myself.

He got out a long pad and, poising a pen over it, asked me quietly, "How long have you had this condition?"

"I guess always. Though I didn't know it until recently."

"I see," he said writing. I fancied him jotting down, *always*. He looked up. "You have never had an orgasm, then?"

Had I? I squirmed with embarrassment. Couldn't the doctor tell without asking me? Wasn't that what they were trained to do?

"I don't know," I said. Did it count, I wondered, that Alport could kiss me to joy? "Anyway, not through intercourse."

I didn't know which embarrassed me more: my confession, or my choice of the word *intercourse.* Impossibly equivocal.

He watched me, waiting. I was grateful for the darkness. I knew I was expected to continue, but I didn't know what to say. The more I wanted to please him, the more impossible to speak. I counted the holes on the telephone dial and was astonished to find ten, one for each of the sins I had come to confess.

"How long have **you** been married?" he asked at last, helping me out. Such a considerate doctor.

"Three years." I thought he would write down *three* and give me respite, but he didn't. He waited for me to proceed as deliberately as I waited for him to produce the next question. At last, thoughtfully fingering his beard, he leaned back and said kindly, "Why don't you tell me a little about yourself, Sasha?"

Of course I was licked before I even started. I had never been one to explain myself. The very things I needed to confess, I couldn't. I couldn't even select a vocabulary. Intercourse was out. Fucking? Relations? Having Sex? Fornicating? Sleeping with? Going to bed with (even if there were no bed)? Each was wrong in its own way.

"I find it difficult to talk," I started honestly, "about my problem."

"Oh, that's all right," he said. "Talk about anything you like. Anything at all."

But each thing I thought of to say was sure to convey the wrong impression or strike a false tone. I tried to think of something both intelligent and shocking, something telling and rare, something to make this doctor know that I was not, in Dr. John Watson's memorable words, just another ordinary "quacking, gossiping, neighbor-spying, disaster-enjoying" neurotic frigid woman—a textbook case; but I could not. I said nothing.

At last Dr. Webber interrupted my interminable silence to announce the session nearly over, time to arrange for appointments and fees. "What does your husband do?" he was careful to ask.

"He's the Haversham Ellis History Fellow at Columbia this year," I said, instantly ashamed of the pride in my voice. "I'm a receptionist," I added for penance.

Mother had offered to help with the bills, but I didn't mention that. I hoped the fee would be low enough that I wouldn't be forced to turn tricks at lunchtime, which might further damage my psyche.

Finally we settled on a fee. A bargain, considering. The doctor waited as I put on my jacket. When I finally left through the larger of two mysterious doors, I wondered if he was observing my ass, and if so, what he thought of it.

More parties, more contempt. It was enough to make one cynical! In Columbia waters I had to swim carefully to avoid being caught in the net laid for nonconforming traffickers in capitalism. I had worked in a bank, then in a trading-stamp company: clearly suspect. Unless I was careful to denounce them (yes, even Trixie), I was sure to be judged guilty. As to my other activities, reading poetry on the subway was the certain mark of a dabbler. Starfish were as unacceptable at Columbia as they had been in Baybury Heights. Like the Ugly Duckling, I seemed always to be swimming in the wrong part of the bay.

Again, I surmised the safest mode was silence. As more of our friends took advanced degrees and wives, I camouflaged my reading matter in plain brown paper covers and withdrew further into myself. A closet dilettante, biding my time.

I was seeing Dr. Webber regularly, Mondays and Thursdays, after work, and though I tried to do what was expected of me, I found myself talking about everything except what really mattered. In fact, it was by observing what I was unable to say that I discovered what really mattered: whether or not he found me beautiful.

I was frantic to know but could not bring myself to ask. Even if I could someday manage the question, how would I make him answer it? And if he should miraculously answer, how could I know he was telling the truth? I couldn't even ask him if he thought me *pretty*, an easier, an almost innocent question, and one common courtesy would dictate he answer yes. But like one obsessed, I could not ask. (*Aha!* he would have said had he known my obsession, *why do you want to know?*) Instead I tried to captivate him. I concocted dreams with secret messages for him to decode. I drenched him in anecdotes and plied him with metaphors. I gave him my favorite poems to read. Leading him to the well of my beauty if he'd happened to miss it, I told him of my various conquests and seductions, exaggerating to inspire him to drink.

"It's interesting," he observed, "that the only man you say you loved is a father, as old as your own father, and forbidden to you by the mother, his wife." He ended on a question mark, hoping I would pick up the thread. But I wouldn't. I found his tiresome moralizing silly.

"I loved Alport before I knew he had a wife," I said. "I've been to bed with older married men with more children than he. And not for love."

Sometimes I rebuked him for the *genetic fallacy*: taking cause for value—which only proved to him that he was probably "on to something"; and sometimes, planting my profile smack in his line of vision, I penalized him with silence.

I would wait, smoking cigarette after cigarette, until he came up with a question. Usually it was, "I wonder why you are feeling hostile today?" or else it was his second-favorite conversational gambit:

"What about Frank, your husband?"

"What about him?" I would return. My husband, like my marriage, bored me, as, no doubt, I bored him. We no longer had any life in common. He was full of *no's* and *don't's* while I liked to think I lived by *yes* and *do*. Frank did nothing but study during the week and see his friends on Saturday nights. He varied neither schedule nor sentence structure. The baby talk he had always used for addressing me in public he now used in private as well. Deceiving him had led me to avoid him, and since being in therapy exempted me from his sexual advances ("I'm still frigid, Frank, so don't touch me"), our contact was minimal.

"You hardly ever mention him. Don't you think that's rather . . . uh . . . unusual?"

And then I told him once again that, not believing in romantic love and finding my husband sufficiently tolerant of my idiosyncrasies to permit me a modicum of freedom, I considered my marriage satisfactory. Apart from the sex, of course, which was my own problem.

"And Frank? Does he consider it satisfactory too?"

"He doesn't complain," I snickered. It was wrong of the doctor to call him Frank and take his side.

"Don't you think he knows about your . . . uh . . . activities?"

"Oh, no!" I was shocked. "Do you think I should tell him?"

The doctor said nothing. I knew my "activities" had no bearing on Frank. They might have, if I ever pursued them for love. But I never did. Frank, however, couldn't be expected to understand that. A conventional fellow, he would feel himself wronged and required to do something if he knew.

"What do *you* think, Sasha?" Dr. Webber asked, enigmatically stroking his beard.

"I think it would upset him terribly to know, and I'm really not out to hurt him, whatever you think. It would mess up all his plans. He'd probably feel obliged to leave me."

The doctor nodded. He seemed to like that speech better than my other one, the one in which I weighed my own ten reasons for leaving Frank. That one made Dr. Webber break all his principles and actually give me advice:

"If I were you, Sasha, I wouldn't make any drastic changes right now while you're in the middle of analysis."

He seemed to feel that the known was better than the unknown, another man would prove no better for me than this one, and a crazy nymphomaniacal penis-envying castrating masochistic narcissistic infantile fucked-up frigid bitch like me was lucky to have hooked any man at all.

Actually, Dr. Webber seemed less interested in the practical questions surrounding my marriage than in the theoretical. Over the months I had been working painstakingly at getting him to reveal his premises, but with little success. Until one day, while I was discussing a dream I'd had the night before, a chance remark I made caused him to reveal his entire theory.

That night I had dreamed a chess game in which I, a plain red pawn, had so yearned to reach the eighth rank and become queen that I had refused gambits, squandered opportunities, betrayed my team. Alone and unprotected, I went on trying for queen despite certain defeat.

"What does being queen mean to you?" asked the doctor, suppressing a yawn.

I couldn't tell him about the Bunny Hop. Knowing I had once been considered beautiful might prejudice his own answer to the question I still hoped one day to ask. "The queen is the most powerful piece on the board," I answered. "She outdoes everyone. She can move almost every way there is to move." It was rich with symbolism and also true.

"The *most* powerful? Is she more powerful than the king?" he asked with an insinuating smile.

Either he didn't play chess, or he was after something. I went along.

"In the world a king may be more powerful, but in chess the queen is more powerful. That's why as a little pawn I wanted to be a boy and as a woman I enjoy playing chess."

I was pleased with my answer, but nothing like Dr. Webber. I could tell by the way he sat up and began to scribble that he was through yawning for that session.

"Can you think of what the dream might be saying?" he prodded.

I considered. Frank had applied for a Fulbright for a year's study in Germany. I was excited at the prospect of going abroad, but apprehensive as well; perhaps the dream took on that dilemma. As I was about to suggest something along those lines, Dr. Webber, impatient to share his revelation, leaned forward, reading from his notes.

"Even as a little pawn you always wanted to be a boy. Yet you long to be a 'queen,' " he said. "You have 'betrayed your own team'—your own nature?"

Dr. Webber's crude "hints," which I had always felt free to pursue or let lie, now came thickly. He was like a prompter, trying not to be heard, yet unwilling to let the lines be lost and the play ruined. The more I ignored his interpretation, the more certain he became.

Didn't everything, he asked, reduce for me to queen versus king? My belligerence, my seductions, my willfulness? Did they not all point to a profound conflict within my nature? Was I not always attempting to conquer where I should yield? take where I should give? Did I not identify with my father instead of my mother? Were not my very ambitions (to be a lawyer! a philosopher!), my rejection of maternity, my fantastic need to excel, my unwillingness to achieve orgasm— were they not all denials of my own deepest, instinctive self—my feminine self?

I had never before seen Dr. Webber so animated, not even when he was advising me to do nothing rash. I felt the time had come to plunge in and pose my own question. Catching him off guard in an expansive moment seemed my best chance of getting a truthful answer. After all, self-knowledge was what I was paying for.

He was still waiting for me to agree when, as casually as I could, I said, "Do you think I'm beautiful, Doctor?" If I could learn the truth about myself now, it would be worth all this painful analysis.

Dr. Webber pounced on the question. "Why do you ask?" he asked.

"I don't know, I just wondered," I said, looking intently at the telephone and mentally dialing a number. He was impossible to pin down; already I was sorry to have asked.

He examined me closely while my cheeks went red and my hands went damp. Then he said, "We have just come to an important—a breakthrough!—discovery with this chess dream. Even if you don't acknowledge it openly, unconsciously you do acknowledge it. You ask, *Do I think you are beautiful?* You mean, *Do I think you are a woman?* Don't you see? Yes, Sasha, I think you are a woman. I *know* you are. Now *you* must begin to accept this in yourself."

In his enthusiasm, he sounded positively Viennese. He was clearly too wrapped up in his breakthrough to spare a thought for a poor red pawn like me. My spirit sank as I realized I would never get a straight answer to my question.

He ranted on. "There is nothing the matter with you, Sasha. You are no 'freak.' You are exactly what you were born to be, if you will only open up to Frank and let yourself."

It was all so unfair. *I* was his patient, *my* father was helping to pay for his vacations, and yet Dr. Webber seemed again to be taking Frank's side. I began to cry.

"Yes, Sasha, I have no doubt now that you will soon achieve orgasm on the deepest, most fulfilling level. Cry, go ahead. You are on the threshold of woman's greatest fulfillment. You are at last beginning to feel. Yes, cry. Feel. When you are fully able to do that, you will be able to give yourself totally to your husband and have that blissful union with him you long for."

I stopped listening and blew my nose. My skin would be blotching. I sensed my time was up, though Dr. Webber was too engrossed in his theory to notice. Well, perhaps he wouldn't notice the blotching either, or the clouds of skin puffing up around my eyes. As I put on my coat, I heard him say,

"—quite certain that someday you will even feel deeply enough to think about having a family."

I turned to leave.

"Not yet, of course," I heard him say as I neared the door—I was nowhere near ready yet—but someday, when I wanted to.

❈

There was nothing to do on shipboard but drink brandy in the bar or snuggle under a blanket on a deck chair rolling with the great waves and try to read until the next meal. Now the next meal would be the last.

The homeward voyage was different from the outward journey. Back then when the waves rocked the ship I had struggled to keep my balance. That voyage was to have described the largest of the concentric circles on which I had been expanding my universe since that first train ride through the Adirondacks back in the forties. Stuffing the sleeves and pockets of all my clothes with a year's supply of Tampax (Regular and Super) in case the remote corners of Europe were unsupplied, armed with a select list of people to look up in all the cities of my choice, I had gone to plot my future, rising early each morning to play shuffleboard and participate in the drama of the morning sea.

And now? The concentric circles were shrinking. My future was doubling back on itself. The seven days at sea (like the summer in Rome, like the year abroad) had come and gone with the salt spray, leaving only a residue of abandoned plans. From Genoa I had written Roxanne of my return, swearing her to secrecy. "Don't tell Frank I'm coming," I wrote, and lapsing into our old idiom: *"In a minute there is time for decisions and revisions which a minute will reverse."* But with no one on board to save me, it was clear even before we sighted the Statue of Liberty standing catatonic in New York's filthy harbor that I'd be living with Frank again that very night. End of journey. Unless . . .

"I've been watching you. Do you mind if I talk to you?"

At last! I looked up from my book.

It was the soft-spoken engineer from Brooklyn, seven days too late. I had hardly noticed him since our brief introduction at the champagne sailing party; we had evidently signed up for different sittings.

"Why should I mind?"— I said. He had a gentle, a respectful air.

"You're always so preoccupied when I see you up here. I've been afraid to intrude. But since we'll be docking in a few hours, I figured it was now or never. My name's William Burke, in case you don't remember."

It was a straightforward, low-keyed pitch. I smiled at him.

"You must be eager to be getting home," he said, looking off at the deep waves. From out on the ocean we all called it home, no matter how we felt.

"Not really," I confided. "I'm actually dreading it. In fact, I have a strong impulse to stow away some place on board and go right back to Europe. What about you?"

He looked straight into my eyes. "My impulse," he said softly but without the slightest hesitation, "is to follow your impulse."

The sentiment, so softly expressed, was enough to trigger the appalling flow of lust. I lowered my eyes. It took so little. However often it happened, I was always unprepared; abashed to discover that so-delicate mechanism reacting despite me.

A confused shout and a rush of passengers to the rail came to my rescue. People began hugging one another and leaping around like children.

"Someone's sighted land," said William Burke.

"Do you see it?" I asked.

"No. But then, it's not what we're looking for, is it?"

Again. Sinking stomach, confusion. How crudely my body behaved. "We'd better go down for breakfast," I said, not really wanting to leave the deck but desperate to say something. Why hadn't he come forward a week earlier?

My chivalrous friend touched my elbow and led me down.

We exchanged addresses. "Maybe we can get together in the City," said William Burke.

"You know, I'm married," I answered, liking my candor but loathing my message.

"Oh? Where's your husband?"

"We've been separated," I said, trying to salvage something. "He's in New York. We're going to try to work out an arrangement."

"Well, if you do, perhaps he'll join us for lunch, then."

Not until much later, on the dock awaiting customs inspection, did we see each other again—far too late to be of any use. Once I got home I would have to behave myself—or else what was the point of going back? Indecision was unpardonable at this late date. Anyway, I had tried it alone and failed. From under our respective letters, B and R, we waved to one another; after that I avoided looking over at him.

"Anything to declare?" asked the customs inspector.

I wasn't prepared for declarations. He looked from my two suitcases to me and back again. Since Spain, my two bags contained all I possessed.

"Nothing. Six packs of Bleus," I said, opening my purse. He gave me an indulgent smile and chalked my bags without examining them, leaving me free to re-enter New York.

I looked quickly around the cavernous dock. Afraid Frank might be lying in wait for me. No one in sight.

With a last gesture of independence I avoided the redcaps and lugged my bags outside myself, but I knew I hadn't the muscle for an independent life. The taxis and trucks were speeding along Twelfth Avenue exactly as they had before I left. Everything was exactly the same—as though I didn't exist. No matter how grand my schemes or fanciful my ambitions, my year abroad hadn't dented the universe.

I hailed a taxi, gave the driver Frank's address, and headed uptown to the mate, as the saying goes, I deserved.

# SEVEN

"Who's William Burke, Sasha? We're invited to a party," said Frank, examining the invitation.

"Burke? I don't know. A party? Let's see."

I had been back less than two months, but it felt like years. Frank and I each had new jobs—he teaching at N.Y.U., I clipping and filing in an ad agency. We had a new apartment, spacious and rent-controlled, with a freezer compartment for me and a study for Frank. But though we had vowed to "try harder" and "start again," our hearts weren't in it.

The formal invitation was from someone named

Hector Crockett announcing a party for "friends and associates" of him and William Burke, to celebrate their partnership in a new business firm. R.S.V.P.

"He must be the man I met on the ship coming home."

"A business party?" sneered Frank. "Did you take up with a businessman? "

From a matrimonial dead end a party is at least a place to turn around. "If it seems like slumming to you, I'll be glad to go without you," I returned.

The day of the party, I bought a new dress—a black silk sheath I'd been seeing in the window of a little shop on Lexington Avenue—and against all my principles, desperate to be new, I had my hair done in a beauty parlor, molded into a smooth French twist. Though Frank scoffed suspiciously at my primping, when we set out in the snow for the subway he took my arm with the old pride.

We were both a little intimidated when someone opened the door and invited us in. I was wearing clumsy galoshes over my elegant Italian shoes, and did not know whether to leave them outside or take them in. I'd never before seen East Side bachelor quarters, though I'd been working in New York offices for years. A new country, only blocks from work. A bar in a corner, fashionable people, white furniture, flowers.

Hector Crockett introduced himself, and Frank told him what we were drinking. As I took off my coat, aware of my hair twisted artfully on my head and my first resort to mascara, I sensed new possibilities. Was this party perhaps a bonus from my genie? One extra last chance?

William Burke was carving turkey in the dining room. As soon as I saw him, I took Frank over to introduce them.

"Hi there. I'm so glad you came." He clasped both my hands as though we were dear old friends before retrieving one of them to extend to Frank for the ritual male handshake. "Glad to meet you," he said. "I've heard about you."

"How do you do, William?" said Frank.

"My friends call me Will," he smiled, "or" (to me) "Willy."

The table was spread with ham, potato salad, seeded rye, gherkins and olives. Frank popped an olive into his mouth, then asked awkwardly in the donnish voice he reserved for inferiors, "What sort of business are you starting?"

"It's a consulting firm. Computer systems. I suppose your wife told you I'm an engineer. Hector's the brains of it; I'm only a technician. Hector says it's the coming field. You should really ask him."

Hector approached with our drinks, "Are you the Franklin Raybel who wrote that piece on the German Question for *Intersection?*"

Frank's eyes lit up. "Yes."

"I'm glad to get a chance to talk to you," said Hector, swiveling Frank around; and in a moment they disappeared as though by prearrangement.

As soon as they were gone, Willy started to feed me turkey. First he took a perfectly carved slice of breast, rolled it skillfully around a gherkin, and slipped it into my mouth. "Surprised to hear from me?" he asked.

I swallowed the turkey, my heart tripping, then rolled one for him. "Very."

Then he rolled another for me, and I for him, until it seemed an improper way to carry on.

My antennae picked up Frank in a corner keeping me under secret surveillance. I excused myself. For the next hour I stayed out of the dining room so Willy wouldn't think I was looking for him, but at the same time, I tried to stand where I could be seen.

It was a good party, even though I was too self-conscious to enjoy it. The records were mostly old jazz and blues—Louis Armstrong and Bessie Smith, Hector's specialty I later learned. There was a man there who had programmed a computer to play chess, and a woman who had tended bar in Paris, and a lot of funny stories going around to which I paid less attention than necessary and laughed overlong.

Once, a little before midnight, I walked into the kitchen for ice and unexpectedly came upon Will there. I behaved like a child caught at the cookie jar.

"Oh! Excuse me!" I felt myself flush.

A sprig of mistletoe hung only three feet away, at the entrance to the dining room, but nothing came of it. Hastily I got my ice and retreated out the same door through which I had entered.

I flipped through a pile of records for something to do.

"*Soothe me with your caress, sweet lotus blossom,*" bellowed Jimmy Witherspoon to Omer Simeon's clarinet. "*Even though I know it's just a fantasy—*"

"What's a lovely thing like you doing off here in a corner?" asked someone as though I were single and available.

A couple we had known years before at Columbia walked in late in the evening. They were old admirers of Frank. "What are *you* doing here?" they asked me, and "How was Europe?"

"You look sensational, Sasha," said the husband. "Travel evidently does more than just improve the mind."

"I love your hairdo, Sasha, I love your shoes," said my enemy his wife.

"Where's Frank? I hear he's teaching downtown now."

"He's around here someplace," I said scanning the room. And then suddenly I caught sight of Willy Burke laughing his big, good-natured laugh in a corner with a pair of women I didn't know and I wanted to leave.

Frank was sitting bored and superior on a sofa. "Let's go soon, okay?" I said.

"I'm ready to go any time you are," he answered with that indifference he tried to pass off as accommodation.

After we found our coats and galoshes, we approached Hector and then Willy for goodbyes.

"It was good to see you again," said Willy. "Maybe we can all get together for lunch one of these days."

"Sounds great," I said. Frank beside me smiled his all-suffering smile and turned to the door.

That night before going to sleep I put a net over my hair, hoping to preserve the professional French twist one day more. It didn't work. I must have had torturous dreams, for when I woke Sunday afternoon, hairpins were scattered on my pillow and my hair was undone. Hearing Frank typing in another room, I surmised we wouldn't be going out that day anyway. I took the rest of the pins out of my hair, piling them on the night table beside me. Pulling the covers over my disheveled head, I retreated into sleep, sorry I had awakened.

*
* *

Each time the phone ran in Clayton Advertising's "research library," where I sat with two women named Joan clipping competitors' ads from magazines, I rushed to answer it. For three days it was only the account executives demanding instant information. "Hi, doll. Get me a list of all the urban markets in Illinois with over 35,000 population. And hurry. I need it before two. In triplicate. That's a good girl." But on the fourth morning—a cold, wet Thursday—it was he.

"Sasha Raybel? This is Willy Burke."

I was already smiling when I picked up the phone, hoping it would be he.

"Does your name have a C in it?" he asked jovially.

"No. No C. How did you find my number at work?"

"I have my sources. I'm calling to ask you, are you free for lunch?"

"Today?"

I wanted to say no. I had expected to have some notice. I knew I didn't look the way I had at the party, and he would be disappointed. There were weekday circles under my eyes and other imperfections. I had on a coarse white turtleneck perpetually dirty at the cuffs, and my hair, pulled carelessly back, was tied with a shabby scarf. A ghastly quarter of a century old. Nevertheless, feeling that itch it was hypocritical to deny, despite my qualms and vows, I accepted.

"I'm free. But I don't have much of a lunch hour. From twelve to one exactly."

"I'll pick you up in the lobby of your building at twelve sharp. So long, lotus blossom."

We sat across from each other in one of those little restaurants too elegant to hire waitresses, where the waiters recite the menu and place on each table a basket woven of pasta filled with *pommes soufflées*. The headwaiter knew Will and was so discreet in overlooking me and my wedding ring that I figured he was used to such lunches.

"If you put yourself in my hands, I'll see that you have a delicious meal," said Will.

"But can't you see I'm already in your hands?" I answered coyly. However shabby my sweater, I could still use my eyes with the old bus-stop swagger.

We flirted outright over a martini. ("Do you usually have lunch with married women?" "Hardly ever. Do you usually go to lunch with single men?" "Never." "Then shall we make it our secret?") Until quite unexpectedly, staring deep into the hole in the olive in my second drink, I saw straight through to the inevitable end and wanted to leave.

"What do you want with me?" I asked with an impermissible seriousness.

"I? Why, to enjoy you," answered Will.

His answer, appropriately airy, made it worse. I was sick of affairs; I had grown old being enjoyed.

"Let's enjoy this lunch and then forget it," I said, straining for levity. But even that was presumptuous, for he had not yet suggested anything more than one lunch. Squeezing the universe into a ball, I had lost my appetite.

"Don't be silly. I expect to be waiting for you in the lobby of your building tomorrow at noon."

"Well, don't," I said, "I really don't want to see you again." *Oh God,* a voice inside reproached me, *must you women always get so serious? And on a first date, too?*

"You seemed to be enjoying yourself well enough until approximately two minutes ago. What happened?" He looked puzzled.

"Nothing."

It was too absurd for me to sit there pouting. Martinis were the end of me. How could I explain that

I was only a fake adventuress?—a nice girl who wanted all or nothing.

On Will's face was the same incredulity I had seen whenever I'd tried to say no. Jan Pulaski had had it, and Mr. Winograd, and Leonardo, and others I couldn't remember. It was a look that made me feel obligated to sleep with any man who had taken the trouble to buy me a cup of coffee.

Suddenly an unexpected insight lit up Willy's face. "Why, you're the poor little rich girl. Your trouble is you've obviously never been pursued. So lovely and so neglected. Well, lotus blossom," he announced, breaking into a confident smile, "get ready for a new experience. I am going to pursue you."

The next day when I arrived at work, on my desk was a slender green bud vase sporting a single long-stemmed American Beauty rose. ("Hmm," quipped one of the account men, "did the rose come in on the breakfast tray?") The note beside it said, "see you at lunch." Will wouldn't reveal how he managed to get it there, or how he sneaked in the fresh rose each succeeding week. "I have my ways," was all he would tell.

We lunched that day on roast beef sandwiches Mr. Romance brought in a paper bag. We ate them on a stone bench in Rockefeller Center where, touching knees, we scintillated like the lights on the giant Christmas tree, toes tingling with cold and lust.

"I'll be here at five to take you to dinner. First, champagne cocktails." He grasped my arm firmly as we walked back to my office.

"Not tonight," I laughed. "I have to go home after work."

"Why?"

"I have a husband waiting for his dinner, remember?"

"Do you want to go home and cook his dinner? Rather than eat with me?"

"No."

"Then why do it?"

Though it was my kind of argument, I had no answer. There had been reasons for my return to Frank across an ocean and a continent, but at the moment I could barely remember them. (I had tried to explain them to Roxanne. "I fell in love in Spain. Love, beautiful sex, everything. I was even trying to figure out how to make it last. But then I got sick and everything collapsed. I had a terrible scare. I could get sick again. Or get fat. It was an awful discovery. Now with Frank, whatever happens to me, he'll just have to take care of me." And Roxanne had answered flatly, "You'll never get fat.")

"Come on," urged Willy. "Call him up and say you're not cooking tonight."

So glibly said. Blow my setup for sex and a dinner? "That's easy for you to say. You have nothing to lose."

"Neither have you. Not if you trust me."

Trust him—it was a luxury so hazardous it was the last thing I would do! "I could even lose my job if I keep getting back late from lunch," I said as we entered the Advertising Building lobby and I saw the clock.

"Quit your job. Come work for me. I'll teach you all you need to know about the programming business."

"I did manage to learn a thing or two before I met you," I snapped. "You act as though you're the first man in my life. Actually," I said, trying to deflate him as I entered the elevator, "if you get that far, you'll be

my thirtieth." I rounded to the nearest ten, hoping to
match his audacity.

"As long as I'm the last," he smiled.

Late that afternoon I received a phone call from
Western Union. A telegram. BE IN LOBBY AT FIVE
EVERYTHING ARRANGED. It was signed, NUMBER THIRTY.

I left work fifteen minutes early that evening, running all the way to the subway. Elementary tactics: *One
must flee in order to be pursued*, I remembered from
junior high.

*

* *

"You're early," said Frank.

"Sorry," I said, "I had a headache and wanted to
beat the rush hour. But don't feel you have to drop
everything just because I'm ahead of schedule." I was in
no mood for rote conversation anyway. "Go on and
finish what you were doing. I don't mind."

"Perhaps I will, then," said Frank politely. "Actually, I have a tough lecture tomorrow, and I'll probably
be working late tonight. I'll do a little more now, then
take a break at six when the news goes on."

I cooked smothered pork chops that night; I remember chopping the onions. Each morning before leaving
for work I set to thaw our nightly meat purchased and
frozen on Saturdays, and that morning it was pork
chops. I remember feeling ashamed to be crying even
though it was only from chopping onions.

For once I was glad Frank turned on the news at
dinner. With my mind in a turmoil of traitor thoughts I
was glad to be relieved of our matrimonial pleasantries.
Later, after the news, while I was doing the dinner

dishes with Frank off in his study again typing out his lecture notes for the following day, the question suddenly intruded on my mind. *What am I doing here?* and again, as in Europe, I could think of no answer.

I had not asked that question since I had returned from Europe full of fresh vows. But of course even the best intentions change nothing. After Frank and I had each taken new jobs and moved into our new apartment, after he had presented the "German Question" and I had cooked the new European recipes for our old friends, we were approximately where we had always been. Many of our friends had moved up a rung on the familial ladder while we were abroad: the single ones had married, the married ones had reproduced; only Roxanne, living divorced in a Grove Street tenement with little Sasha and working as a secretary in a publishing house, had moved in the other direction. Otherwise, it was the same scene as before. The men discussed exams administered instead of exams suffered, the women spoke of recipes instead of restaurants, the students at N.Y.U. were younger than the ones I remembered from Columbia, but it was the same empty life, stretching as far as one could imagine in both directions.

"How can you go through life just preparing for your old age?" Roxanne had asked me. She had climbed out of a bad marriage through a messy divorce, and with a baby besides. How could I hope to make her understand?

"Listen, Roxanne," I had answered her, "the men I went out with in Europe only cared about one thing. One told me that was what he'd gone to Europe for, to get laid, honest to God. They told me about their unobliging wives and the loves they'd left at home—I was just a last resort. Which makes me think I've already entered my old age." Nothing new to Roxanne. "To tell you the truth," I had even confided, remembering the unmentionable clap, "I wouldn't mind living the rest of my life without sex. It's not such a big deal. Lots of people live without it."

"*Those* people," Roxanne had answered caustically, "have got God, or politics, or somebody else."

Somebody else. I finished the dishes and put the pork chop bones outside to rot, but the question kept returning. *What am I doing here?*

I threw in the dish towel and telephoned Roxanne.

"Do you think I could spend a night or two with you? I can baby sit if you want to go out."

"What happened? Did you and Frank have a fight?"

"No, no fight."

"Of course you can come here."

I went into the bedroom and packed a bag. Then I put on my coat and walked back to Frank's study.

"I'm leaving," I said from the doorway.

He looked up over his glasses, surprised. "Leaving? Where are you going?"

"To Roxanne's."

"What for?"

"For good."

He did a double take out of an old movie, then stood up and thrust his hands in his pockets. "You're leaving for good?"

I nodded.

"But why?"

"That's the wrong question. The question is, why stay? There's nothing for me here. So I'm leaving."

He began walking back and forth in front of the typewriter. "Nothing for you here? What about the apartment? What about me? I love you."

"You do not." It all sounded vaguely familiar, like snatches of an old play. "You don't even know me."

Frank nervously lit a cigarette. "Your trouble is," he said, puffing himself up into his classroom stance, "you don't know yourself. You're one of those pathetic people who squander their lives not knowing what to do with them. What a waste you are. Nothing satisfies you."

I didn't want him to start calling me the names again. But I couldn't resist saying, "Maybe you can suggest something interesting for me to do with my life, Professor? Paint perhaps? Pursue a hobby?"

"It's your own choice, baby. If you were willing to do something, to have children like normal women—"

"Then," I cut in, taking one long stride into the hall, "it would be a lot harder for me to leave you!"

(Normal women. "You look perfectly normal to me," Roxanne had said, scrutinizing me the first time I had visited her after my return from Europe. "What do you mean?" I had asked. "Your letters were very confusing. So high, and then so low. From the way you described yourself, I really thought you'd be disfigured or something. And then Frank told me you'd got sick and gone crazy." "Crazy!" I had gasped. "A man thinks you're crazy if you don't want to spend the rest of your life with him!" We had laughed over that, but it was true.)

"I'm sorry I said that," said Frank following me to the door. "Please don't go."

"What I don't understand," I said, "is why you would want me to stay? We have no life together. You know you'll be much better off without me." I was uncomfortably aware of Frank's lecture waiting to be typed. It was getting late. "I'm sure there are women around who would be happy to be your wife and have your babies. But not me."

"Don't be obtuse." He shifted out of focus. "It's you I want."

I knew better than to ask why. I'd heard it before. It was his problem now. I picked up the bag again. "I'll give you six months before you find someone else."

"And just how long," he asked archly, turning his pleas to accusations, "will it take *you* to find someone else?"

"I'm not looking," I answered equivocally.

I opened the door. Even though I was leaving, I felt guilty to be consuming so much of Frank's good working time on my personal problems. "You can call me at work if you need to. I'll be in touch with you."

Downstairs I suddenly realized I had forgotten to pack my diaphragm. I pushed the elevator button for our floor, rode back up, and let myself quietly into the apartment. Down the hall in the study I heard Frank already typing away. I tiptoed into the bedroom and slipped what I needed into my purse, then left again without disturbing him.

\*
\* \*

I didn't tell Willy I had moved out. Whatever I might have said, he would certainly have thought I'd left Frank for him, and then he might never have called again. When I found myself being steered by the elbow through the Advertising Building's revolving lobby door as though to an ordinary midtown lunch and instead into Willy's Chevrolet waiting at a hydrant, I wondered if he had found out anyway.

"Where are we going?" I demanded.

"Don't worry, someplace nice. Leave everything to me," said Prince Charming and headed west across town into the crush of Christmas shoppers. "Don't count on going back to work this afternoon, though."

On the West Side Highway I discovered Prince Charming was a maniac driver.

"At my office they fire people who take long lunch hours," I said half-heartedly. Ladies in distress were supposed to protest only up to a point.

"You don't have to worry," said Will, looking more frequently at me than at the road, "I'll take care of you."

There was nothing to do for self-protection but keep my foot poised over an imaginary brake and think positively. I was too nervous for a true adventuress.

The Harlem River was the northern boundary of the world to me, so when the Henry Hudson Parkway crossed the Harlem into the Bronx, I stopped wondering where we were. I was out of my element; for all I knew, the next stop was Canada. It was a terrifying drive on those icy highways, but as the old saying has it, at least I knew I was alive.

We speeded along in silence, cutting a wake of white through the barely plowed roads. I tried to remember the condition of my underclothes as outside, sunlight glinted off icicles.

An enchanted region. If the Hudson River was the moat, somewhere lay a castle. Up past the shimmering Tappan Zee Bridge, at last, I spotted the redwood motel suspended on top of a mountain.

"There?" I asked.

"There."

"With Manhattan full of hotels, you pick a motel up some icy mountain," I teased.

"You could walk out of a Manhattan hotel," said Will, leaning over to kiss me.

Our tires spun as we climbed toward the craggy top where a dragon waited to be slain.

In the dining room facing across a chasm into distant snowy woods, we ate our lunch. Rather, we faked lunch. For even after two fast martinis to steady our knees we were too nervous to try the impressive shrimp salads the waiter placed before us.

"I can't," I said, looking at it regretfully.

"I can't either," said Will.

He signed the bill with a room number ascertained in advance, and wrote in a tip. The waiter smiled. Will held my arm as we proceeded slowly down the corridor with admirable restraint to our room.

I was wearing a perfectly simple black wool dress that zipped up the back, and my hair was pinned in a sort of bun. In those waning years of the fifties long loose hair was a secret to be revealed only in the bedroom. With such ceremony as Rapunzel might have shown, I drew the pins slowly out of my hair and shook it loose over my shoulders while Will bolted the door. Then I stepped down out of my shoes.

"My love," he breathed, taking an awkward step toward the center where I stepped to meet him. No witch intruded. He wrapped me in his arms and kissed my eyes and mouth with princely grace.

The largest wall of the room was a picture window. Outside, snow was falling heavily. It would feel strange to make love in the bright light before the open woods; nevertheless, retrieving both my hands, I lifted my long hair off my neck and presented Willy Burke with the zipper.

I had always considered independence and commitment mutually exclusive options. I had gone for independence in marrying, but now I was ready to reconsider. With Frank and without him, my independence had proved illusory, not to mention boring; in fact, I suspected I was already suffering from emotional rickets.

Could it be that I'd been living by a mistaken premise? An excluded middle? Was it possible that the poets, and *not* the philosophers after all, had the right of it? I had sought ten good reasons to marry and ten again to leave; but maybe one compelling reason was enough. My husband's profession had made little difference to me. Maybe commitment would make more.

Now, if Willy Burke were as devoted as he claimed ("All I want, Sasha, is to make you happy"), there was still time to switch my bet. It would take a large risk and an act of faith, but theoretically, at least, it could be done. Four years to thirty, the game wasn't over yet.

Weeks before the first buds of spring Willy and I moved into a tiny two-room Village sublet on Perry Street. Paying my last respects to independence, I insisted we split the rent (too high for me to manage alone), but in everything else we attempted to become what Willy called "one person."

"Reading! With me home? Close that book!" said Willy, bursting in on me with an armful of quivering sticks.

"What are those?"

"Quince." Aping the prophets, he announced they would spring to life before my eyes if I only had faith.

"Those sticks?"

"Buds, flowers, fragrance, seed—just wait."

"Like us," I laughed, closing forever my book.

"Like us."

It was a risky business, this commitment. People had been known to die of it. There was always the chance that Willy, invariably late, would wind up a no-show; the possibility that after I had given up my apartment, my salary, my swagger, my cool, my wicked eye, he would turn out his pockets with a sheepish smile, head for the door, and leave me with nothing but dregs of wine and ashes of roses pressed between the pages of some abandoned book.

But I determined to risk it. I had scoffed at romance through the entire five years of my first marriage, resisting all pressure to adjust. And what had it got me? Sneers and lies. Now, I was starting from scratch, five years behind everyone else, without even Roxanne's resources to live alone. If there was to be a second time, it had to be radically different. If Will was the man, and his style Romance, well, it would be a refreshing change from the indifference I was accustomed to. Between the champagne cocktails and the flowers, there might at least be some fun in it.

★

My dearest darling Sasha,

Your father and I were stunned to learn you are getting a divorce. Even before I opened your letter something told me it was going to be bad news. What can I say, except to tell you how much we love you and how truly sorry we are?

From the time you entered your teens I have worried about how you would manage. You had a difficult and painful adolescence, always full of surprises. But I never for one instant lost faith in you. Even in the worst moments I believed that if we just gave you

your rein and loved you, eventually you would justify
our trust and settle down. You were always such a
fine, clever, and basically considerate child with all
the potential of a devoted wife and mother, capable
of making someone truly happy. Though I was surprised when you chose to marry Frank (at last I can
say he never seemed to me really worthy of you),
still I trusted your good judgment.

And now it's to end in divorce. I constantly ask myself: where did I go wrong in raising you? What did
I do to make you wind up unhappy? Lord knows I
tried my best to be a good mother.

If we had been a little wiser, maybe we would have
known how the wind was blowing. When you wrote
you were going off to Spain without Frank, I said to
Abe, this is not right, though I would never have
dreamed of saying it to you. (Maybe I should have.)
If you had only had children, this tragedy might have
been averted. Without a sense of purpose and respon-
sibility even the cleverest woman is bound to be unful-
filled. Dearest, there is nothing that cements a marriage like children. In fact, when we offered to help
pay for your psychiatrist, it was in hopes that you
would come to want a family. But it was not to be.

Well, what's past is past. I am sure you will marry
again and make a wise choice. You are fortunate to
be young enough for a second chance. (I know a young
man right now—the son of an acquaintance of mine
who lives in New Jersey—who would probably be de-
lighted to meet a girl like you. Let me know when I
may send him your address.)

Now to other news. I am happy to write that your
brother Ben has just opened a new branch of his store,
this time in Medina, Ohio. That makes it a real chain,
and of course, we are terribly proud of him. With
Marnie pregnant again (and little Michael ready for
school—can you believe time goes so fast?) it is almost too much good news at once. It would be
awfully nice if you could find the time to drop Ben a
note of congratulations. He has always been so fond
of you. After all, you are only a year apart in age.

Even now he seems as much concerned about you as we are.

Your father wants to add a few words, so I'll close now,

With all my love,

*Mother*

Dear Sasha,

As a lawyer I think your announced decision to let Frank sue you for divorce is hasty, if not downright foolish, and I urge you to reconsider. For the time being you must be very careful with whom you are seen in public and where, for until you are legally separated or finally divorced, your husband still has rights. Even though you and Frank are living apart, your character can be damaged and your settlement jeopardized if you are indiscreet. It may not, as you claim, matter to you now, but it does matter to the world. For this and other reasons, it will matter to you eventually, whether you recognize it or not. Better for you to divorce him. Think it over.

We would be very happy if you decided to come back to Baybury. Your room is still here, and it is such a long time since we've seen you. We always miss our little girl, but especially now. We are frankly uneasy thinking of a beautiful girl like you living alone in New York City.

Let us know what you decide.

Love,

*Dad*

Another letter to hide, another piece of me to lock in a drawer for solitary contemplation—perhaps in the nightmare hour each evening between the time I arrived home from work and the time Willy, armed with flowers and excuses, appeared for dinner.

❖
❖

### W.B.'s Favorite Veal Scallops Marsala

Marinate wafer-thin slices of veal in marsala, garlic, pepper. Precook mushrooms in butter; season. Sauté veal in butter; add mushrooms, basil, strained marinade. Just before serving, squeeze in juice of one lemon, sprinkle with parsley. Serve with noodles.

### Hollandaise Sauce for Asparagus

Melt one stick butter. In blender put three yolks, two tablespoons lemon juice, salt and pepper. Cover and blend for an instant. Turn to low speed, uncover and gradually add hot water. Yield: three servings.

We went at our thing with a vengeance, prepared to turn inside out to change. Loyalty was our credo. Not content to stand bare before one another like ordinary lovers, we stripped off secrets, then skin, as though we hoped by mingling our innermost nerves to become one flesh. Each observation one of us made became the other's illuminating insight; each casual metaphor became the other's poem. Believing words could bind, we found it impossible to give promises enough.

"Promise me we'll never spend a night apart."

"I promise. Swear you'll never glance at another man."

"I swear."

By Schubert and candlelight we drank perfectly chilled white wine, dipping artichoke leaves into a single bowl of melted butter, then slipping them into one another's mouths. We drank *café filtre* out of our own tiny porcelain cups, bought for Valentine's Day. By shamelessly juggling history we discerned that despite a world of striking differences, we had in fact been born for each other, all it took was faith.

"Always," we whispered, and "forever." Until midnight or so, when Will turned me on my side, set the alarm clock for more love in the morning, and tucking his knees behind mine to make us like a pair of spoons stacked in a drawer, snuggled us off to sleep.

♥

The ride from the new Cleveland airport where Ben picked me up in his Bonneville sedan through the periphery of town was jarringly disconcerting. So much new. "But where's Clark's? Is that another Halle's?" I asked. Ben, proudly proprietary and with no sense of loss, pointed out now a new shopping center, now abandoned corners. The broad, once deserted Route Eighty, where we had had our "chicken" races in high school in souped-up Fords and where the boys had driven us to neck, was now lined with neon drive-ins, car lots lighted like Christmas trees, glass motels. Ben too—bigger, flashier.

Once we ascended the hill into Baybury Heights, however, everything was magically the same, as if some fairy had cast a spell. Pungent autumn leaves raked into piles on tree lawns, rock gardens separating driveways from next-door lawns, basket hoops on garages with nets torn from overuse, folded evening papers carelessly tossed on welcome mats by some ambitious new version of Ben—all preserved. I held my breath so as not to disturb it.

"Before I drop you off, Sash," said Ben, lowering his voice conspiratorially and slowing the car as we turned onto Auburn Hill, where I had been pantsed, "there are a couple of things I think you ought to be aware of. The folks are really very upset about this divorce, more than they'll show. Mother's done a lot of crying. I'd appreciate it if you try and act normal. For their sakes."

"Normal! You're kidding, Ben. This is 1958—millions of people get divorced. It's not an abnormal thing to do nowadays!"

"Calm down, will you? I'm not saying you're abnormal, honey. Personally I couldn't care less. I happen to think getting divorced may be the smartest thing you ever did, though it's none of my business. Myself, I never thought Frank had the balls, if you'll excuse my language, to handle you, and personally, I don't see any reason for a couple to stay together if they don't have kids. For my money, you can live any way you damn please, you can be a prostitute if you like, it's your own business. But the folks are kind of old-fashioned, that's all. Let's face it, this is a conservative town. I'm not saying you're abnormal. I'm just saying, try to stay off the subjects that might upset them, that's all. 'Cause they're understandably a little shaky about you. Living alone in New York and all."

"I told you, I'm *not* living alone."

"Listen, Sasha, it's your first visit back in what? five years? So why not try to make it nice for the folks? I mean, you don't have to mention the guy you're living with."

I held my tongue. *In a minute there is time for decisions and revisions which a minute will reverse.* Ben looked at his watch.

"If you can manage till after dinner when I bring over Marnie and the kids, I'll take your bag in then. I promised to see a salesman at the Baybury store and I'm already late."

Why argue about who carries the bags? Why disturb the universe?

"Sure, Ben. See you later. Sorry I held you up."

"It doesn't matter, hon," Ben laughed. "This time I'm the customer, and the customer's always right."

I stepped out of the car onto the sidewalk. So many more cracks to avoid treading on than I remembered. So few unmarred surfaces. Slowly I walk up the front path through the red Baybury leaves. They rustle like music, smell like incense. It is almost twilight. Mother will be in the kitchen whipping cream for Ben's hot chocolate, expecting him to return any moment, cold and ravenous, from his paper route. Then she will go upstairs to "freshen up" for Daddy while Ben and I stretch out on the floor before the radio with our secret decoders ready for action. Exactly on time, he'll come in puffing a bit from the hill and after a little tease present Chiclets to me and Ben. He'll brush my hair out of my eyes and tousle Ben's as we—whispering, "Shhh!"—move in closer to the radio. "Now what do I smell for dinner?" he'll say sniffing at the air playfully. If it's before six, he'll get no players, but if it's six or after, Ben and I will throw him off the track with transparent subterfuge. "I sure hope it's not liver!" Finally he'll settle down in "his" chair, open the evening paper Ben ceremoniously presents to him, and send us off with a kindly, "Okay, kids, I'm going to look over the paper now. Call me when dinner's ready."

I push the bell. Chimes ring in the hallway. I feel a chill run through me, knowing how warm and light it will be indoors. Tonight someone has already taken in the evening paper. The porch light goes on over my head. They have heard me. The same chimes, the same light they had installed in 1938 to replace the ones that had been ripped out by the vacating occupants. "Why'd they want to do that? What good could it do?" my father had asked sadly, discovering every window in the house broken and every light fixture demolished on the eve of our moving in. "Why would anyone want to do a thing like that?"—shaking his head. Who? I had wondered. Why?

The house, like all the houses in the neighborhood, had been a Depression bargain, bought cheaply from a bank that had foreclosed on some unfortunate's mortgage. We were lucky to be able to buy it, my father said. But like every Depression treat—even the ice cream cones with double cups, four scoops, and chocolate sprinkles, all for a nickel—our luck was someone else's loss, our treat someone else's hunger. And even the miraculous hummingbird in the hollyhocks behind the house—at whose expense did she come to us? What would I have to pay?

Footsteps, and now the door. My face, still tanned from the summer, feels split like the sidewalk. I pray she will know me, even as for an instant she looks and hesitates.

"Sasha! Darling Sasha! Come in! Abe—where are you? It's our Sasha!"

In a rush of joy she hugs my shoulders and kisses me, cheek at a time, then both together, demolishing time and distance. "Abe! Abe! Come down!" And to me: "Come inside. Give me your coat. Let me look at you."

There she stands, gentle, aging, still beautiful. How strange that I should have to bend down to kiss her. "But didn't you expect me?" I ask. "It was Ben who dropped me off."

"Yes, I knew you were coming. But expecting you isn't having you. Oh, Sasha, I'm so happy you came. You look so lovely, so sophisticated. Why, you're skinny as a reed, and I've put on all this weight." She touches her hand to her generous bosom in a gesture of hopeless apology.

What can I say? If the sample of my urine Willy took to the lab after dropping me at the airport stimulates a frog, this talk is all gross irony.

"It's the dress, maybe, mother. I always weigh the same."

But at once I realize my skinniness is there only as an ideal, and quickly I take my cue. "You look beautiful to me, Mom, you don't look heavy at all. You still glow, you never change." We reserve this kindness for each other, and partly out of sympathy, partly out of love, we almost believe in it.

"She's right, you know," says my father coming in and throwing one arm lovingly around each of us. "You really are quite as beautiful as you ever were; you look like a girl."

My mother and I both smile awkwardly, looking away, not quite sure which of us he is complimenting, not quite wishing to know.

"*Still* negative? Are they sure? Shit, Willy! Then why haven't I got my period?"

"I can't exactly say, but I'm sure there's a reason."

Maybe a mustache again or the clap? Oh no! Must my body pay every time I fall in love?

"You can go to your doctor and find out as soon as you come back to New York. I'd have thought you'd be glad it isn't positive."

"If it were positive, at least I'd know what to do about it. I'm so sick of this! There is never a time when someone I know isn't suffering over a fucking missed period! It's disgusting! Anyway, I don't even have a doctor."

"We'll find you a doctor."

"I hate doctors."

"For Christsake, Sasha, don't worry. Don't I always take care of you?"

"Yes."

"Well, I'm going to get you out of this one too. You just have to have a little faith in me."

"What did you do last night? It was practically unbearable here without you."

"Went to a movie."

"Alone?"

"With Hector."

"What are you going to do tonight?"

"Go to a movie."

"And tomorrow?"

"Another movie."

"Do you miss me?"

"What do you think?"

"I think I'm going to come home and see."

"I think that's a splendid idea."

"Aren't you going to the club with Ben and Marnie? Don't you want to meet some young people and see some of your old friends?"

"No."

"Let her alone, Laura, let her do what she wants," said my father. "If she wants to be different, let her. She hasn't changed a bit."

I withdrew into a book as I had always done—only this time I went gingerly, encumbered by recollections. All my early tutors were still here, quietly waiting on the bookshelves to be singled out and posed a question. It seemed years since I had asked one; my time to question had passed. Dipping again into Aristotle and Watson was like the first drag of a cigarette after years

without smoking. Dizzily, I pondered again my childhood puzzle of which one to take to a desert island.

On my brother's block I bumped into Sally Harris, a
childhood friend. Her face was worn; it was a shock to
see her. (It shouldn't have been; we were all closer to
thirty now than to twenty.)

"Sally Harris?"

"Yes?"

"It's Sasha. Sasha Davis."

For a moment we stood scrutinizing each other. She
had more lines near the eyes than I, none around the
mouth.

"Of course! Sasha! But your hair is so long now!"
she said. She still wore hers short, as we all wore it in
the high school yearbook, "I'm Sally Colby now."

"Buddy Colby?" I asked.

She nodded, giggling. "How long is it since I've seen
you? I remember the class predictions: you were going
to be a lawyer. Did you make it?"

"No."

She looked too hastily at my hands. "You're married
too, of course. Do you have any children?"

"No. Do you?"

"Oh yes, we have three. But you will, you will," she
said generously.

We eyed each other, comparing. "You really haven't
changed a bit!" we lied to each other.

She recited who had married whom, and how many
children they had.

"Joey Ross? Who did he marry?" I inquired.

"Joey? He married a girl from the West Side. Martha something. I don't think you'd know her. Sweet
girl. It turned out she couldn't have any children, so
they adopted a couple. A boy and a girl."

"What does Joey do now?"

"We don't see them much. I think he's still in the shoe business."

Things were more or less as I remembered them at home. Upstairs I went from room to room touching things as though they were alive. The woods in the back had shrunk and I could see from the window in my mother's room that the treehouse was gone. On the wall over my mother's dressing table (even more crowded with jars than when I had lived here) all the photographs had been carefully rearranged. Color photos of Ben's children indistinguishable from baby pictures of us; all the graduations; generations of weddings; Ben in a football pose, me at the pool. The pictures of Frank had been discreetly removed, but there were several Frank had snapped of me in Europe.

I was pleased with how little I had changed in the photos. Surprised, too, considering that never, not even in my prime, had I photographed well. Even the face in the mirror was passable: if there were creases lurking, they hadn't surfaced yet. Perhaps, I thought, I ought to consider cutting my hair again; short hair had always been so becoming.

My mother walked in, made-up and dressed. "Do you like my rogue's gallery?" she asked. She was wearing an expensive pajama set, and her skin had the pink smell I remembered. Had she dressed for me? When I was a child she had always, even in the midst of vacuuming or doing the laundry, put on a girdle, stockings, and a dress just to run out to the store.

"Quite a collection here," I said.

"Yes. The family keeps getting bigger and bigger."

I thought of the parasite perhaps even now clogging my womb, like the Kotex clogging the toilet, the monthly nightmare: How, oh how, to get rid of it? At the bottom of all my bad dreams was one or the other, an overflowing toilet or a bloodstained chair. I wondered if my mother still menstruated, if she and my father still made love—if they ever had.

"Is it your perfume or powder that smells so nice?" I asked.

"On me? I don't know. I use both." She began opening bottles for me to smell.

"Do you really use all this stuff?" I asked.

"From time to time, yes. What do you use?"

"Nothing much. Sometimes a little mascara."

"And nothing at night?" She looked alarmed.

"No."

"You should use something on your skin at night, Sasha, you really should!" She lowered her voice. "When a woman gets past twenty-five she should think about her skin. Things change so rapidly if you don't take care." As she spoke her hand fluttered to her throat, where make-up is useless. "I never go to sleep without putting some of this on my face." She held out a bottle to me, an offering. "And for a woman my age, I still have a remarkably good skin. Want to try some? It feels very good. Go on, dear, take it with you. You're leaving today and the stores are closed: I can always get more."

I had been so proud of her beauty. And now to see her reduced to this, hooked on medicines, careful of light, trying to warn me of what was coming. I wanted to put my arms around her, to hug and console her. Perhaps the weakening of the senses of the aging is an adaptation for survival. Perhaps we grow weak in the eyes and hard of hearing the better to preserve our illusions.

♣

Roxanne told me about a way to abort myself with a speculum, a catheter and syringe, sterile water, and a friend. (Not till months later did I learn it could be lethal.) "There's nothing to it. I've done it twice myself. You just have someone squirt a little sterile water into the uterus, you wait, and in a few days you abort."

"What if you don't?"

"Then you do it again."

When I told Willy, he hit the roof. "Are you kidding? That's insane! We'll find a proper doctor to do it, thank you."

"But Roxanne's done it three times," I said exaggerating. "She says it's easy."

"Just thinking about it makes me sick."

"Come on, Willy. You'll help me, won't you?"

"Not that way. I'm going to find you a doctor."

Roxanne knew an intern whom she got to do it at his apartment in the Bronx. He pulled all the blinds and locked the doors while she boiled up the instruments.

"What a tight little twat you have," he said as Roxanne directed a flashlight between my legs. Each leg hung over a kitchen chair instead of being fitted into stirrups. I was ashamed. "It's a pleasure to work on you after the gaping smelly cunts that come into the hospital. If you could see them, you'd never want to have children."

"What do children have to do with it?"

"Believe me, having babies wrecks your plumbing. Now hold still a second. I don't want to hurt you if I can help it."

An instant of pain, and the catheter was in. "I wouldn't want to have children even if it was good for my plumbing," I said flatly.

"Don't you like kids?"

"I love kids. Other people's."

"Hey, will you relax? That's better. Don't you have any maternal instincts?"

"I have an instinct of self-preservation."

"You'll feel different when you fall in love. That's when they all want their babies. Now hold very still one more sec. Here comes the water."

"But I am in love."

"I doubt it," he said.

It was a familiar line, about love and babies. I'd been bucking it all my life. If it were true, as the scientists claimed, it would be smarter to live without love. The only power a woman had against a man was the possibility, never more than problematical, of leaving him; with babies even that defense vanished. No; plumbing aside, maternity was vulnerability itself, sentencing a woman at best to the plight of Mrs. Alport, and at worst to grubby isolation.

Sensation without pain, I felt the liquid enter me. "When I'm in love," I told him, "I rely on my convictions."

The very night I decided to try out my mother's lubricating skin lotion ("What's that godawful smell?" said Will as I got into bed. "Just some face lotion." "Well for Christsake, Sasha, can't you go and wash it off? You smell like a filling station!")—it was that very night, sometime after midnight, that I awoke with unbearable cramps. I was exploding, coming apart at the seams. I rolled around and doubled up and moaned.

"What's the matter, Sash?" asked Willy in his sleep.

"Nothing. Go back to sleep."

I thought it was food poisoning or appendicitis. Then at last I felt I had to take an enormous crap.

"Where are you, Sash?" called Willy, feeling me absent from the bed.

I sat on the toilet and pushed and pushed. Then out it popped, my first baby.

I looked down. It was suspended over the water in the toilet bowl, swinging from my body, its head down.

"Oh my God! Oh my God! Oh Willy!" I cried. I covered my mouth and screamed.

A nightmare. I looked again. It hung there like a corpse.

"Willy, please! Come quickly! It's a baby!"

I couldn't understand what was happening. I had thought at two or three months it would still be a fish with gills, or a tadpole. But it was a real baby, with a human head, only blue.

"Oh God! It's hanging here! Please help me."

"Now listen, Sasha," Willy was saying softly, "you've got to pull it out of you."

"Did you see it?"

"Yes."

"It's a baby, Willy!"

"I know honey, but you've still got to pull it out."

"Oh I can't." I was all atremble.

"You've got to."

"I can't."

It was too awful: the first baby I produced in this world I deposited like a piece of shit straight into the toilet.

"Try darling. Pull it out. Trust me."

At last, I pulled it out of me and dropped it into the water. It had always lived in a liquid medium. I couldn't look at it, my own child. I flushed the toilet.

Then I dissolved on the bed in a shudder of tears and afterbirth.

"It was a baby. I can't believe it. It was a baby," I moaned. Will stroked my back as I wept and bled.

"Do you think you'll be all right for a few minutes while I get the car? I'm going to take you to a hospital."

"I'm all right," I sobbed. "I'll get blood all over the car."

"Fuck the car," said Willy.

"I'm all right," I repeated. "I don't need to go to a hospital."

"Do as I tell you!" he shouted.

When we got to the hospital, a doctor prescribed three kinds of pills and a bed in the maternity ward.

"Don't leave me here, Willy. I don't want to stay here."

"Don't worry, honey, I won't leave you."

"I'm sorry, sir, but you're not permitted on the ward," said the nurse. "You can visit tomorrow."

"What are you going to do to her?" Will asked the doctor. "Can't you do something now so I can take her home?"

"Can't do anything till tomorrow," said the doctor.

"Why not?"

"I've ordered some pills to control the bleeding, and antibiotics and a tranquilizer. If she'll stop with the hysterics there may be a chance we can save your baby."

"But there is no baby, doctor," said Will. "She miscarried."

The doctor looked skeptical. "You sure?" he asked.

"Of course I'm sure. I saw the fetus myself."

"Did you bring it with you?"

"Bring it? No!"

The doctor shrugged and turned away.

"It's flushed down the toilet," said Willy frantically.

The doctor shook his head. "That's really too bad," he said, "If you'd brought it with you we might be able to clean her out tonight. But if she's not hemorrhaging and there's no fetus and I do a D-and-C at three A.M. with no one from the regular staff around, I could get into a lot of trouble. You understand. I wish I could help you out—"

"Take an X ray," said Willy desperately. "You'll see there's no baby inside her."

"We can't take an X ray."

"Why not?"

"An X ray might damage the fetus."

❧

At the end of that winter my divorce came through. Though I had sometimes talked of staying single ("Why do we need the paper? We've got our love"), it wasn't a week before I was carrying red roses to City Hall, already knowing the next step.

Babies.

Why? For the very reason I had refused them in the past: babies could bind.

The abortion, though we seldom spoke of it, had exposed my bluff. I had demanded it in the name of independence, yet ostensibly I had renounced independence. If my commitment to Will were serious, the best way to prove it was by making a baby. Without a career, I no longer had a reason not to. Willy expected it, poets encouraged it, it was part of the package. And as a job, motherhood seemed to offer more possibilities of advancement than the Clayton Advertising Agency's research library.

"Make it a good wedding, won't you?" said Will winking at the J.P. "The last one was just practice; this one is going to count." We wanted all the cement we could get to make it stick. Flaunting our devotion, we proselytized for second marriages. I was twenty-seven: unless the rust of my life had wrecked my plumbing, I had three years left to change. And Willy, a ripe thirty-one, had the rest of his life to help me.

We never celebrated our wedding anniversary, arbitrarily determined by the date of my final decree. Instead, at least till our second child was born, we celebrated the anniversary of that season we met, replaying those days like the album of a favorite show, complete with costumes.

"Don't ask questions, just try it on," said Will, presenting me with a large box from Lord & Taylor. "I saw it in the window and had to buy it for you. It's like the dress you were wearing at Hector's party that first night in New York. You were so beautiful I couldn't take my eyes off you. Go on. Try it on."

As usual, Willy was right. It was like, but better made than, the one I had bought for the party. It was perfect for the occasion. Starting with champagne on whatever liner was moored in the harbor (a fifty-cent donation to the Seaman's Fund would get us on board), progressing to turkey and gherkin and Jimmy Witherspoon at Hector's on the first Saturday night of each December (with me in a black silk dress), we repeated the steps of our marathon. Our first lunch together at the restaurant with the *pommes soufflées* (I in my off-white turtleneck), the American Beauty roses, our first champagne cocktail at the Monkey Bar (same sweater), our miraculous chance meeting at the Museum of Modern Art where, lunching in brown wool with Roxanne, I had spotted Will sitting alone across the room watching us. ("Is *that* him?" asked Roxanne. "Yes." "He looks all right, but you'd better be sure.") And then finally our first embrace at the Motel on the Mountain in Tarrytown, New York, in the other black dress that zipped up the back. Precisely three days before Christmas, only months after I had resigned myself to a life without love.

"Goodnight, I love you," said Willy every night, molding us into spoons. And though I had said the phrase to others out of courtesy or caution, now for the first time in my life without feeling sly or dirty or had, I too could affirm before closing my eyes, "Goodnight, I love you."

# E
# I
# G
# H
# T

Without daring to reconsider, we made Andrea in the new year and I bore her in the fall, entering the park world in the winter, bundled up. The books I had taken from the library in preparation proved, like *The Questions Girls Ask* and *Girl Alive!,* to be mere parodies of life; but there was nothing else to go on. Child care was neither discussed in society nor taught in school. However contemptuous I'd been of the prospect of Spock, I was grateful for him now. He had the latest word and a good index.

It would be good news for every baby weighing 10 pounds or more to be outdoors, when it isn't raining, for 2 or 3 hours a day, as long as the temperature is above freezing and the wind isn't bitterly cold. (Dr. Spock, *Baby and Child Care,* Section 244.)

The old lady who fed pigeons peered into the carriage, but otherwise I was alone on a deserted bench, paralyzed by the fragility of my overwhelming charge, afraid to move for fear of waking her, afraid to take my eyes off her lest she sleep and die. During her brief sleeps I studied her like a difficult text, trying to fathom each mysterious tremor and start, praying she would not wake too soon. When she did wake—always grievously ahead of schedule—I leaped to jiggle the carriage as I had seen the neighbors do, trying to shake the sobs from her throat and the knots from my gut.

If you live in a city and have no yard to park the baby in, you can push him in a carriage. Long woolen underwear, slacks, woolen stockings, and galoshes make your life a lot more pleasant during this period.

In summer it would be different. She would be older then and I would not fear her death so much as her life. But now each sob my Andy suffered was on my hands. In my breast lay the power to soothe or torment her, but also dangers. If ten minutes of jiggling the carriage didn't get her back to sleep, that would be ten wasted minutes, six hundred useless sobs tearing at my raw conscience. It would take ten more minutes to get home from the park, and another ten to get the carriage up the stairs and our wraps and clothing off.

What do you do if he wakes as soon as you put him to bed or a little later? I think it's better to assume first that if he has nursed for 5 minutes he's had enough to keep him satisfied for a couple of hours, and try not to feed him again right away. Let him fuss for a while if you can stand it. (Section 127.)

The baby carriage turned out to be an unexpected aid in stopping traffic. "Pedestrians have the right of way!" I roared indignantly from the middle of Sixth Avenue, and for once even the long-distance haulage trucks stopped for me. But it was still a good half hour between whimper and feeding—a half hour that took months off my life and left yellow milkstains on my nursing bras.

It may start leaking from the breasts when you hear the baby beginning to cry in the next room. This shows how much feelings have to do with the formation and release of the milk. (Section 102.)

If I had stayed home with her instead of going to the park I could have put her to suck the instant she woke, forgot the clock and the dangers.

The treatment of fretfulness seems clear to me. . . . The baby should be allowed to nurse as often as every 2 hours, for 20 to 40 minutes. (Section 122.)

But I so wanted everything to be right for her, and the park was the preferred milieu. Constant feeding was contraindicated. If my breasts were never more than partially emptied, which could result from putting her to suck too often, then they would not be properly stimulated to fill up again and I would dry up with no comfort for my helpless daughter.

If the breast-milk supply is insufficient at all feedings, you will need a bottle at all feedings, whether you give the breast first or not. (Section 126.)

I knew I shouldn't be offering her bottles yet, but how could I risk starving her? Her life was in my hands. I nursed her around the clock every two hours for half an hour at least, watching her tiny fists clutch spasmodically at my long hair and her toes curl in the joy of sucking, until she fell asleep at my breast; then gingerly I tried to roll her onto her stomach without waking her.

> There are two disadvantages to a baby's sleeping on his back. If he vomits, he's more likely to choke on the vomitus. Also, he tends to keep his head turned toward the same side. . . . This may flatten that side of his head. It won't hurt his brain, and the head will gradually straighten out, but it may take a couple of years. (Section 248.)

During the mornings and late afternoons, when I had the diapers and laundry, the bottles and bedding to do, I let her sleep on our bed between feedings. Does a tree falling unobserved in the forest make a sound? Does my child live without me there to see her? I carefully slipped rubber padding between her diaper and our sheet, sometimes leaving her bottom bare to help her diaper rash. ("Jesus, Sasha, isn't there anything else you can use on her diaper rash besides Desitin Ointment? It smells worse than shit; our bed stinks of it," said Willy.) But at night, when I longed to share with her my brief interludes of sleep, I couldn't risk keeping her in bed with me. Even if Willy hadn't protested her little body coming between ours, it was a dangerous place for her. A carelessly flung arm could snuff out her fire like a breath a birthday candle; not to mention the

> chance that he may become dependent on this arrangement and be afraid and unwilling to sleep anywhere else. (Section 250.)

No; better to follow (Section 251) the doctor's better

> sensible rule not to take a child into the parent's bed
> for any reason (even as a treat when the father is
> away on a business trip);

to suffer now than pay later.

The conspiracy of silence about motherhood was
even wider than the one about sex. Philosophers ignored it and poets revered it, but no one dared describe
it. The experts who wrote articles for magazines ("Ten
Steps to Restore Muscle Tone"; "Before You Call Your
Pediatrician"; "Take the Time to Stay Interesting: Six
Shortcuts to Keeping Informed") spoke in euphemisms;
as to the real dangers, their best advice was to consult
still other doctors. Why didn't the women speak? Evidently they were too busy.

"Roxanne!" I cried. "Why didn't you warn me?"

"But I did, Sasha. I told you everything. I honestly
thought you knew."

By summertime Andy sat up unsupported and charmed
us with her laugh.

"Boy or girl?"

"Girl."

"Oh. What's her name?"

"Andrea."

She purred and giggled as I suckled her. She had her
preferences, did my daughter, and when something
made her cry she broke my heart with her great stores
of tears that flooded her enormous green eyes and
overflowed their thick banks of black lash like swollen
rivers. How, I wondered, could Willy bear to be away
from us? Why did he leave us promptly every morning
and return late every night?

"Sasha," called Willy, "she's started crying again. I was just sitting here with her and she started screaming for no reason."

I dropped the spatula and ran to the living room, oblivious of Spock's warning to parents who

always anxiously pick him up when he fusses: . . . the more they submit to his orders the more demanding he becomes. (Section 282.)

"Give her to me, Willy, for God's sake, don't let her cry like that!"

If your baby is sensitive about new people, new places, in the middle of his first year, I'd protect him from too much fright by making strangers keep at a little distance until he gets used to them, especially in new places. He'll remember his father in a while. (Section 348.)

I took my baby in my arms and walked her, patting her perfect back the way I had when she was a newborn. The sound of her crying was always absolutely unbearable to me.

Many mothers get worn out and frantic listening to a baby cry, especially when it's the first. You should make a great effort to get away from home and baby for a few hours at least twice a week—oftener if you can arrange it. . . . If you can't get anyone to come in, let your husband stay home one or two evenings a week while you go out to visit or see a movie. (Section 278.)

The trouble was, Willy didn't get home most evenings till eight or so and couldn't have helped me then if he'd wanted to. Oh, he was thoughtful in many ways. He telephoned the Diaper Service from his office to yell at the delivery man for me when the fouled-up deliveries drove me to phone him, sobbing, at work; he was comforting in emergencies. But he too had changed when Andy was born. A family man now with responsibilities, he buckled down to work.

"Honey? I'm in a meeting now that I just can't leave. Better eat without me."

His work and ego prospered—for us, he said. But how could he possibly learn on Sundays the intricate rhythm we had established during the week? How could he relieve me if he left us in the morning and returned late at night, or if he were away, as the omniscient Spock had divined, on a business trip?

"Hold it—" said Will, opening his lens on us.

I tried to hold it.

"Okay. Relax now."

Us at the fountain in Washington Square, us lying naked on the bed, us playing pat-a-cake, us arty under the Brooklyn Bridge.

"You have no idea how breathtakingly beautiful you are with that child," he said, holding the negatives up to the light for scrutiny. "You're going to love some of these."

He kept us like a credit card in a window of his wallet and blown up splat on his office wall. As I sat in the doctor's office waiting Andy's turn or stood in line at the checkout counter, I liked to think of us on Will's office wall silently watching him work, decorating his life. Our sepia eyes followed the viewer all over the room. Hector had a penchant for pretty clericals from good colleges, and I wanted our presence felt in that place. Not that I mistrusted Will, but I remembered how far I could have been trusted as an unattached clerical. Overnight, it seemed, I had switched alle-glances: suddenly I found myself siding with wives and parents against insurgents. Marxists were right: we follow our class interests.

Once every two weeks I hired a daytime sitter and tore myself from Andy as Spock advised. I planned to slip off to the library and read a book or arrange to meet a friend at the Museum of Modern Art. But somehow the hours were too precious to use up on personal frivolities, and instead I took to dropping in on Will for lunch (as in the old days), doing everything I could to live up to my photographs. Flat-stomached supermother uptown between feedings. "Please tell him Mrs. Burke is here," I said with authority to the current receptionist. Not for nothing had I insisted on living in Manhattan.

I took more care dressing for those office calls than when Will wrenched me away from Andy at bedtime to accompany him to the movies or a party at Hector's, where I watched the world go spinning on as though babies were a recent invention. Couples stood in line at movie theaters holding hands, oblivious of the consequences; old friends gathered at Hector's with new girlfriends to exchange news of charter flights and recent books, as though Dr. Spock's *Baby and Child Care* had not been written for them. "How's that baby?" asked informed singles. And when Will proudly displayed the latest photos of me and Andy he had carefully enlarged on weekends in the darkened kitchen, they saw no prophecies, heard no warnings. "I told you; I thought you knew," Roxanne had said, yet not even I had caught the message. Then how could these party girls be expected to understand what was in store for them? I was not about to admit exhaustion or plead anxiety to them, waiting like harpies for just such a signal that Will was carrion. Nothing provokes attack

like the smell of defeat. Instead, I joined the general
snicker at the profession of housewife and kept a
careful eye on Willy. And determined to do stomach-
muscle exercises if I could steal the time.

That first summer I took Andy to the crowded playground every day, carrying her up the slide and sliding
her down on my lap.

"Wheee! Andy," I said; and she after me, "ee."

I strapped her into the baby swings, swinging her,
singing to her, anything to hear her delicious laughter.

> *I had a silver nut tree, nothing would it bear*
> *But a silver nutmeg and a golden pear.*
> *The King of Spain's daughter came to visit me*
> *And all for the sake of my little nut tree.*

From the tilt of her head, her sounds, the way she
held out her hands to me, I knew which songs she
loved, which games she wanted. We spoke in a secret
code. Her laugh and cry was the pitch pipe by which I
tuned my days.

> *I skipped over water, I danced over sea,*
> *And all the birds in the air could not catch me.*

From a park bench I watched her at my feet intently
tearing up a leaf, her mouth open and brows knit in
concentration, her pudgy fingers moving with careful
grace. Though I always took a book to the park I
didn't dare read for the dangers; couldn't read for the
distractions. Anyway, most books were now irrelevant.
Instead, I searched around to see which of the other
mothers, multiparous and knowing, could tell me
things about my daughter I ought to know. Some of

them were limber and accomplished, some foul-mouthed and acne-scarred, no doubt with mean lives and husbands to match, and I wondered as I watched them fitfully sunning themselves on the benches—their skirts or dungarees pulled above their knees to reveal legs laced with varicose veins and stubble, their hair in rollers on Fridays, their hips spreading, their ankles puffed with edema—I wondered that some of them had ever managed to land and hold husbands at all. I listened to them entranced. Their complaints were auguries, their advice oracular. I hung on every casual comparison they made of Andy with their own like revelations. My daughter's life was on my hands.

"Slow down, Willy!" I screamed as we rode the bumper of the car ahead. I yelled for Andy, and all the others Willy was bound to kill, it was only a matter of time. He was surely the most reckless driver in New York City. Always rushing to make the turn, pass the car ahead, get into the tunnel first, make it through the light on yellow, as though restraint were defeat. I half wished he'd crash and get it over with. ("There, you see? Now you've killed our baby!")

With a certain acumen he labeled my criticism "disloyal," and forbade it. "I've told you: this is the way I drive. If you don't like it, then don't drive with me!"

I couldn't fault his position. But aware of Andy asleep in her carcrib in the back seat, I couldn't control myself either. Her enemy was my enemy.

"I'm sorry, Will. I mean, *please* slow down. As a favor. I don't know what I'll do if she wakes up now."

He threw me an exasperated look and dropped a few feet behind the car in front before pulling out fast to change lanes. I clenched the armrest and closed my eyes. "Oh please, Willy," I pleaded.

He stopped the car short in the parking lane.

"You're impossible! If I'm going to creep, I have to be in the slow lane. Why don't *you* drive?"

But I had long since given up driving except in emergencies.

"I'm sorry, Willy. Go on. I'll keep quiet."

I dreaded angering him. My stomach had knots enough. If we continued to break faith with each other we would turn sour like any other couple, and then— The mere thought of Andy fatherless could make me panic.

Will started the car again, his mouth set against me. There was never time any more to talk things out as we once had done. Misunderstandings lingered. I always seemed, he said, to be pushing him away, when what I needed was to bind him close.

I was more helpless than ever in the passenger seat. yielding to nature's temptations had put me in Willy's power as surely as it had once put me in Joey Ross's. Only this time I couldn't escape by moving out of town.


I began each day solemnly with resolutions:

Today I will make myself lunch; I'll brew myself a cup of tea between breakfast feeding and diaper delivery.

I will *not* pick her up whenever she cries today.

I will be *calm* when she spits out her food.

The horror of my predicament was: everything counts. Each tiny mistake I made was destined to reverberate through all eternity.

The first time I yelled at Andy she looked at me unbelieving; betrayed. Her chin puckered, her lip trembled, then tears gushed from those green eyes all over her hands. I sank into a week-long depression. (Only a week and I had damaged her forever! More than a week and who would have fed her?) The weeks became records of my guilt, the months stages to weather and survive. No wonder my poor mother blamed herself for all my foolishness: I felt responsible for all of Andy's. Willy was pissed at my state of mind; I wasn't the carefree woman he had married. I lived by the tick of a clock not the beat of a pulse.

It's possible that you will find yourself feeling discouraged for a while when you first begin taking care of your baby. It's a fairly common feeling, especially with the first. You may not be able to put your fingers on anything that is definitely wrong. You just weep easily. Or you may feel very bad about certain things. One woman whose baby cries quite a bit feels sure that he has a real disease, another that her husband has become strange and distant, another that she has lost all her looks. (Section 16.)

Exactly as I had once imagined but forgotten, when my child was born my fate slipped through my fingers into the bay. I was hers now.

If you begin to feel at all depressed, . . . go to a movie, or to the beauty parlor, or to get yourself a new hat or dress. . . . (Section 16.)

A new locale, a new hair style, could solve nothing any more. We swam around sifting plankton, hoping for some huge uplifting wave to come along and carry us high and wide; but there were only the usual ripples and currents and erratic seismographic disturbances to be recorded on the precision instruments of oceanographers. It all went down somewhere in a book;

caprice was a memory. Even Roxanne had been stuck until Sasha began school. At least until Andy reached puberty, I noted, I was no freer to kill myself than a barnacle.

*Notes in a Baby Book:*

*December 14*: First smile. More delicious than the sneeze.

*January 2:* She discovers her thumb.

*April 5:* I laid her down on her stomach and picked her up on her back. Ergo: she has learned to turn over.

*June 21:* First tooth through. Though not yet visible, I can hear it clink against her spoon. At last an explanation for her fretfulness as good as Will's hypothesis that I am overprotective.

*August 17:* She learns to stand.

Thinking her still asleep in her crib at naptime I had gone next door to borrow some diapers from a neighbor. When I returned, I heard her screaming in her room. (Was it my fault? "Look, honey," Willy had warned, "this is the third time you've run out of diapers. What happened to the emergency supply I got you? You need better planning. If you won't increase the regular order, you'll just have to use the ones you have more sparingly.")

An accident? Had I forgotten to raise the side of the crib?

A baby, by the age he first tries to roll over, shouldn't be left unguarded on a table for as long as it takes the mother to turn her back (Section 349.)

I rushed to her room to find her standing in her crib clutching the bars terror-stricken, her fat knees buckling.

"Standing! Look at you!" I cried. She sobbed with exhaustion and victory. A star!

I unhooked her fingers one by one from the bars and scooped her up into my arms, my bumblebee, pressing kisses all over her shining face. "You can stand. You can do anything." I rejoiced. When she kicked to be put back again, I sat her down in the crib; then up she climbed on her little legs once more, crowing with pride.

She had learned to stand not for a moment or a day, but for all time. I knelt before her crib. She looked so much tinier upright than sprawled across her mattress. She was one of us now, though she didn't come up to my knees. As I knelt adoringly before her, trying to kiss her nose through the bars, she began to shake her little body furiously, rattling the bars, laughing until her chin puckered, her lower lip protruded toward me, and once again, the deluge.

Down again with my help to sitting, then up on her own. For an hour and more we did our joyful dance while the tide waited.

"William Burke, please."

"Just a minute, please." A new voice at the switchboard.

"Willy? She can stand up!"

"What?"

"Andy! She can stand up!"

"Alone?"

"Yes. She holds on, of course, but she can get up by herself."

"Hey! That's great, Sash! Great! It's about time, isn't it?"

"No, Willy. She's only nine and a half months old. Spock says it happens any time in the last quarter of the first year. But she's so happy, Will," I went on, imploring him to rejoice. "Like she *knows*. She stands up and laughs that way she has, as though she's the wonder of the world. And you know what? She is! The minute I sit her down, up she goes again. I thought you'd want to know about it."

"Sure do, honey. Thanks a lot for calling me."

When I hung up I chastised myself for having phoned him with the news. I ought not to have told him at all. I should have let it happen for him as a surprise, as it had happened for me. And when he finally did come home, I overdid it, searching his face for a joy that could not possibly appear. And filled up like a Hoover bag with resentments.

*October 10:* First step unassisted.

*October 28:* First word: *pity* (pretty).

The experts would have agreed I expected too much of Will: infants' progress is fit news only for ladies' magazines. Andy's triumphs were everything to me— elating, exonerating—and only bonuses to him, which somehow diminished them. They were like the figure skates I had wanted for my ninth Christmas because my best friend had asked for skates and I imagined us learning together. We each got our skates, but Jackie got skis as well. She skated occasionally, but spent most of her Sundays on the Baybury slopes with other friends, while I settled for the school pond, alone. I acquired considerable skill, but what I had wanted was my friend.

Willy tried. He brought home quince in the spring and roses often. But even with the living room a garden, he sat at the window and looked out. I could see he felt trapped inside with us, whereas I, trapped too, could barely be induced to leave.

On Sundays he was gallant, taking us to Central Park, first to the zoo cafeteria for pancakes, then to the carrousel, where he waved to us from a bench each time Andy and I rode by. But in between, though I never actually caught him, I knew he looked at the carefree New York girls.

> Ride a cock horse to Banbury Cross
> To see a fine lady upon a white horse.
> With rings on her fingers and bells on her toes
> She shall have music wherever she goes.

Everyone but me was on best behavior, sitting still and enraptured in the darkened Hunter Auditorium as the Budapest String Quartet (with an extra cellist) unfolded Schubert's Quintet in C Major. To me, it was the most exquisite music in their repertoire; of the five concerts in the series, this was the one I'd been most eager to hear. Yet already the opening movement had gone by while I sneaked nervous glances at my wristwatch, and now, with the adagio approaching, I feared it would all be over before I could begin to listen. Another waste.

"Give me a dime, Willy," I whispered between movements, unable to contain myself.

"What for?"

"I'm going to call home."

He glared incendiary darts into my heart. "No!"

"Give me a dime!"

"Shhh," said people around us as the music commenced again.

Trapped mid-row. If only he'd thought to buy aisle seats! I glanced at my watch. Time stopped. The exquisite slow movement was interminable!

For my twenty-ninth birthday Willy had bought tickets to the entire Budapest series. Once, I noted bitterly, it would have been the perfect gift, the music stopping time for us in a different way. But now, the tickets were a burden, the music a snare. For two concerts in a row Andy had refused to be left with a sitter, and when I threatened to stay home with her again tonight, Willy was enraged.

"Are you a wife or a fucking nanny? Why do you allow that child to tyrannize us?"

Talk of tyranny! As though it were my fault that child care precluded entertainment! As though I should share his mad priorities! I had been working for weeks on getting her to sleep without having to sit with her in her darkened room for an hour, and I knew leaving her at bedtime with a strange sitter would set me back days.

> The cure is simple: put the baby to bed at a reasonable hour, say good night affectionately but firmly, walk out of the room, and don't go back. Most babies who have developed this pattern cry furiously for 20 to 30 minutes the first night, and then when they see that nothing happens, they suddenly fall asleep! The second night the crying is apt to last only 10 minutes. The third night there usually isn't any at all. (Section 284.)

With Andy, it had been a half hour the first night and an hour the second, and I wasn't going to try any third.

It's hard on the kind-hearted parents while the crying lasts. They imagine the worst: that his head is caught in the slats of the crib, or that he has vomited and is lying in a mess, that he is at least in a panic about being deserted.

By then Will bristled at the mere suggestion that he get someone else to go with him to a concert. "Now tonight you do as I say! You put her down in that crib and close that door and *leave,* do you hear? Or else *I'll* do it!"

Though I trembled with hate (her enemy was my enemy), I couldn't fight him. He forbade me to over-rule him as he forbade me to go for the mail in my night clothes or tell secrets to Roxanne. He was too strong. I couldn't handle Andy and him both; things were difficult enough. If he threatened to leave us, if he *left* us, we couldn't survive. ("Don't be so fatalistic," said Roxanne. "I could probably get you a job. I know a few angles by now.") I gave in as often as I could; when it came to a fight I always ended in tears and apologizing, like someone without resources. ("The best thing about a divorce is, afterwards you get to say and think anything you want," said Roxanne.)

Finally, the applause. "Excuse me, excuse me, please," I said, pushing past the others in my row all applauding ecstatically.

At last the aisle, only seconds ahead of the intermission crush. Now for the lobby and the phone booths. If I couldn't complete my call or couldn't stand the message, Willy or no, I would leap into a taxi and break for home!

When I felt the flutter of life in me anew, I kept the thrill of it to myself. Something told me to be careful. I did my quota of nesting, washing Andy's outgrown

layette and making extensive lists of details to attend
to, but I was careful not to burden Will with them.
There was something about the way he picked up the
newspaper and then put it down again, the way he kept
going to the refrigerator and the window for something
that wasn't there, that told me to keep my nesting
secret. He was too restless around us, as though we
were keeping him from something important and elsewhere.

I did my best to avoid sensitive topics. I hid my
child-care pamphlets among my recipes as I had once
hidden my beauty charts and *Seventeens*. I knew they
were considered vacuous, like the talk of formulas and
play groups that blighted cocktail party repartee—unless it issued from some doctor. But they dealt with
matters too important to leave to chance. I knew I
risked the worst contempt for reading them, but I had
more than my own ego to consider: there were the
children's. How else was I to learn the pitfalls of sibling
rivalry or the symptoms and cure of croup? I had no
models, no advisers for child care. Like housework, it
was something charming people didn't discuss and rich
people didn't do.

Once I had tried to read Will an urgent paragraph
from the "Parent and Child" feature in the Sunday
*Times Magazine* supplement. Tearing it away from me
he had cried, "Why do you read that trash and let it
upset you? It's just bullshit!" as, during my earlier
pregnancy, he'd forbidden me to read about the limbless
thalidomide babies, saying, "You'd be a nervous wreck
if you didn't have me to protect you."

I too was protective. Too vulnerable to rebel, I
always tried to have Andy's bath finished and her toys
picked up before Will came home, to put on perfume
and music at dinnertime, so things would be cozy. I

could never have risked Roxanne's guerrilla tactics. But however carefully I spared him our disorder, he still used every excuse to come home late. No matter how endearingly Andy greeted him at the door, once home, it seemed, Will couldn't wait to get out of the house again.

> Men react to their wife's pregnancy with various feelings: protectiveness of the wife, increased pride in the marriage, pride about their virility. . . . But there can also be, way underneath, a feeling of being left out . . . which can be expressed as grumpiness toward his wife, wanting to spend more evenings with his men friends, or flirtatiousness with other women. (Section 18.)

Of all the experts I'd ever consulted, none—no Watson, Webber, or Spock—was unequivocally on my side. They made us do it, then blamed us for it, another case of damned if you do and damned if you don't. They found nothing more hateful than a clinging wife—except a dominating mom.

> Some fathers have been brought up to think that the care of babies and children is the mother's job entirely. But a man can be a warm father and a real man at the same time. . . . Of course, I don't mean that the father has to give just as many bottles or change just as many diapers as the mother. But it's fine for him to do these things occasionally. . . . Of course, there are some fathers who get goose flesh at the very idea of helping to take care of a baby, and there's no good to be gained trying to force them. Most of them come around to enjoying their children later "when they're more like real people." (Section 20.)

From the confines of my cell I tried to thwart Willy's wanderings. It was my duty. By turns I tried confrontation and subterfuge, and for penance I suppressed my terror in the face of his driving and my gloom at his playing knight to every lady. And when I ran out of coffee or snapped at him in my regular early morning panic, I kicked myself for driving him off to Riker's Restaurant for breakfast, the *Times* tucked under his arm as he walked out the door. And when I finally went to the hospital to give birth to Jenny, I could no longer hide my obsessive conviction that once Will was free of us, with me away and Andy gone to stay with his mother and nothing in the world to keep him at home, he would simply pack up his things and leave.

"What a beautiful child! I never saw such eyes."

"Thank you." With a pang for pale Jenny asleep in the carriage, I beamed at Andy. Picking the chocolate off her Good Humor, oblivious of praise, she was indeed beautiful.

"I mean, her eyelashes, What *we* wouldn't give for lashes like that, eh! Too bad they're wasted on kids." She smoothed her white uniform, sighing with fatigue, then peered into my face. "Where'd she get them—from her father?"

"N-no," I stuttered, brushing my hair back self-consciously. "I mean I don't think so. Her father's fair." Should I explain? "Actually, I once had eyes like that myself."

"You did? When you were a kid? See what I mean?" she said, shaking at once her head and the carriage in her charge. "What a waste."

The ice cream was dripping down Andy's fat arms onto her overalls. I reached down with a diaper to catch it, but, too fast for me, she squirmed free. "Come back here, monkey," I shouted, taking off after her. "Take that stick out of your mouth when you run!"

Too late. Jenny was awake and crying. I caught my screaming Andy and tucked her under my arm. She replaced the stick I snatched from her mouth with her thumb.

"I've got to go now," I said to my companion, hooking Andy into the baby seat atop the carriage.

"You mustn't let her suck her thumb, dear. Her teeth will come in all crooked and ruin her face. She'll need braces."

"I don't believe in that," I said.

Whether thumb-sucking displaces the teeth or not, you naturally prefer to have your child give it up as soon as possible. (Section 324.)

"See that? Your little girl's eyes are even brighter now she's been crying. What we wouldn't give."

I gathered our plastic belongings and Andy's strayed sneakers, then pushed the carriage toward the ramp leading out of the playground. Jenny quieted as soon as we were rolling, but there was still no time to waste.

"See you tomorrow," I called back. My milk was already letting down.

"The man I work for," the woman called after me, "is a professor at the university!" She could have been his wife for the pride in her voice. "He won't let Charlotte suck *her* thumb!"

We rolled down the ramp and out of the park.

"Pedestrians have the right of way!" I yelled.

"Pedestrians have to right away," mimicked Andy.

What would the park nurse have thought if she knew that as soon as I put Jenny to my breast, Andy took hold of her sister's tiny foot, rubbed it on her cheek, and watching me with her great green eyes, sucked her thumb inconsolably?

"Don't you think that's a creepy scene, Sasha? Don't you think it's bad for her?" asked Will. But whatever I did about it was bound to be wrong, damned either way. And who but a stranger would have the heart to stop her?

I had just walked in with the groceries when the phone rang.

"Surprise," said Roxanne.

"What is it?" I asked.

"Guess."

We hadn't spoken in ages. We still confided in each other, loved each other, but since I had become a mother I'd seen and spoken to almost no one.

"Let's see," I tried. "You're getting married?"

"Married! Don't be crazy! Once was enough. Guess again."

"You got a new job?"

"Getting closer. But it's better than that. Guess again."

"You sold a poem."

"Yes! Four poems, to be exact. To *Intersection*. They're going to feature me. Their Lady Poet. But I don't care—it's a start."

"Roxanne! How wonderful!"

"All it takes, ladies and gentlemen, is freedom, determination, and very hard work. And to think," she added, "I was once foiled by zygotes."

"Wait till old Franklin Raybel sees one of *us* in his *Intersection*," I said. And though it was probably mean, I couldn't wait.

Will came leisurely into the kitchen, distributing kisses. He gave Andy a large, plush, multicolored ball from FAO Schwarz, peered at Jenny in her Infanseat, presented me with a bakery box, set a bottle of champagne in the refrigerator, and got down the long-stemmed goblets he had courted me with.

Andy's second birthday and I hated him. He'd said he'd be home at six thirty, and as usual he arrived at an entirely unrelated time, pretending nothing was wrong. As usual he came swathed in gifts when what I needed was love.

I couldn't let it pass. Crippled by vanity and two babies I had only two choices: to care or not to care.

"Where have you been?"

He stiffened, setting his jaw for the defense like a bull lowering his horns. "At the office. And then picking up these things."

Presents and a lie. No one had answered his office phone for hours.

It was the way we always started. Not with a difference to be resolved or an unkindness to be forgiven, but with some absolute and crushing betrayal. To be obliterated by a new total commitment—or divorce.

"I've been calling your office for hours. No one was there."

"I was in the back room. Or maybe I'd already left to get the stuff."

Another lie. Schwarz's closed at five thirty.

"Did you stop at Schwarz's on the way home?" I asked, laying a trap.

I could catch him, or he could answer skillfully and escape; either way I lost. I prayed he would have some half-believable explanation to prove that despite all his treachery he might still love me.

"No. I got the ball on my lunch hour. I had a drink with Hector and picked up the champagne. Are we going to have an inquisition over the birthday cake?"

A drink with Hector! Me here, waiting, and he has a drink with Hector! If it *was* with Hector.

But as always, it was too risky for me to follow through. Mothers of very young children are not in the best position to press their hunches. Anyway, Andy was already watching us. And we were dealing only in words, which didn't matter.

I opened the cake box. Frosting flowers: sweet deceptions.

What did matter were facts. The fact of me here alone with the girls, always alone, waiting for him, going crazy. Of his being ever poised to flee. The incessant subterranean battle. Whatever time $t$ he said he'd show, he showed at $t + x$.

His defense: "Can't you be flexible? Must I know in advance and report to you every step I'm going to take?"

No way for me to calculate $x$ without being small-minded. No possibility of retribution. For every $x$, the salad would be wilted, the entree spoiled, the children ready for bed or asleep. Complaints too mean to voice. My complaints deemed trivial, while his:

"Can't we do anything spontaneously any more?" My back a trampoline for his spontaneity.

Small-minded? On the contrary, my mind soared, exploded, with resentments! (*A disaster-enjoying woman of thirty will be, unless a miracle happens, the same at 40 and at 60*: Dr. Watson.) My mind, my faculties, universally disregarded since I had become a housewife, were tuned to detect the minutest discrepancies. They never worked better! No sooner did the key turn in the door than the smile I summoned turned to snarl or sob, as in he walked, a torment to his wife, a stranger to his children, bringing gifts and excuses and romantic pretense to make it worse.

> *Happy birthday to you,*
> *Happy birthday to you,*
> *Happy birthday, dear Andrea,*
> *Happy birthday to you.*

The flashbulbs and the champagne cork made Jenny cry during the ceremony, but at least Andy didn't cry—even though I had to help her blow out her candles and it was long past her bedtime. With her endearing unpredictability she was the model celebrant, chasing the ball gleefully around the room, perfectly nesting the set of nesting boxes I gave her for a challenge, my precocious pumpkin.

There we were, except for the absence of a little boy, the perfect family (flash! snap!). Lacking only an audience to make us real.

"Sit still, darling. I'll put the birthday girl to bed myself tonight," said Will, elevating Andy to his shoulder. He whinnied like a stallion and cantered her off to bed.

"Don't forget her poem—she can't sleep without it," I called. "And two diapers for night time." (The sleep crises of Section 284, long since resolved by ritual poems, had been superseded by other crises, other Sections.)

"This whole family needs jollying," said Will, returning to the living room to lift dozing Jenny from my arms. By the look in his eye and something in his voice, I knew he planned a bedtime treat for me as well.

All forgiven. For once I would leave the dishes on the table till morning and go to bed unclothed. We would take it slow and all over, calmed by champagne, kissing and rolling, forgetting the formula and the new receptionist. Though I was no less exhausted than other nights, no less tense with the children in the next room ready to waken before we'd finished, still tonight I would try to relax.

"Relax, will you? Where's the fire?" Will had often urged, popping in and out of me in the early mornings as I lay poised to answer the baby's first cry. It was as it had always been. If I wanted to kiss and snuggle and embrace, I had to be prepared to screw. One thing had to lead to another, whether there was only a little time or a lot. Touching and holding, for which I yearned, were only prelude for men. As Baybury girls learned at twelve, *boys always go as far as they can and never backwards.*

"Kids are God's contraceptives," Willy quipped to his friends, "always waking up just when you feel horny." Tonight, though, I would back Willy in letting them cry if they woke too soon. For once I would not fake orgasm in the interests of my offspring, but with the abandon of former days that made sex into love, I would try to scale with Willy those treacherous peaks we had once managed to climb so perfectly together.

Unless Jenny switched to her panic cry, or Andy asked to be taken to the potty.

The main cue for the mother is to remain friendly, encouraging, and optimistic about tomorrow. She can talk about how she, Daddy, brothers, sisters, friends, use the toilet, how the child is growing bigger every day, how nice it feels to be clean and dry. I don't mean a whole sermon every day, just a reminder.

All this takes a lot of patience. Some days the mother will be irritated and angry that no progress is apparent. If you see you are making no progress, drop the effort for a few days or weeks. It's better not to punish. If encouragement doesn't work, stronger methods will only set you back further. (Section 379.)

# N
# I
# N
# E

Leave it to the philosophers to have a weighty German name for the question of whether or not to procreate. *Zeugungsproblem.* An aspect of axiology, a branch of ethics. Hear the learned professors contemplate the consequences of birth for the race of Man, the metaphysical implications of existence, and not one word about the effects of procreation on a woman's body.

Schopenhauer, the profoundest of pessimists, meets the gloomy Byron on a holiday stroll through Venice. The two giants greet each other, remark the shimmer of the air, the futility of life, while their inamoratas, each leaning on her lover's arm and shifting her weight from foot to foot, looks the other over, smiles sweetly, twirls her parasol, straightens her skirts. Ah, sighs Lord

Byron, how painful this life. Aye, nods Schopenhaner, we must put a stop to it. They part, the one to suicide, the other to misogyny.

But see what the tiniest baby will do to the woman. Stretching her belly and waist into the ghastliest shapes before it even emerges from the womb, ruining her breasts, turning her pink nipples brown. Producing spots at the hairline, dark hairs down her midline, bleeding gums, stretch marks, varicosities, blues, alterations of the hormones and perhaps the DNA—and that's only the beginning. In time comes the ugly crease in the brow between the eyes hewn by incessant anxiety and sporadic rage, the rasp in the voice, the knot in the gut, the regret. Fear alters the features, and in time the sweetest child will make a shrew of her.

Schopenhauer, the misogynist, resolves his *Zeugungs-problem* by remaining a bachelor and sometime celibate. He rises punctually each morning to write his books, blames his mother, takes his meals in his favorite restaurant, in a temper shoves an old woman down a flight of stairs, and discourses at length on the futility of life and the deception in women.

📖

It was partly because of the way Willy noted the girls on the street that summer, partly because of the new fashions, that I finally decided to cut my hair. The sixties had started while I was having my babies, and I felt I had to do something about it. The threat of abandonment or another woman had crept into the nursery, and I was going out of my mind.

I did not act on impulse. I spent a long time thinking it over, studying the ads and my old photos, before I finally made an appointment with a hairdresser and hired a sitter. And even then, I would never have had the nerve to go through with it if Willy, who had declared himself against the haircut, hadn't left town for a week to supervise a computer installation in Waterbury, Connecticut. He said.

At first I tried to reach Andrew, the man who had regularly cut my hair when I was at Columbia before I had married and let it grow long. He would have known exactly the look I wanted. But I was told on the phone he had long since left to open a shop in Queens, and I accepted an appointment with a Mr. John instead.

Standing on an Eighth Street crosstown bus edging through traffic, I was fairly optimistic about the results. My reflection in the bus window was not unattractive. It skipped the details and gave no hint of texture. Depending on how I chose to focus, I could see at a single spot on the windowpane my nose or a building across the street.

I had never been one to dwell on my failings. Rather, since the miraculous removal of my braces back in 1945, I, raised on Emerson, had always believed that whatever faults surfaced, there was always some cure, some program or remedy to apply, to reverse the symptoms. A diet, a haircut, sun, sleep, exercise, a change of scene, a new lover, a husband, determination, suicide if all else failed. Through the years I had found my own standards more exacting than others'; and examining my reflection as we stopped to take on passengers, I was reasonably confident of the expedition's outcome.

The moment I sat down before the beauty parlor mirror, however, surrounded by regular customers and Muzak, I knew I was making a mistake. Reflections in a dirty window are one thing; in a fluorescent-lit mirror another. There was a crease beside my mouth it was useless to deny, and other shocking imperfections. Not in my skin only. My very bones had shifted: narrower cheeks, more prominent cheekbones. The hairline was new, and there were several small, as yet inconspicuous moles destined to enlarge. I had evidently undergone some reversal of luck.

The operator covered me—hands, purse, and all—in a green smock, then looked me over in the mirror. "A Cap Cut, I think," he suggested.

"Okay," I said, "but short enough that I won't have to set it."

"Aren't you down for a shampoo and set?" He checked his book.

I did not believe in hair setting. It was a fraud, like a wig or a padded bra. They all corrupted the user, robbing her of dignity. The women in the mirror surrounding me, staring at their green-smocked reflections, their hair wrapped in towels, set in rollers, teased, straightened, frizzed, dyed; eyebrows red from plucking, lips foaming with peroxide, hands soaking in softener—they had all been robbed, like the mannequins in Rome and the secretaries in offices.

"No. Just a cut."

"Well, I'll wet you down then. You could use a styling. With that much hair I'm going to have to charge you for a styling anyway."

I suddenly recalled the sorry fate of Veronica Lake and her famous "peekaboo bang." When the peekaboo bangs of thousands of women working in factories during World War II began getting caught in the machinery and fouling the War Effort, the Department of War asked Miss Lake to set an example by changing her hairdo for the Duration. A patriot, she complied. It ruined her. Directly she changed her hair, she fell into obscurity and then oblivion.

Mr. John sprinkled water on my hair and my fluff flattened, leaving only my naked face.

Under the circumstances, I thought, a haircut might prove a disaster.

He reached for his scissors. I gripped the arms of the chair underneath my smock. I tried not to wince as Mr. John picked up my long front lock and made his initial snip; watched horrified as pieces of me fell to the floor. Remnants of my past, to be swept away by a porter's broom, too late to get back.

"Remember," I cautioned, "very short. But soft. Not severe."

Though I aimed to convey only reasonable concern, something in my manner must have betrayed anxiety, for Mr. John, holding scissors poised midair, gently reprimanded my reflection with:

"Why don't you wait till I finish before you judge?"

A new operator, I thought, inexperienced. Too late to change, and Will expected home tomorrow. I held my head absolutely still as he proceeded to cut, my features frozen as though caked in mudpack.

Mr. John hummed with the Muzak, then paused to examine his work.

"Shorter at the ears," I instructed. "I'd like a more tousled look." No going back.

Mr. John ignored me, pursuing some ideal of his own.

"I may have a picture here of the look I want," I admitted at last. And as casually as I could, I brought out from under the green smock my old graduation photo that had been reprinted years before in the Cleveland *Post* with the Former-Prom-Queen caption. With pride and shame I tried to present the picture as though, despite its yellowed crumbling edges, I had clipped it from some ad in last week's *News*.

"More like that."

Mr. John glanced at it quickly without recognition and shrugged.

"Of course, I'll cut it any way you say, but frankly, your ears are not the daintiest."

There was a blinding flash as for an instant the mirror lit up with revelations.

*My ears, never before worth noticing, were suddenly to be regarded!* Like my skin and my hair, heretofore unobjectionable, suddenly my ears, too, were factors in the total picture. How the considerations proliferated!

> *The clothes you're wearing are the clothes*
> *    you wore,*
> *The smile you are smiling you were smiling then,*
> *But I don't remember where, or whhhh-en,*

sang Mr. John to the Muzak, snipping away. Of course I was glad to have escaped detection in that old clipping, but I was vexed to discover that we no longer bore any recognizable resemblance to each other. Perhaps, as Mr. John suggested, it was time to be restyled. All the magazines proclaimed times had changed. The sixties were news. What had been in was out; what out, in. Taking the clipping out of my drawer the night before, I had even then sensed an anachronism, like my paltry total of twenty-six lovers on the coded list beside it, now regularly surpassed by every industrious contender, like the four-minute mile.

I made no protest as Mr. John severed my remaining locks, wrapped the stumps in tissues and rolled them on rollers, then stuffed my ears with cotton and shoved me under a dryer.

"Want me to bring you some magazines?" he mouthed, as a barrage of hot molecules battered my ears, drowning out the opening strains of Muzak "Stardust."

Oh, why had I neglected to bring a book? The truth was, years had passed since I had read a book. I had looked things up and read reviews on Sundays, had even browsed in bookstores on Eighth Street with Willy after the movies. But in my daily life of clutter and climax my attentions had been so splintered, my concerns so manifold, that the concentration required to read a book through had evidently atrophied in me, and except for survival manuals like Dr. Guttmacher's and Dr. Spock's, never intended for reflection anyway, books were but titles to me, like lovers' names, documents of my biography. Even the tiny volumes of the Little Leather Library, now collectors' items, were stored safely away with the baby clothes to be handed down to a daughter. The most I managed was now and then a poem from a quarterly, to commit to memory and replay for solace.

"I said, would you like some magazines?" repeated Mr. John, raising the headpiece for a moment so I could hear him.

"Yes, thanks."

He returned with a handful of slick paper. And within moments, there I was under a dryer leafing through magazines, without even a book to distinguish me, as though I too had come to be patched and repaired, styled, shampooed, and set. Rather than simply trimmed.

*Does she . . . or doesn't she? Hair color so natural only her hairdresser knows for sure.*

Starting at puberty in *Seventeen* magazines all my life I had noticed ads for skin care and hair rinses, but I had never understood them. Not that I had been smug—I had simply not believed in cosmetics, not known what all that talk of pores and textures was about.

*Radiant color that never rubs off on pillows, towels, collars, or him.*

Suddenly under the influence of the extremely hot air, the pages of *McCall's* and *Glamour* yielded intelligences I had frankly never suspected. At last, in my thirty-first year, I began to understand those ads for the first time in my life.

*Can a cream really make dramatic improvements in aging skin? Is such an achievement possible? Today, Science tells us, the probability exists as never before.*

Perhaps such things, like sex and motherhood, can be understood only when it is too late. Are not the products promoted in the magazines intended to halt precisely those developments that cannot be halted? Afflictions like acne have nothing in common with this other condition, despite surface appearances; one, time alone will cure; the other, time will only worsen.

*Gives you back that flat tummy of your teens.*

*Gone forever that flaky caky feeling, washed away with Beauty Bar.*

Suddenly under the dryer I saw that those very remedies I had come to count on—haircuts, diets, sun, lovers—would produce in time such terrible symptoms of their own that more cures, more tricks, more devices would be necessary to control them. Bleach your hair and it will turn out coarser: shave your legs and it will grow in thicker; have a mole removed and two more will pop out. My own once-radiant skin had begun to show imperfections which to camouflage would be to aggravate. It would dry out in the sun, hang loose if I dieted, puff up if I slept; and even if I did nothing at all, the pores would enlarge, hairs sprout, dimples crease, pimples scar. The whole process was out of control. Once the grey got a start in my hair, it could only spread. And a lover—the ultimate cure—a lover was absolutely out of the question for the simple reason that I could not bear for him to see my thirty-year-old thighs quiver!

It was all coming startlingly clear. The hot air waves bombarding my head and burning my ears were no doubt transmitting cosmic messages. In the *Ladies' Home Journal* at last I began to see the necessary connections between causes and effects that had eluded me in all my study of philosophy. Perhaps every stimulus, as Dr. Watson testified, had its response and every act, as Spinoza maintained, its consequences given from the beginning of time, but the responses and consequences were not those I had grown to expect. Who would have predicted that the crooked smile I had artfully cultivated for its power to charm would leave an entirely different mark beside my mouth? The particular fate I had spent a lifetime fleeing across two continents and decades had been here waiting for me all the while I was looking back over my shoulder. Neither course I had followed had saved me from it. To find myself at thirty locked under a dryer eagerly studying ads in magazines while I worry about the sitter and my husband is away on a business trip; now, after my schemes and triumphs, my visions and dares, to be, without income or skill, dependent on a man and a fading skin—it can only be the fulfillment of a curse!

\*
\* \*

Beverly Katz and her big bust float into the dryer. She is dressed as a bunny. Her face is a large clock; her hair is teased to resemble ears. Seven little bunnies hop behind her.

"I told you so," she throws at me, her black eyes flashing disdain.

Her bunnies begin pulling at her tail. "Stop it, now. Stop it or or I'll tell Daddy!" Then to me: "I told you you couldn't get away with that shit forever, it was only a matter of time."

I smile, and my cheek cracks in a jagged line beside my mouth, like a crack in the sidewalk.

"That should teach you to smile," she says.

"Why you little bitch," says the Blue Fairy, suddenly materializing. Her blue gown is sadly out of date. By now she is my mother's age. She grabs Beverly by the tail and, pinning her second hand, washes her mouth out with soap (Beauty Bar). Give it to her, Blue Fairy!

Meanwhile, with their mother otherwise occupied, the little bunnies have begun trading cards and pulling at one another's tails. Each time a trade is consummated, they multiply. Soon there are fourteen. Or is it twenty-eight?

"I'm sorry! Glub glub!" shouts Beverly, her mouth filled with soap.

The Blue Fairy, with a touch of her wand, transforms the soap to a special-formula antibacterial anti-acne unguent (twenty-seven dollars the quarter ounce) with which she gently swabs Beverly's face. The second hand stops. The minute hand stops. Only the hour hand continues on its inexorable course.

"Blue Fairy, the anti-acne unguent works like magic," says Beverly gratefully. "Oh, how can I ever thank you enough?" She spits several soap bubbles from her lips, then says: "I know what! I'll get my patron, the eminent Dr. I. Friedman, to put in an extra large supply for Valentine's Day. At fine cosmetics counters everywhere."

Yes, I decide, I must have some! But there is no time to run out for so much as a gram: the judging is about to begin!

Onto the table we march in chronological order. The judges sit in a row below. "Cinchy," I think when I see their faces: I have slept with them all.

There are Spinoza, Emerson, and Alport, all nodding their heads sagely. There are Nietzsche, Schopenhauer, and Dr. Watson, withholding judgment.

Spinoza looks forlorn, like poor Geppetto.

"What's the matter, Mr. Spinoza?" I whisper respectfully, leaning over the edge of the runway. "Or is it *Doctor* Spinoza?"

"Nothing, my dear, nothing," he says, pausing to wipe his spectacles. "Actually, I am serenely happy. As should you be. Because of your dedication to Truth, your shiksa nose has not grown in the slightest. If your ears are not the daintiest, it is because you do not perceive them under the aspect of eternity. But if you stop to listen, you will agree, their essence partakes of the ears of God. Hearken to the divine Muzak and you will hear for yourself. Q.E.D."

As I stand up he gives me Winston Churchill's $V$. (Or is it Roosevelt's?)

"Go on out there, baby, and trust thyself," says Emerson, more sanguinely. As usual he is using his time to good purpose. He is practicing the knots in the Boy Scout Handbook, open on his lap. I fear he doesn't really care about us.

Alport beside him, his long legs getting in his way, smooths his mustache and tracks me with his eye. I go limp. He says nothing, but I know he is pulling for me. How I love him!

Nietzsche, Schopenhauer, and Dr. Watson, however, don't even seem to recognize me. "Hi, boys," I say, waving a handkerchief and smiling.

My cheek cracks a little more each time I smile, like a split lip. I apply Chap Stick. I know I ought to let it heal, but I also know I can never win with a straight face.

"Hey—don't you remember? It's me! Sasha!" I shout. "We had some beautiful times!"

But they are straining to see the contestants coming up behind me. I try to gain their attention by several bumps and a grind. All I get, however, is Watson, pinching my ass and pushing me aside. "Seen one, seen them all," he spits out contemptuously.

"Keep your filthy hands off me, you old letch!" I sneer, "and don't be disrespectful!" But if he hears, he does not seem to care.

"Fellow eminent judges," he begins. "Science says a thing of thirty is a bitch forever. Unless a miracle happens."

They applaud.

"Tell you what," he continues. "I'll get my friend and colleague, the celebrated Dr. Spock, to send us up some youth. He's got them divided up by age into hundreds of sections. In any case, science says this number"—he points to me—"is *dis*-qualified."

At least, I note, it gets me some attention. I begin waving again, gaily, wildly. But now when I smile I feel the crack deepen dangerously, as above it my bones begin shifting. The crack is a veritable fault in the landscape. Perhaps we will have to evacuate the area.

"Her ears are not the daintiest," says Schopenhauer.

"Burn them off," says Nietzsche.

"Why not allow her to dispose of them herself!" interrupts my friend Emerson.

"That's not really fair, you know," I protest (softly).

But already Beverly's bunnies have taken over the table and are multiplying to beat the band. I am clearly outnumbered. Already in a single season they have far surpassed my lifetime record of twenty-six, and they have barely begun!

Watson wastes no time lining up all the bunnies in neat regular columns as fast as they can reproduce. At a nod from Watson the orchestra lets go with a drum roll, then launches a treacly rendition of "Stardust"— all strings and woodwinds, no timpani or brass.

"One-two-three ready?" says Watson, as the bunnies settle down to pick up their cues. "Now.

> "Science says hands up
> Science says hands down.
> Hands up, hands down,
> Science says hands down.

"You, you, and you. Disqualified. Ready? Now, once again:

> "Science says legs down
> Science says legs up
> Legs down, legs up
> Science says legs up."

I play the gane too, but my heart isn't in it. It lacks tenderness. And my ears are burning: no doubt someone is talking about me.

"Didn't I tell you that you were disqualified? Why do you always have to be different?" says Watson, grabbing me by the shoulders and shaking me with all his might. (He doesn't believe in spanking.)

"But I didn't miss," I protest.

"Maybe not. But you have made the toilet overflow. You have an ugly pimple on your chin. Your time is up. You are ready for your comb-out."

Gail the sitter was still out with the children when I got home. Thank God. I went straight to the bathroom, ran water on my brush, and, ignoring the underwear I had left soaking in the sink, began brushing my hair. It had been teased and sprayed like an uptown matron's. All a waste. I had to undo it.

I brushed and shaped the short ends, urging them over my curved fingers till they dipped on my forehead and rose pertly at my crown as I remembered. The water mixed with sweat. In the bathroom mirror under ordinary indoor incandescent light, my skin was again passable, but my hair, which didn't depend on light, was not. No, not even after I finally got it right, caught exactly the tousled Baybury look; then my face was wrong.

I should never have cut it. Suddenly I understood why older women wore their hair in styles of decades past. They were not ignorant; they were trying to objectify their memories, like women living through their children. But neither could be done.

No, it was not hair after all that made the difference. It was something else, something elusive. Talent? Skill? Perhaps—but they were past developing. Skin, then? Could a little make-up used sparingly help after all?

Though I had always had contempt for make-up— always considered it a frivolous indulgence or a deceit—I decided the time had come to reconsider. At least to experiment. A secret-formula unguent to protect against weather, a cleansing lotion to remove it, a touch of mascara on the tips of the lashes, something odorless and lubricating at night. A quarter ounce of prevention to be applied daily, for a start, to touch me up like a photograph.

Of course, I would conceal the jars among the babies' Desitin Ointment and cotton balls. What I did with my skin was no one's business but my own.

\*
\* \*

Andrea rushed in, spilling acorns. "L-l-look, Mommy, l-look," she said, "for dow and de squirrels." My Andy: she stammered, she talked like the Bible, and she had a plan, all at once. She brought so much to observe and sort out, there was room for almost nothing else.

Jenny was in Gail's arms, fussing.

"I would have come back sooner, Mrs. Burke, but the baby was asleep and I didn't want to wake her," said Gail. "Did you have your hair cut?"

"Yes."

"It looks nice."

Jenny was holding out her arms to me, squirming for me. "Uhn, uhn, uhn, uhn." I took her.

"Thanks, Gail. How did it go?"

"Oh, fine. The carriage is in the hall. I changed Jenny twice. The only problem was, Andrea talks so fast I can't understand her, and it makes her mad."

She said it as though Andy were deaf. "I know," I said. "Here, watch Jenny a second and I'll go get your money."

I put Jenny down on the floor and instantly she began to cry. I felt the knot in my stomach. Andy trailed me to the bedroom, tugging on my skirt and trying to explain something. "In a minute, pumpkin," I said.

I opened my purse, saw the clipping, put it back in my drawer, got out the money, and with Andy still dogging me returned to pay Gail and snuggle the baby.

"Now, Andy," I said, sitting on the floor with Jenny in my lap after Gail had gone, "now, darling, tell me."

It was mostly at beginnings that the stammer came. As though she wanted the words to come out not in sequence but all at once as angels speak, under the aspect of eternity. The stammer was just a stage, of course, and would pass in time, like everything else. But it had to be handled properly all the same.

She told me her plan. Acorn cakes and sugar-water tea. These things and many more. I understood her perfectly.

> *Peter, Peter, pumpkin eater*
> *Had a wife and couldn't keep her.*
> *Put her in a pumpkin shell*
> *And there he kept her very well.*

We practiced consonants in the guise of song; drank tea and baked acorns in mime; bathed and fed Jenny; ate; read together; prepared for bed. And in all that time, Andy, who plucks a speck of dust from the air, who sees the single blade of grass growing miraculously out of a brick, who divines moods before they erupt and catches discrepancies as they occur—in all that time Andy never once noticed my haircut.

Or did notice but didn't care.

Even if I had recaptured exactly the glow and look of the Baybury Queen, would Willy have started coming home in time to join us for dinner? I doubt it. A highchair did not go with candlelight, nor mashed bananas with white wine. Our island life was hard for him to adapt to. We talked baby talk and read picture books, by common standards primitive. We cried unpredictably and often, stifling him. We had tantrums and provoked wrath. We lacked spontaneity. We read recipes and stammered. We examined Jenny's stools. We bugged him, we bored him to tears, we were united against him.

Perhaps when the girls were older, as Dr. Spock suggested, and more conventionally charming? But then I would be older too. And if Andrea never stopped sucking her thumb? If the children died?

No. It was all there in black and white in all the texts I had ever studied. *Baybury boys are taught it is weak to need a woman, as girls are taught it is their strength to win a man.* It was as clear as the girls Willy watched on Sundays in the ads in the *Times Magazine* and on the paths in Central Park. Times were moving; so were we all.

◥

"Well?" I asked, smiling weakly, already knowing Willy's response.

He looked injured.

"Oh God, Sasha. What have you done?" He raised his hand to his eyes as though warding off a blow.

"I *told* you I was having it cut," I said in my defense. An extenuating circumstance. Could it really be *that* bad? It had once looked so right short. It had never been particularly luxurious long. "Don't you like it at all?" I asked.

"How could you do it?" he whispered.

Were those *tears* in Willy's eyes? That was going too

far. "Christ, Willy," I cried. "it's just *hair!* It'll grow in again!"

But it was only out of habit that I reassured him, for I knew after it grew back in it wouldn't really be the same.

I turned my back to him and left the room. And felt his eyes on me still as I picked up the phone and called Roxanne.

## ABOUT THE AUTHOR

With the appearance of her first published writing (a section of this novel) in the feminist literary journal APHRA, in 1969, ALIX KATES SHULMAN began devoting much of her energy to writing. She has, since then, published three books for children, a biography of Emma Goldman, and a collection, which she edited, of Emma Goldman's speeches and writings; she is now at work on a second novel.